TEN THOUSAND MILES OF CLOUDS AND MOONS

These translations first published by Honford Star 2025

Honford Star Ltd.
Profolk, Bank Chambers
Stockport
SK1 1AR

honfordstar.com

ISBN (paperback): 978-1-915829-31-3
ISBN (ebook): 978-1-915829-32-0
A catalogue record for this book is available from the British Library.

Printed and bound in Paju, South Korea
Cover art: 《又见山水系列》一幅 by Xiao Xianghui, used with permission from Artand
Cover design by Xiao Yue Shan
Typeset by Xiao Yue Shan
Cover paper: 250 gsm Vent Nouveau by TAKEO, Japan
Endleaves: 116 gsm NT Rasha by TAKEO, Japan

1 3 5 7 9 10 8 6 4 2

Ten Thousand Miles of Clouds and Moons

NEW CHINESE WRITING

EDITED BY
ZUO FEI, XIAO YUE SHAN, & SIMON SHIEH

Honford Star

CONTENTS

EDITOR'S LETTER

≋

In China, writing is a calling. We go where the language goes. Literature is the means of our discovery, our determination, and our desire. As the nation tangles with currents of rapid change, hurried now by intelligent technologies and pursuits of economic development, it is important to remember that the dedications of its writers are ancient. They say to us: as long as there is the impetus to put a mind into language, there is someone to hear those words—across time, across demarcations, across divides. This anthology is the acknowledgment that the world is listening.

To select from the Chinese language's vast repositories… Well, it's anything but simple. For as long as it has existed, literature in China has always been something of a grand occasion, with each of its innumerable contributors an essential element (imagine an ocean being separated into droplets). In our past curations, we've faced this vastness with equal parts reverence and trepidation, knowing that at any time, an extraordinary voice could be emerging amidst the canals and rivulets of the literary landscape. As the saying goes, masters are hidden amongst the masses. So in addition to lauded authors, we also read widely in search of singular, independent approaches to the Chinese language—artisans who work in the exquisite methods of gemstones, porcelain, silk. This is the wishful thinking we indulge in as editors, but also as readers and intimates of letters.

For this compilation, we only set ourselves a few guidelines. The work had to be excellent; the writer had to have a point of view that is under-explored in the Anglosphere; there had to be a balance of genders; and the language must be so special that it has the potential to torture translators. This final aspect came only from our love for the Chinese language—which, like all languages, has a singular soul, a force drawn from its age and its malleability throughout time. The more a writer is able to tap into that soul, the more difficult the piece would inevitably be to translate. We loved the lines that made us think: "How could this ever be said in English?" We looked for voices that made us consider Chinese in its ever-changing, ever-individualizing forms, because that is how writing transcends textuality to present itself as a wonder of the mind, emerging in such surprising forms… Also, we knew our translators—themselves writers, poets—would be up to the task.

We considered what would be the most impactful, surprising, or moving for the purveyors of world literature. Admittedly, we wanted to change the way that English readers approach Chinese writing. Beyond the expected stories of revolutionary tragedy, soulless oligarchy, or oriental romanticisms, we set our focus on choosing works that embody the contemporary spirit of experimentation and stylistic flair, intending to introduce textual inventions that indicate towards the nation's sheer variety and polyphony. And to tell you about these pieces…

It must be acknowledged that every writer working in the Chinese language is held to account by the vast annals of history, and the three who have taken this task to heart are San San, Chen Chuncheng, and Li Hongwei. San San's period piece, "Lady Wei's Dream," seems at first typical of a classic work, but soon cracks open to reveal a treatise on destiny and a formidable account of feminine strength, drifting from lush poeticisms to startling revelations. On the opposite side of time, Chen Chuncheng has his eye cast on the future. In his story, "Mass of *Dream of the Red Chamber*," he poses a hypothesis: if the most cherished tome of the Chinese canon were to be destroyed, what would happen to us? Elements of science fiction and fantasy are used to deconstruct and reconstruct the reverberations of iconic works, building an enthralling narrative of epistemological and political conquest. As for Li Hongwei, his piece, "Pulling Thunder," ranges across the tenets of Daoism, Buddhism, and divination in a story of mystical technique; this profound story questions the role of human life amidst the uncertainty of magic—which is perhaps something we've invented only to extend our own curiosities.

Our stories must rest just above or beneath reality, without mimicking its contours exactly. What one expects from literature is a degree away from direct experience, a distance by which we are given some room for discovery. The excerpt from Huo Xiangjie's novel, *Stellar Corona*, recounts the tale of a southern family and their development across generations, from the first colony to the latter half of the nineteenth century, when Chinese culture experienced tremendous shifts with the influx of external influence. Through his incantatory prose, the intricacies of an enormous, interconnected world are forged through a single clan's ancestral presence. Similar complexities also appear in the excerpt from Lu Yuan's novella, *The Large Moon and Other Affairs*, which sees a new world held within the apocalypse; celestial phenomena merge with dreamy phantasmagoria to portray a global collapse that is, despite its strangeness, still all too vivid in our era of climate devastation and international crises. Lastly, in "History in Bomi Time," the young writer Li Jiayin constructs a narrative around the fictional Bomi tribe, applying anthropological methodology with the micro-histories of independent invention, reflecting the contradictions within our contemporary evaluation of history.

Daily life often finds its way into surrealism and absurdity, and the two writers who most closely approach this chaotic tableau are Suo Er and Da Tou Ma, exemplifying their profound ability to soar unimpeded across narrative boundaries. While it initially appears to be describing the pedestrian routines of a married couple, Suo Er's "Man and Wife" veers in its latter half; turns out that the young people trying to make a living in the city are still harboring nostalgic thoughts of a profound, rural order. As for Da Tou Ma, the young, tired characters of "Catcher in the Rye" are similarly awash in the urban tide, attempting to find some enduring meaning amidst the nihilism of spectacle. Salinger's presence in the title is part of a greater puzzle in the author's 2020 collection, *Nine Stories*, in which she takes on the themes of nine Western literary works, intuitively rendering a collision of cross-cultural themes.

As for the six poets we've selected, they range across four generations of writing. The first is Ma Xu, born in the late fifties, who has applied his incisive consciousness to avant-garde poetics for the last forty years. Guided by his distinctive style, readers can pass through the lines to arrive at the center of his thinking, which, in the topography of poetry, is also a peak by which to look over the linguistic vistas. Representatives from the next generation—poets born in the seventies—are Jiang Li and Du Lulu. Jiang expresses a clear dialectical intelligence in his pieces, cohering imagery with philosophical practice. Du, who has been active in many channels of Chinese-language poetry, writes of the deceptively true paradoxes of contemporary life, substantiated through her presence as a proud woman poet. Fu Wei and Jia Wei are born in the nineties, and as such, their elegant, surprising work characterizes both a deep immersion in poetic tradition and the urge of any contemporary writer to free themselves from past convention. As for the mysterious poet Tan Lin, when we felt the need to incorporate a poet who writes in form—someone approaching modern aspects with the ancient temperament of ephemerality, precision, and perfection—he came immediately to mind.

Additionally, we've included two essayists in this volume. Mao Jian has long been renowned for her cultural and film criticism, and in her moving memoir, "No One Sees the Grasses Growing," she recalls the eighties and nineties, a time of unconstrained artistic prosperity for both the nation and the author, then a university student in Shanghai. As for the writer Hei Tao, his pieces are paintings of Jiangnan's dense and vivid hues. Since its very beginnings, China has distinguished between its northern and southern regions, and here, Hei draws our attention to the warm valleys and waters that raised him, the residences, courtyards, tools, plants, relatives, and sages that appear now as if in a dream. They are elegies for the lost things of the south, and through them passes not only sorrow, but a profound love and reverence.

In bringing all of these writers to the page, we are profoundly grateful to our translators, who have worked tirelessly to untangle images from their representations, emotions from their grammatical constraints, and philosophy from that strange liminal space between the word and the ineffable. Their effort indicates a truth that literature can learn from physics: nothing is ever destroyed—it simply changes forms.

Perhaps to absolve ourselves from what Baudelaire called the ennui of modernity, there is only literature—its creation, its translation—because this work still requires equal parts passion and intelligence, dedication and discovery. It demands that its practitioners draw harmony in isolation, negotiating between the mind and some kind of light in the distance.

The human ability to bring forth pasts, futures, visions, dreams, alternative realities, and unconquerable landscapes... Well, it used to be a power belonging to the gods, and here we do it with only words.

陈春成

Chen Chuncheng

**TRANSLATED BY
XIAO YUE SHAN**

《红楼梦》弥撒

MASS IN DREAM OF THE RED CHAMBER

PRELUDE

On a spring night in the fourteenth year of the Wanli Era, something strange happened in the palace. Emperor Shenzong dreamt of a white crane landing beneath the sophora tree in the courtyard's northeastern corner. There, it turned into a crippled old priest and circled the tree once before seeing a spot on the ground, upon which he exclaimed, There it is! Then he bent down and began digging at the dirt with his hands. The emperor saw him from the shadows and shouted: Who's there? The priest looked to him with a smile, then turned back into a crane and flew away.

When the Emperor woke up the next morning, he felt the dream lingering, and ordered his attendants to dig up the ground by that same sophora tree in the northeastern corner. What they found was a case made of stone, with a jade cup inside. Exquisite. Prismatic. Smoke whirling within it, as if from another realm. When Shen Shixing, a scholar from the Wenyuan Pavilion, was summoned to examine the object, he said that during the Hongwu Era, Timur had sent his envoys to the capital with a cup as tribute. Named the Cup of Worldly Illuminations, it holds a penetrating light, and if a saintly person were to take hold of that radiance, they would know the world. It had been hidden in the palace and eventually lost—but perhaps this was that Cup. Shenzong was smitten, he couldn't put it down, night after night he fondled it under the moonlight until suddenly, he glimpsed in its depths some mirage, and came to realize the truth of all creation.

In the following decades, he persevered with a tireless neglect to unsettle the empire's foundations, opening the Ming Dynasty to utter decline. To quote directly from the history books: "The Ming Dynasty perished by way of Shenzong." On his deathbed, the emperor hallucinated countless figures of foreign calvary swarming in through the breaches of his empire, and the face of a man—whose name was Cao—blinked briefly amidst the crowd. He then knew that the secret mission of his life was complete, and he died in peace.

I

After a perfect victory, a prison inside Taozhi Mountain was discovered by my troops. Over half of the peak had been hollowed out by this structure, but its entrance was well-camouflaged. In Jiao Datong's time, the fortress held detainees while they awaited trial, and when the doors of hundreds of caves were pried open one by one, it was discovered that most of the inmates had long perished. On an autumnal afternoon of November 4876, I received instructions to leave my formation in the peace parade and fly my plane eastward. By the time I arrived at Taozhi, it was sunset, and the peachy walls of the cavern had been dyed a deep rust by the dying light. The grasses languished in the wind. The land languished within itself. After leading me into the reference room, the officer in charge handed me the relevant documents, and after dinner, I went through the prisoners' papers. One particularly thick file, labeled "HXH," caught my attention. The name of the prisoner had been redacted, and his year of birth was marked as 1980. Assuming this wasn't some bureaucratic error, that birthdate would make him the longest living creature on earth. I thought of an old rumor: around sixty years ago, in a museum, an ancient man named Chen Xuanshi suddenly woke up from his vegetative state. Afterwards, he wrote a novel dedicated to the then-global president, Jiao Datong. Jiao gave the work high commendations, and the news reported of people trying desperately to get their hands on it. I did a bit of research to see what had really happened, discovering that the text had only gone through one edition, and most of the copies were forcibly distributed to students. It was not held in high regard, and has since disappeared from circulation. There hasn't been any word on Chen Xuanshi since. When I checked the publication date of that book, it was only two weeks before the day that this unnamed prisoner entered these confines.

In a dim, musty room of stone, I met that ancient prisoner. His large face was mostly buried beneath a filthy mound of hair, and he was nearly blind. Still, I hoped that he would feed me some long-lost pieces of the past. He was dazed and took a while to issue his responses, as if he had just wandered back into his body after a lengthy escapade, but still, he spoke smoothly. It didn't seem like he had been alone for so many years, but perhaps he was simply accustomed to his own company. He told me: My memory is getting worse and worse, and now I only remember two stories—my life, and that of a novel. The first is unremarkable, worn out by the years, and passes in a blur; the second is incomparable, growing ever-longer in the dark, and has yet to come to a close… Rather than that unnamed novel, I indicated that I'd like to hear the story of his life. Our conversation, interrupted several times by his physical condition, lasted seven days. The following is the transcription of what he said to me, and in order to maintain its original form, no errors, omissions, or temporal inconsistencies have been corrected.

ONE

After breakfast, a well-mannered young man came by my bed to see me. He gently asked how I was doing, and if it was a good time to answer some questions—they wanted to understand some things about our generation. I said it was fine, and followed him out of the patient room, heading towards the door at the very end of the hallway. The lights glinted all silver, and the ornaments along the walls seemed technologically advanced, like we were inside a spaceship. No windows. I walked and thought of what I would say. I could sing some old songs that were popular in my day, or talk about that one time I met Eason Chan, or even recite the names of over two hundred Pokémon. That last one might be of some value, I thought, because when I woke up in the gallery of objects from the twenty-first century, there was a Pikachu figurine in the display case next to me. Maybe it's become a kind of divinity, like the qilin. Besides, I knew nothing of the turbulent international relations or the socio-economic developments of my era. Maybe I could put on a Tang Lusun impression, and talk about the food we ate back then.

There were two reasons that the room shocked me as soon as I entered it. First, it was clearly an interrogation room, and second, interrogation rooms apparently have not changed for thousands of years. A large mirror took up nearly an entire wall, and I knew that behind it, someone was studying me. The walls were made of soundproof materials, and there was an extremely bright lamp on the steel tabletop. They asked me to sit—a few faces submerged in brightness. They were piercing. I turned my head, and saw a skinny man looking back at me from the mirror. I used to be fat, but they said that I had shed all the weight in my sleep. It all felt like an illusion, like watching a film starring someone else. The nightmare of not knowing what would happen next. A voice coldly asked:

Have you ever read *Dream of the Red Chamber*?

Huh? Yes.

How many times?

Once or twice.

Is it once or is it twice?

Once in high school. Then re-read some chapters in my second year of university.

They seemed to get worked up. One of them hurried out, not even bothering to fully close the door, and I thought I could hear the low sounds of cheering. The same young man who had led me here asked with great gravity: Can you repeat it? I thought he wanted me to repeat what I just said, but he interrupted me. Then I understood: they wanted me to repeat *Dream of the Red Chamber*. I told them that this was impossible, that it's a story with a great many intertwining narratives, and anyway, so much time has passed. They seemed to be prepared for this response. A few of them came and held me down, fitting some kind of machine on my head. An electric current passed through my temples, and it was as if a million little golden snakes were darting around my brain. This will help you remember, they said. I was screaming from the pain. They were shouting in unison: Focus your energies, think of *Dream of the Red Chamber*! And with that I could almost see towers and pavilions, suspended in cloud-smoke, a group of men and women walking in the gardens, they were laughing, sighing, cursing, reciting beautiful lines of poetry, anxiously weeping, then disappearing into a flurry of snow... I managed to spit out a few words: Nüwa, daoshi, Jiayu Village, stone, a serene and wealthy village... And then I lost consciousness.

After keeping me on the machine for a few days, they finally determined that I was unable to systematically recite the entire novel, and even my summarizations were jumbled. So they began another line of questioning: What is the central idea of *Dream of the Red Chamber*? I said: I don't know—is there a central idea? They weren't convinced, and pressed on: It's said that in your time, *Dream of the Red Chamber* was a mandatory text for students, and countless studies have been done on it, so someone must have brought up a central idea—even if it's just your guess. With a hint of kindness, the young man said to me: You see, *Dream of the Red Chamber* has been lost for a long time. Now there are only a few stray fragments drifting amongst the populace. It's very unusual that it wasn't saved, because some people still herald it as a great work, and certain anarchist groups even consider it a bible. My bosses are hoping that you'll be able to help us restore the text—of course we want to maintain its original integrity, but we'd also like to clean it up a bit, trim it, and use it to propel some positive energy into our new era. If we succeed, it'll be the event of the century, and a great boost to our president. Which country's president? I asked. The world's, the young man replied. At the moment, the project seems like it'll be difficult to accomplish. We'll have to just use the major characters and narrative pieces you gave us, and write a new *Dream of the Red Chamber*. The experts are on it, so don't worry about that. Your job now is to remember the central idea. Still perplexed, I asked him why. He hesitated and looked to another person, who said: Tell him.

The young man then continued: There's some evidence indicating the existence of a theory—or a formula or a proverb—hidden inside *Dream of the Red Chamber*. Some people believe that if we're to carry such a concept over to state affairs, to economic or technological development, it might have some miracle effect. No matter if that's true or not, management has asked us to pry the idea out of you, so please be cooperative. With that, he pressed down once more to activate the machine.

The little golden snakes bit at me, and in the pain, I indistinctly recalled a half-sentence I had read in my school days. Stuttering, I recited: Evidence that a decaying feudal society is destined to perish. . . I'm not sure why, but they grew furious at this, as if the words had stomped on them. They said I was speaking nonsense, and increased the currents. Once again, I was gone.

TWO

The first time I saw her, it struck me that beauty really does connect the present with the past, that it is immune to time. The ancient, tired metaphors suddenly awakened against her figure: autumn waters, white jade, hibiscus buds, new gleam of frost. She came in, and the door closed silently behind. Paired with that face, the slate grey of her military uniform shone with the wonder of dissonance, like a flowering branch sticking out of a trash heap. She walked up, put her bag to one side, and began to undress. I could guess the intentions behind the act; *Dream of the Red Chamber* may have been lost, but the trappings of loveliness are not. After a thousand years of sleep and several days of interrogation, it was as if my body had forgotten how to exercise its instincts, but the glaciers were beginning to thaw. I started to unbutton my shirt, hoping she wouldn't force me to give her the central idea of *Dream of the Red Chamber* prior to the act, but soon saw that beneath her uniform was a bodysuit of some kind, more suitable for diving than for fantasy. She rolled her eyes and said: Behave—I just came to save you. I stared at her. She knelt down and looked at her wrist, where an image similar to a watch face floated up. Then she opened her bag, took out a lipstick, and drew a circle on the ground. I looked over suspiciously in time to see the red outline turn suddenly black, beginning to emit a noxious smoke. She stood up, stomped her foot, and that whole round piece of flooring fell away. A piercing alarm rang out from somewhere. Footsteps came thundering from outside the door. I carefully stuck my head into the hole, seeing only waves beneath us. It was only then that I realized—I've been on a spaceship this whole time, passing over some lake or sea. She took hold of me and jumped.

I said to myself, If this is a dream, the descent will definitely wake me. But the feeling of her hair against my face was so gentle and clear. In the middle of that thought, I suddenly felt cold all over.

THREE

As for the assets, it wouldn't be right to say that I lost them alone. Actually, my grandfather and father (may they rest in peace) also played their roles. The 2008 financial crisis had finally put an end to the Chen family's precarious comforts, and to repay our debts, I had to sell yachts, planes, and even auction off the estate upon which we had lived for generations.

When I cleared out our collections, going over the exquisite pieces that had surrounded me my whole life, I couldn't help but get emotional in front of the household staff. As I wandered around, a box made of white jade caught my attention. It sat in the shadows behind a grandfather clock of ebony wood and a gilded bronze incense burner, looking like nothing I'd ever seen before. When I picked it up, it felt like ice in my hands, and upon lifting the lid, a fragrance and a chill wafted out in one wisp. Inside was a little vial, lustrous and green. About the size of a snuff bottle, it looked like a container for medicinal oils. Also inside the box was a sheet of wax paper printed with a cloud pattern, inscribed with the fine ornate characters of my grandfather's unmistakable hand: "Purchased in the fall of 1950 and said to have come from a stone chamber at the western foot of Taihang Mountain. Ingredients unknown, but suspected to be what is called a 'mountain wine.' Dates back thousands of years, likely spoilt. Not for drinking, for admiration only. Chen Qiaowang."

The cap of the bottle seemed to be intact, but a slightly bitter, herbaceous perfume leaked temptingly from the mouth. Impelled by my natural inclination for greed and hedonism—not to mention the despair of bankruptcy—I opened the bottle. The contents had already congealed to the texture of jelly, and dissolved easily in my mouth. A shudder ran through me. Afterwards, I had the vague vision of moss flowing along the carpets, lichen dangling from the chandelier. A few elk jumped in my direction, nipping the grass at my feet. Then the ground suddenly began a soft collapse, and the walls hurtled towards me. Before passing out, the last vision I had was of the ceiling's patterns, their elaborate symmetry.

FOUR

The moon was out, and the ginkgo gave off a careless perfume, the soothing scent of aged books. I slept awhile in that fragrance. When I woke up, a golden-yellow shadow was spread out before me, interspersed with sparks, and in my daze I deduced it as moonlight, split first by the branches and again by the fallen leaves, scattering as finely as frost. Beside me came the sound of her breathing. We had been lying side by side upon the thick carpet of gingko for who knows how long, but soon she said in a low voice: We can head up now. Then we climbed out from the piles, brushing the speckles of foliage from our bodies, and in that nebulous lunar glow, she led me towards the forest depths.

This woman with the name of Xi Chunhan had pulled me out from the waters a few hours prior. I didn't think that the current would be so strong, and despite knowing how to swim, I'd swallowed quite a few mouthfuls of water. We burrowed through the dense woods, heading to the mountains, and she told me that this river, which she called the Rapids, flowed into twelve tributaries. She had purposefully jumped at the point where it split, and any troops they send after us would have to follow each individual stream in their search. I followed her through the trees, over a hill wrapped in mist. After walking for an hour in a chasm cracked into the cliffs, an immense mountain range, glittering gold, appeared before me. Nearly all the surrounding peaks were replete with the thick trunks of gingko. Their fallen leaves came up to our knees at their most shallow, and could swallow us whole at their depths. She seemed to know the way, traversing the forest with the acuity of a deer, and despite tagging closely behind, I still managed to step into a hollow patch. As I treaded fiercely with all four limbs, I sank deeper and deeper. She had no choice but to stop and come back, but suddenly a faint sound of wings came fluttering through the dying light, and she suddenly twisted and tackled me. We fell together, disappearing into the leaves. Just as I was about to struggle, she whispered into my ear: Don't move, and don't make a sound. It's a Greenbird. What kind of bird? A drone shaped like a bird.

We held perfectly still until it was dark. It felt like something from one of Pu Songling's ghost stories—being alone with such a woman on a desolate mountain night. The events of the past few days had been so ridiculous that if the woman were to reveal herself as a fox at that exact moment, it would've been of no surprise to me at all. Such nonsensical thoughts spun through my head until fatigue caught up. The dim fragrance of the gingko, along with the crisp sounds that crackled whenever our bodies shifted, it all came to feel like we were asleep in some old book, one of those long-forgotten texts that no one ever finds. So when she urged me to get up, I hesitated, taking my time. She called me twice, loudly from above, until I finally stretched out my hands. She grabbed them and pulled me to the surface.

After walking for another half hour, the woods grew even denser. Only silver threads remained of the moon, quivering between the leaves, and a chill came over the air. A bird sang its gurgling song, sometimes far away, sometimes near. Occasionally, more leaves drifted down, and when their shadows passed through the moonlight, they briefly shone. It was as if they made up a real river and we were wading through, with the ground rustling beneath us. Seeing the apparently infinite expanse of ranges, of ginkgoes, I couldn't help but comment, I didn't think that the environment would be in such good shape. She casually responded, It's because the Second War cut the human population by half. The Second War? I was shocked. Wasn't the Second World War ancient history? The Second Interplanetary War, she said. It ended thirty years ago. We fought back the alien colonizers and rebuilt everything. She suddenly stopped. We've arrived.

Ahead of us was an empty field—a small void within the thickets. We'd come to the utmost depths of the forest, and the silver trees around us were abnormally giant, as if stretching all the way up to the gilded skies. A few leaves glistened at the places where moonlight could touch, and apart from that, the entire forest was weighted in darkness, like a palace stripped of its gold veneer. She walked up to one of the ginkgoes, knocked a few times against the bark, and leaned close into a small peephole, carved into the trunk at her height. Softly, she said: I've brought it back. No one in pursuit. From the hole came a startling voice, deep and masculine: Lucid dream-speak, a cauldron's tea-smoke veering to green. Xi Chunhan replied: Slant wind-force, a window's bamboo-shade lending down the cold.

I felt a slight tremble beneath my feet, and in that empty field, the leaves piled along the ground began to slowly rise. Like the sands along a dune, they slid down the sides of a structure emerging—the yellow ceramic tiles of a sloping roof. Gradually, it rose up until an entire temple stood facing us, whole. The leaves kept pouring along its angled shape, drops of a yellow rain. I looked up to read the plaque above the door, its black lacquered text inscribed not with the name of a temple, but "The Village of Yellow Leaves."

The doors opened, and a crowd of figures darted out to greet us.

FIVE

As for the disappearance of *Dream of the Red Chamber*, it started almost as soon as the text was finished. Everything after chapter eighty had been lost while its author was still alive, and only two mysterious individuals named Zhi Yanzhai and Ji Husuo had ever read the manuscript in its entirety. In our time, many editions circulated simultaneously, and each was different. We called this phenomenon Chaos. The disappearance seemed to have occurred simultaneously in print, in virtuality, and in memories, evolving surreptitiously for several generations. This was called the Age of Diffusion. Several conflicts exacerbated the process, and after the First (Interplanetary) War, the text became extremely difficult to understand because many passages had gone missing. When the authorities decided on a rewrite, they also took the opportunity to redact some of its more obstructive elements and any morbid passages, aiming to transform it into a classic that could rouse the spirit of prosperity and urge its readers towards self-improvement. The leading scholars and writers of the time were gathered in a committee to complete this task, and later on, researchers would point to this as the definitive Final Destruction of *Dream of the Red Chamber*. On the same night that the rewrite was to begin, many households who had kept copies of the text reported a sound like porcelain cracking apart, coming from their shelves in the smallest hours. The next day, along the pages of *Dream of the Red Chamber*, there remained only a mess of strokes and radicals, like corpses rotting at the site of a great battle.

In the very many years that followed, there were several half-hearted attempts to revive *Dream of the Red Chamber*. This is what we called Terminal Lucidity. About fifty years after the Final Destruction, while chiseling a piece of jadeite, a craftsman found eight faint characters of sigillary script in the outer layer of the gemstone, as if they had been growing there since the ancient days: "Near, close, keep me and live forever young." Some people thought it was a trick planted by the Red Chamber Committee, intending to publicize the text's miraculous nature. One morning, ten years later, a panda in a zoo suddenly pulled out the bamboo from its mouth and recited to the onlookers, "I've seen this young maiden before." Then it went back to eating as if nothing had happened. Even though a considerable number of people attributed the incident to hallucination, the panda underwent a meticulous examination, which returned only results of the most definitive normalcy. Afterwards, it only ever made panda noises. Around the same week, an astronaut was walking around on Pluto, and noticed a series of irregular white scars along the surface of the ice. He took a photo, and upon returning to Earth, he connected the impressions on the image with a pen. What came out was a strand of writhing text, straight from chapter nineteen: "If I had known that they would all go, I would've never come." The few elders who had been alive prior to the Final Destruction claimed that they had seen these lines before, that they perhaps came from *Dream of the Red Chamber,* but it couldn't be verified. The appearance of such lines were utterly unpredictable, incomprehensible, as if they had materialized from the very depths of matter. Some believed that these events constituted a prelude to the text's resurrection—a few slivers of verdure gesticulating from a forest reduced to ashes—but the truth was that they were the echoes of a grand symphony, because nothing similar would happen ever again.

And those words, so much like scripture, could only be kept in the mind, passed from mouth to mouth, and inscribed from memory. Secretly they traveled the world in the form of remnants, and it alarmed the authorities, who confiscated and burned them upon discovery. The edict forbidding the private discussion, research, or worship of *Dream of the Red Chamber* was issued at that time.

SIX

Yan Tongbei was sitting alone in the foyer, drinking tea from a gaiwan. Seeing me, he asked: Why are you awake? Couldn't sleep? I replied: I thought I felt an earthquake. After being on the road for most of the day, I was exhausted—as soon as I got to the guest room, my head hit the pillow, and I was out. I wasn't sure how much time had gone by, but I suddenly felt the boards of the bed shake slightly before stilling again. Unable to go back to sleep, I thought I might as well take a look around. Yan Tongbei said, It's not an earthquake. The ground shakes a bit when we start up, but it stays steady during normal operations. He told me that the temple was actually a subterranean carrier—it could move underground, and also occasionally surface in the guise of a secluded temple, which helped with air circulation. Most of the time, it was in motion. Frequent location changes were necessary for security reasons. Turns out that the group of people who put the machine on me had never stopped going after the Red Chamber Committee, of which Yan Tongbei was the vice president. He looked mixed-race, but had a Chinese-style distinction to him, a Chen Daoming type. Everyone was introduced to me by Xi Chunhan. The president was named Hong Yiku—he was old, with one eye. The secretary was Li Mangmang, chubby and kind. The carrier was piloted by two monks whom everyone called Captain Mu and Pilot Hui, their Buddhist names being Ben Mu and Ben Hui. Most of the directors were women: Zhang Miaomiao (Li Mangmang's wife), Shexing, Tanyan, Fenhua. These might've been aliases or code names, and I wasn't given many opportunities to match them with faces. Apparently this group was just the permanent staff of the base, and there were plenty of other members, typically roaming around undercover, each with their own false identity. Xi Chunhan told me that the Red Chamber Committee became an underground organization after being heavily persecuted in the thirty-second century. Something similar to the Ming Cult or the Tiandihui, I thought.

Yan Tongbei poured me some tea. I raised my cup for a taste, finding that the flavor was slightly different from what I remembered of my time—sweeter. We talked for some time, and came to the topic of my deep, enduring sleep. I explained that it was like I had taken some kind of strange medicinal wine. Zhongshan wine, he nodded. It's said that drinking it freshly brewed can keep you drunk for three years. You must've had a strong, aged batch.

He told me that in the past few thousand years, my metabolism had slowed down exponentially, similar to that of an animal in hibernation. Originally, I had been laid up in a medical institute, and they fed me intravenously while conducting their research, hoping to salvage the formula of Zhongshan wine. Nothing worked, however, and when the institute went bankrupt, I was sold illegally to a private collector, eventually ending up in a special exhibition hall at the museum, enjoying national-treasure status as an ancient corpse. Slapping a hand down on the table, I exclaimed, No wonder. I was thinking about how I woke up with a piece of jade in my mouth, all dressed up in a golden burial suit. So they thought I had died. He responded, Because previously, it was determined that there was no chance of you waking up, so even though Jiao Datong had deluded himself into thinking that he could use *Dream of the Red Chamber* for his own benefit, he never thought of the twenty-first century body sleeping right in front of him. I said that the name sounds peculiar. Who's Jiao Datong? The president of the universe? He nodded and replied, He had a lot of hope when you unexpectedly woke up. I heard that he thought of you as an auspicious omen. I mentioned that they wanted to create a new version of *Dream of the Red Chamber*, which sent Yan Tongbei into a rage.

Suddenly the thought recurred to me, and I couldn't help but ask: So what is the central idea of *Dream of the Red Chamber*? Yan Tongbei didn't answer, and instead he directed a smile past me. I heard a hoarse voice coming up from behind:

There is no central idea of *Dream of the Red Chamber*, because it is already the center of everything. And neither can we extract any meaning from it, because it itself is the meaning of the universe.

A figure, leaning against a cane, walked out from the shadows. White hair, one eye. Hong Yiku.

SEVEN

In our time, people generally thought of the universe as some combination of aimless time and aimless space, and they were at peace with that. But the Red Chamber Committee did not feel the same. Aristotle believed that there was an entelecheia hidden within the world's movements—some ultimate purpose pursued by all beings, which constituted the base driving force. Laplace thought that the Big Bang introduced the first batch of variables to continuous time, which in turn ascertained a second batch, which in turn ascertained a third... As such, the universe in its entirety was determined in that first cosmic instant. The doctrine of the Red Chamber Committee had been forged by merging the philosophies of these two thinkers with their own adulation of *Dream of the Red Chamber*: the meaning of the universe is the text itself. The doctrine posited that there is a guiding thread amidst the darkness, woven from every single individual fate, which emerged amidst the chaos that was the world before creation, and had furtively wound its way between every object, every being, stretching forth across the immense expanse of time. At the moment of creation, it ignited, and that spark continuously pushed itself onwards, passing through the dynasties, burning all the way up towards *Dream of the Red Chamber*'s completion (they call this the Red Point) until—boom—the universe reached its most glorious, most splendid peak. After that, everything headed down a long descending slope, a slow decline. *Dream of the Red Chamber* began to dissipate at the second of its realization, and when it disappears entirely, the universe will follow with its own obliteration.

The Red Chamber Committee believed that everything prior to the Red Point was preparation for *Dream of the Red Chamber*, and everything in the aftermath of the Red Point was the text's reverberation. Which is to say that every flame of the Battle of the Red Cliffs was lit for *Dream of the Red Chamber*; every scimitar raised behind Genghis Khan was aimed skyward for *Dream of the Red Chamber*; the Song dynasty woman weeping for no reason in the dying light of spring, her cries were *Dream of the Red Chamber*; no one had ever perished from war, famine, flood, or despair—everyone had died of *Dream of the Red Chamber*. Before the existence of *Dream of the Red Chamber*, the battles waged could be defined as that of slave-owners against feudalists, feudalists against the bourgeoisie, the many against the few, the north against the south, this man against that man, but truly there was only one kind of fight: forces that benefited the production of *Dream of the Red Chamber* against forces that did not benefit the production of *Dream of the Red Chamber*. Without a single exception, the former was always victorious, a series of triumphs leading towards *Dream of the Red Chamber*. In the same vein, everything after the Red Point was the extension and the prescience of *Dream of the Red Chamber*: the May Fourth Movement, the rise of rock n' roll, the Internet Age, the First World War, even the Ten Thousandth World War, the unification of the Milky Way, the collapse of the galaxies, each insignificant conversation, each ripple in every teacup—it was all initiated by a line or a plot in *Dream of the Red Chamber*. The Ruminations Faction of the Red Chamber Committee thought of *Dream of the Red Chamber* as some gaseous element, floating about the world, cohering into words, then gradually separating, fusing into everything…

The base formation of *Dream of the Red Chamber* is emptiness, then color, then emptiness. The Wuji cliffs of Dahuang Mountain are emptiness, "the white vastness of earth so clean" is also emptiness, and the Grand View Garden holds an aggregation of colors. Doubtlessly, the universe was constructed using *Dream of the Red Chamber* as its model—with the same symmetry. Its beginning and end are of nothingness, and in the middle is *Dream of the Red Chamber*, a masterwork of every hue. The symmetrical structure indicates that the disappearance of *Dream of the Red Chamber* is inevitable. "The white vastness of earth" did not only predict the dissipation of prosperity, but also the disappearance of language. *Dream of the Red Chamber* bounded towards us from the depths of all things, and will, in the end, diffuse back into the world. Because the banquet must end, he told me.

I stared at Hong Yiku's solitary eye. Trembling, I picked up my tea, and took a sip.

EIGHT

With great care, they showed me the remaining fragments of *Dream of the Red Chamber*. Most of it was displaced sentences, copied out by hand, and the longest of the pieces contained several lines of dialogue and a regulated verse of poetry. They also had the very last page of the text, printed with the publisher information and price, and speckled with a few ocher spots of blood. I handed all of it back to them with both hands. When the remnants were returned to their secure location, they looked at one another, and Hong Yiku spoke up with a request. His tone was one of caution, but a hint of pride came through: he wanted me to restore *Dream of the Red Chamber*. It came as no surprise. For all the time and effort they had put into my rescue—not to mention the lecture—they definitely wanted something more than just a new member.

I splayed out my hands and told them it was impossible, that I no longer remembered. They said there was a way, something to bring back the memories. Seeing my face tense up, Hong Yiku smiled and said: Don't worry, no electricity involved.

Yan Tongbei said they had information: a precious object was in the possession of some collector. While Xi Chunhan and I were making our escape, envoys had already been dispatched to make the purchase, and they should be back by now. The fear was of word getting out, as Jiao Datong and his thugs also had their eyes on the object. Just then, as Hong Yiku was absentmindedly preaching the doctrines, I had noticed Yan Tongbei's furrowed brow, his many glances towards the telecommunications device on the wall. So that's why he had stayed up all night—he was waiting for someone.

After thinking about it for a while, I asked Hong Yiku: You all have just said that *Dream of the Red Chamber* must disappear. According to that symmetrical universe theory of yours, before *Dream of the Red Chamber* came into the world, any act that was detrimental to its emergence would have failed; then, with its disappearance, shouldn't anything that diverts from this process also fail? What's the point of trying to recover it? Hong Yiku put down his cup and said, You're pretty smart. Humanity was called to wait for, to suppress, to read, to ignore, to comprehend, to misunderstand, to worship, and to destroy *Dream of the Red Chamber*, right up until its complete disappearance. The turning of one's back on destiny is included in destiny's perpetuations. As for us, we just want to read the work. Even just to recover one line, to read that one line would give us one line's worth of joy. He also said that even though *Dream of the Red Chamber* is the meaning of all things, the work itself is useless. The Red Chamber Committee never thought to sift any power or any new natural laws from its depths—or even to use it as some pretext for overthrowing Jiao Datong. Regimes have no meaning in the face of the universe. They simply wanted to peer at what history has called the most profound, most majestic, most complex, immense, thrilling, desolate, infinite book.

To tell the truth, I couldn't say if I believed this oblique dictum of the Red Chamber Committee, but I wasn't repulsed by it. I was an amateur (in sciences and philosophy), and in my limited knowledge, I thought of each life as having a definitive moment—an instant that everything else seemingly leads up to. This could probably extend to the universe or its creator—there's probably such a point for them as well, otherwise it would be somewhat unfair. It's fine to say that the meaning of the universe is *Dream of the Red Chamber*, it would be fine to say it's Mass in B-Minor, or *Timely Clearing After Snowfall*, or *Slam Dunk*, an icy cola, someone's smile, someone's kiss—it made no difference to me. Perhaps an icy cola is the meaning of some parallel universe, standing in opposition to this one. All to say, I could agree that the meaning of ours is *Dream of the Red Chamber*. I decided to try and help them.

After some more tea, the sky began to brighten, and the other members of the Red Chamber Committee gathered in the hall. Xi Chunhan, having changed into a charming suit of emerald green, stood behind Yan Tongbei. Just as I was about to say something to her, the telecommunications device sounded in a string of beeps, some long, some short. Everyone held their breath in rapt attention. Li Mangmang murmured a code, and a frail female voice answered her. Captain Mu hurriedly raised the base above ground, and we all surged towards the entrance. This was my first time seeing Wu Wan-er. Her face and its Arab features hung with a strange pallor, and stray branches had made tatters of her clothes. She took out a small box from her waist. After handing it to Hong Yiku, it was as if her whole body deflated, and she collapsed.

Yan Tongbei asked, Why are you alone? Where's Mingyun?

Her hands rose up to her face, covering it, and her shoulders began to shake.

NINE

My stomach burned for two hours. When I opened my eyes, all was clear.

The Remembrance Pearl was said to have been in the possession of the Tang historian Zhang Yue, and legend supposed that it could restore any forgotten memory, just by being held in the hand for a moment. Hong Yiku passed it to me and said, Rub it and you'll understand. I took it—a blue-purple thing the size of a walnut. After massaging it for a bit, many things really did come back to me. I took the paths of memory down to my school years, flutteringly thinking of the woodgrain on my old desk, the sweet fragrance of a used eraser, the mole behind the ear of a girl I had secretly loved, right up until the cerise-hued cover of *Dream of the Red Chamber* swung before my eyes—I could see the words on the pages, but only a few lines came through in relief, the others were blurry as if out of focus… Yan Tongbei said that perhaps holding the Pearl in the hand wasn't sufficient to release its full effects. The young woman named Zhang Miaomiao took out a prescription.

The hall was well-stocked with Buddhist statues, incense burners, prayer mats— likely to supplement their facade of being an actual temple. Everyone sat down in a circle. I looked around for Wu Wan-er, but she wasn't there. Perhaps still resting. While making her way back after picking up the Pearl, she and the man named Mingyun (her fiancée) had gotten caught by the subsidiary soldiers of the Department of Indoctrination. In trying to help her escape, he was shot at the scene, while she sustained some light injuries. In the morning, under Yan Tongbei's guidance, Zhang Miaomiao had pounded the Remembrance Pearl into powder, then blended it with some strange medicine. After kneading the mixture to the size of an orange, she put it into a large metal sphere and hit the power switch. Hours had passed since; it was ready to be opened. I asked Xi Chunhan what it was doing, baking? Smiling, she said: You're looking at some very advanced alchemy. I could've guessed—aside from its shiny exterior, that large sphere was built just like an athanor. Xi Chunhan said it was a prescription for the "Elixir Against Losses and Forgetting," passed down from their predecessors in the Committee. It could substantially increase one's ability for recollection. As she spoke, a faint plume of medicinal smoke rose up. Zhang Miaomiao messed around in the smoke for a while, then came back grinning, holding a small pill the size of a fish egg.

With everyone's encouragement, I ate it with considerable difficulty. It was spicy.

By the time it began taking effect, dusk had fallen. As the fire in my stomach gradually burnt out, my mind was suffused with utter clarity, like someone had washed it with new-fallen snow. I tried to bring back some details from the past—they came to me immediately, shadowlessly. I secretly examined the varied days that made up the first half of my life, and saw them as starkly as the lines on my own palm. I saw events and the twinkling karmic chain between the events, weaving a golden, serpentine braid. I understood how my family had fallen into ruins: flashes and glimmers showed me that it was a business partner of my father's who had plotted behind his back. I thought of long-gone naked bodies and their fluttering commitments; the phone numbers of every friend; the things my parents had said to me as an infant; the secrets I buried beneath a maple tree in the west side of the courtyard (Pokémon cards in a metal box); the silhouette of a green mountain seen on a clear morning through the windows of a train speeding by, the clothing of a woman standing on the platform… Suddenly a voice at my side reminded me that while the medicine was taking full effect, I shouldn't let my mind wander. Concentrate on *Dream of the Red Chamber*. I listened. It was easy, like switching to another app on a phone. I closed my eyes and focused my energies. Not long after, that cerise-colored book hung solidly before me. I stretched out two formless hands, and opened the covers.

TEN

At first, *Dream of the Red Chamber* appeared to me as an image. The paragraphs that had been carefully read through, the pages once merely glanced at—all of it was laid out before me, with the folds of the paper, the underlined passages, the stains, revealing themselves in the finest detail. I hurriedly sent someone for paper and pen. Typing would've impeded my observations. I just had to draw the pictures in my mind exactly as I saw them—it wasn't writing so much as sketching. When it came to the characters I didn't recognize, I just traced. I could even start from a word in the middle of the page and stray up or down. Everything started from this one line: "The first chapter Zhen Shiyin communes with spirits in a dream Jia Yucun thinks of his love amidst lonely misery…"

Whenever I finished transcribing a page, I'd put my hand up, and someone would immediately come to retrieve it for replication. Each person was given a copy, and they all sat on their prayer mats, examining the papers in their hands. Save for the occasional sigh of admiration and the soft hisses of breathing, the great hall was quiet. I sat in front of the Buddha with my back to the crowd, writing with furious speed upon the incense table. For several days, I worked from sunup to sundown. They let me rest in the evenings, fearing that exhaustion might negatively affect the elixir's potency, and I happened to discover that even in the late hours, light continued to seep through the various windows. From behind the glass's inlaid patterns came murmurs of recitation— they were staying up all night studying and memorizing the passages I had written out during the day. I couldn't help but feel a sense of shame. The words they regarded as precious were simply a product of my mechanized output. Having only glided along the text's surfaces, I craved that same intoxication. I wanted to submit myself to the deep admiration of this miracle. On the second day, I began using a pen to survey the language, examining every detail that I had merely glanced at back then, and it greatly slowed the rate of my writing. Not long after, I became immersed. I finally fell into *Dream of the Red Chamber*, that wondrous realm, several thousand years after I had picked up the book for the first time.

A few weeks later, I noticed that the temple's residents were gradually increasing.

Every day, as I sat copying in the hall, the space behind me surged with a deluge of bodies, and there were no longer enough prayer mats to go around. The nights saw a great number of people flooding the side chambers, the galleries, the drawing room, and every single individual would greet me with great deference. Xi Chunhan said that the news had spread to members all around the world, and they were gathering with hopes of seeing *Dream of the Red Chamber* in its original form. Those days were sweet, fleeting. After I finished my transcriptions, the hall would be brimming with devout enchantment, with manuscripts crowding the hands of the jubilant masses, like a scene from the days of Shakyamuni preaching his wisdoms. Whenever I put down my pen, flexing my wrists during a break, I could hear whispers streaming in from all directions: Is this the technique of the Golden Needle Searching Darkness? Or the technique of Wu Yi's Nine Bends? It's hard to imagine where such strange language comes from, it reads like something born of nature itself. That random passage from earlier connects here, such incredible foreshadowing—it really is the grass snakes and the grey threads, braiding veins traversing thousands of miles! I felt a sense of achievement like none I had ever felt before, as if I were the true author of *Dream of the Red Chamber*. When the yellow curtains of the hall hung low with brilliantly glimmering lamplight, someone would light a stick of incense, and I would feel a tremendous sense of peace and joy. I thought, thousands of years ago, there was also someone putting down a pen by an oil lantern, flexing his wrists, gazing at the ornate pavilions and the muddled peoples steadily rising from the page, feeling the glory of creation. There was a moment when I felt the gently closed eyes of the Buddha watching me. There was a moment when I felt that the gaze had come from Cao Xueqin.

ELEVEN

They showed up during the fiftieth chapter.

Everyone in the Grand View Garden was gathered to admire the plum branch that Baoyu had taken from Longcui Temple, and a discussion of the poetry was about to begin. The crowd had finished reading the page I just filled, and the hall was full of countless desiring eyes, watching over me. Just then, a muffled commotion sounded from above. Something shattering.

Just then, I thought—could it be that because we've replicated *Dream of the Red Chamber*, the symmetry of the universe has been disrupted, and Judgment Day is being brought upon us? Tiles and clay fell in pieces, and animal shadows swooped down after them. Greenbirds. They shot from their heights, penetrating the layers of earth and breaking the roof above us, clamping their metal claws into each and every shoulder. In no time at all, every member of the Red Chamber Committee had been taken under their custody. One Greenbird perched by my neck and aimed its iron beak in my direction. Despite having come from the twenty-first century, I knew what I saw: the barrel of a gun. Xi Chunhan had told me that all across the globe, millions of Greenbirds patrolled the skies. While serving as surveillance, they were also weapons capable of significant destruction, and had even been installed with broadcasting functions, charged with singing the propaganda of Jian Datong and his grand achievements across city skies. An enormous Greenbird spread its steel wings, landing with a great animal force in the middle of the hall. Three people descended from its back, patting the dust from their grey uniforms: the head of the Department of Indoctrination, the commander of the subsidiary army, and a valiant man named Xue Chi. The rest of the soldiers streamed down from the large hole in the roof, and within a few seconds, the hall was full of them.

As I stood frozen in astonishment, a woman collapsed and began wailing—Wu Wan-er. Mingyun, she shouted inconsolably towards a soldier in the ranks. From her screams we understood everything: Mingyun didn't die, he was captured by the militia. Xue Chi must have used him to coerce Wu Wan-er into cooperating—she was to bring back the Pearl of Remembrance and wait for the Committee to gather, thus making it easy for the group to be captured in its entirety. They would've put some kind of tracking device on her. Together, the Red Chamber Committee stood with their heads bowed, utterly silent. Not a single person spoke out in blame of Wu Wan-er. Mingyun, in his uniform, seemed deaf to her cries, his expression utterly blank. Yan Tongbei stared at him, then turned and bellowed at Xue Chi: What did you do to him?

Xue Chi laughed and said: If it is not a Holy Book. Mingyun immediately answered: Do not read it. Xue Chi then said: Sainthood and sagacity. Mingyun: Can be slowly attained. Xue Chi explained: I promised I wouldn't kill her man, and I kept that promise. I even let him join our troops. But his mind was full of poison, so we helped clean him out again. He then pointed at me and said: Take him away. We'll execute the others on the spot. As soon as the words left his lips, the Greenbird on Li Mangmang's shoulder shot out a flaming beam from its mouth, disintegrating her on the spot into a spray of ashes, a slow fall. Every member of the Red Chamber Committee closed their eyes, and a low hum of recitation began to spread. I understood what they wanted: to die alongside their favorite passage, letting time stop inside those words. Some picked the part in which an evaluation of couplets is being held in the Grand View Garden. Some repeated the lines of "were flowers so eloquent, were jade so fragrant." Some spoke the verses of the Begonia Poetry Society. Yan Tongbei repeated in a clear voice: Even if my life's work were to disappear into an east-flowing stream, there would be not one sigh of regret. Only misguided fools fail to find contentment amidst incomprehensibility. Bang. Bang. Bang. The beams shot in all directions, and the ground wore a coat of ashes.

Hong Yiku suddenly asked me: When everyone was critiquing the poems, my guess is that Xue Yuqin had the best work? I replied: Yes. He follows up: And then how did they honor him? I said: Daiyu and Xiangyun poured a small cup of wine and toasted to Yuqin. He asked: How did Yuqin respond? I said: That's not in the text. Only a joke from Baochai follows—"The three pieces each had their own merit. You two have just tired of teasing me over the last two days, now you've moved on to him." Hong Yiku nodded and said: Right. I was just thinking about how the scene would unfold. What a clever turn. Such a realistic tone. Good. Before his words could land, the beam glared, and Hong Yiku dissolved into nothingness.

The hall echoed with the claps of gunfire. My shoulder was in tremendous pain— the iron claw drew blood. As I spoke with Hong Yiku, I had heard the quiet voice of Xi Chunhan, somewhere nearby. I couldn't discern the exact words, but there was an ancient tranquility in her tone. When I gritted my teeth to turn in her direction, that emerald green shadow had already vanished. Her recitation still held mid-air, trembling. I don't know why, but that voice has since echoed many times within the walls of this stone prison, and the vague perfume of gingko leaves always follows it.

Striding through the hall of ashes, Xue Chi moved towards me. Behind him swelled millions of grey-clothed troops, Greenbirds blanketing the skies, Jiao Datong's vicious grin, and a gently crumbling universe. The soldiers were burning every single fragment of the transcribed *Dream of the Red Chamber*. Xue Chi waved a hand as he approached, and the Greenbird on my shoulder flew to him. Stroking its body, he smiled and said: The new *Dream of the Red Chamber* has been finished—it was recovered under your management. Now we've got quite a few publicity events awaiting your attendance. He whistled, and the Greenbird swooped in, opening its mouth with a spray of blue-grey. My eyes flowered, and I was gone.

TWELVE

I'm not sure why, but after the new book was published, Jiao Datong stopped his inquiries into the central idea of *Dream of the Red Chamber*. Perhaps he thought that if the book truly contained some kind of miraculous force, the Red Chamber Committee wouldn't have been so easily eliminated, and thereby he lost interest. The new edition of *Dream of the Red Chamber* did not seem to achieve the results he had anticipated, and after a few months, they no longer took me for interrogations. Soon, I was forgotten in the stone chambers, with only an old guard, deaf and mute, to deliver my meals every day. After a long time, it seemed that he died, and a middle-aged guard, deaf and mute, replaced him.

After being detained, I was injected with some kind of hallucinogenic, and they had me give a speech—probably with the intent of publicizing that their *Dream of the Red Chamber* was the very same as the one I had read in my time, to signify the complete success of the recovery plan under Jiao Datong's care, and so on. In a daze, I did as they wanted, and my only memory is of a blurred, sweeping crowd nodding along, thundering applause, tall red banners—nothing else. When it was all over, I was thrown into this cell. After spending a few days crawling around, dizzy, vomiting, my mind gradually began to clear. When I thought of the dust and smoke rippling across the great hall, my heart felt as if it was being torn to pieces, and I wept. I attempted to recall the contents of *Dream of the Red Chamber*, and was grateful that it seemed to be with me still. Looking at those clear, unwavering, deeply black lines of handwriting in my head, tears came again to my eyes. They were right to warn me. While the Elixir Against Losses and Forgetting continued to work, I thought of *Dream of the Red Chamber* everyday, but now that the effects have worn off, hardly any of my other memories are within reach, and only *Dream of the Red Chamber* is safe. It remains.

In the days and nights that followed, I lived inside *Dream of the Red Chamber*. My weakened body was thrown into a stifling prison of stone, choking down clouded water, gnawing on god-knows-what, wrapped in a piece of sackcloth that seemed to have been passed down from the Middle Ages, but another me was roaming like a strand of smoke amongst the Grand View Garden. I was fluttering, passing through the floating pavilions, the flowers, the gates, the vermilion chambers and the painted doorframes, the brocade fabrics, the jade ornaments—it's hard to even describe how magnificent it was, this time in my life. After I'd silently repeated the entire text several times, I came up with a game to wile away the days: I would take possession of various characters, following their turns in the narrative—their existence would be my existence. I can't remember how many lives I've lived this way, but this game always begins to ebb at the eightieth chapter. Beyond that point, I would move through the story as if walking underwater, dredged in a kind of sap. It was like something had gone wrong with the texture of the words. There was an obvious fracture, and only then did I remember that only the first eighty chapters were generally acknowledged as being of the original. After some hesitation, I chose to relinquish everything that followed the eightieth chapter, deciding that I would only submerge myself in the pure, absolute *Dream of the Red Chamber*, as a stubborn safeguard of tradition, until the end.

About ten years ago, something strange happened. After I had lived through nearly every character in the text, I began to age more and more quickly. One day, I had fused with a butterfly, fluttering high and low in the wisteria strands of Hengwu Courtyard, and without any warning, I bumped into Cao Xueqin's soul. It was just a tiny flicker, floating beneath the willow shade. I recognized him immediately—needless of reason, without question, just like one would recognize the sun in the night sky. Gathering my slender wings, I chased him in his wanderings around the Garden. He would hide beneath a fallen petal or curve through the crevices of false mountains, sometimes dotting across the icy waters, sometimes descending upon a certain shoulder, as if unhurriedly taking stock of everything he had created with his own hands. I followed him closely, holding on to the baseless thought that if the presence of a soul indicates some kind of regret, then Cao Xueqin, after his death, had every reason to join the world of *Dream of the Red Chamber*—and the more *Dream of the Red Chamber*s there are, the more thinly his soul would be spread across each copy. Since the text has likely been extinguished in the outside world, the eighty chapters I hold in my mind are all that remains in this universe, and as such, the entirety of Cao Xueqin's soul is embedded in me. Were there no more lakes in the world, my small puddle would contain the moon. In the dark, I pursued that soul, that minute light, wavering and drifting, all the way to the end of the eighty chapters. Something miraculous happened there.

I saw every single fate that had been interrupted at the edge of the eightieth chapter. They were growing on their own like vines, chasing one another, intertwining, resolving, then intertwining again, rolling on and on. Immense words streamed through a point of tiny brightness—I struggled to commit them to memory, and realized that there was no need. In my countless circulations through the narrative, I had become so intimate with every line, every connection, and my long immersion in that literary style made me feel as though the words were coming from my own lips… The brightness grew and grew until it illuminated everything. The swaying of the sentences was some holy lyric that had been sung since the waking of the world, and through all the days and nights it had never ceased…

These last ten years have been ones of pure joy. Progress has been slower than expected, but I'm satisfied, because the journey itself has been one of such unimaginable pleasure. A year ago, I reached the hundredth chapter. Last month, I had one hundred and five chapters. I know that *Dream of the Red Chamber* cannot reappear in whole (each universe only has one Red Point), even if it has remade its presence in my mind, because my internal landscape is but one corner of the universe. I can dimly sense that my own life is approaching its end, and it must end before *Dream of the Red Chamber* does. My concern is that my death will be the final annihilation, and the universe will follow in collapse. Your arrival is like something arranged by fate. I know that your memories now contain certain pieces of *Dream of the Red Chamber*, and I hope you keep them well. Even if they too are lost, if you only remember the words *Dream of the Red Chamber*, the universe will remain—because the title, too, is a part of the story.

Now that I've told you everything, I'm going to let all my memories go. *Dream of the Red Chamber* has filled my consciousness end to end, and it will keep developing, at ever greater speeds. I'm certain that I'll never see it in its totality, but as someone once said, to read one line gives us one line's worth of joy. He told me that the banquet must end. *Dream of the Red Chamber* came flooding in from the centers of all things, and will eventually dissipate back into everything that remains. And so death is nothing but a part of its depths.

II

Not long after telling me all this, Chen Xuanshi fell into a stupor. We called the doctor. After a few days of somniloquism and crazed laughter, he died at dawn on November 27, 4876. I had no way of knowing which chapter or which sentence met him in his departure. After leaving the prison on Taozhi Mountain, I took a hard look at the sky— the moon was hanging there, perfectly intact. No sign of damage anywhere upon that face. So it is as he said: *Dream of the Red Chamber* has not disappeared completely, and the universe remains safe and undisturbed. But I can't give full credit to this recording of mine, or exaggerate its importance. What Chen Xuanshi didn't realize is—after he died, the *Dream of the Red Chamber* that had left with him floated on in many other forms, sometimes splintering, sometimes gathering, everywhere and nowhere. The proof came in the next five years, when a few mysterious sentences were found at the bottom of the Mariana Trench, in the embroidery along a butterfly's wing, upon a piece of morning's glow. The scholars all have their many theories and opinions, but I know from where they came.

大头马

Da Tou Ma

TRANSLATED BY
SEAN TOLAND

麦田里的守望者

A CATCHER IN THE RYE

"When a really top-notch boxer throws a punch, his fist is as precise as a surgeon during an operation."

The trainer bobs away from me, then ducks back in. "You hit the target really well," he told me. Without a word, I raise the corner of my mouth. I know I didn't hit the target particularly well, but there was just nothing else to praise. I'm also not training to actually box. I've just joined a daily crowd of nine-to-fiving downtowners who'll change into tight-fitting clothes, head to the cheapest, most obscure piece of basement real estate in a shopping center, and pretend to be boxers. Pretending to be normal people with downtime and physical energy to burn—people who don't act on their excessive, derailing thoughts, who wouldn't just opt for violence at the slightest disagreement.

"So should we get up to something tonight?"

"Sure."

At that time, A and I, L and W, plus W's girlfriend, were sitting among the night-shrouded towers of a busy little residential complex east of Fourth Ring Road. Like we used to do at the H Tech University gardens, we'd been trying to find some place to sit, but failing that, we settled at a barbecue stand outside a small general store. It was just a grill, two tables, and a frosty woman running things. We grabbed one of the tables.

The woman came over about five times, telling us to be a little quieter. "Everyone's trying to sleep," she said.

For real.

We were sitting in the square, surrounded by tower blocks. The wind was a bit strong, and the table could've flipped over at any minute. We had no choice but to ask for a few bottles of beer, their weight lending us a bit of stability. The floors of the buildings were overwhelmingly dark, only a light here and there. In that splendor, we were tempted to do something.

To do some damage.

There have been many times when we'd tried to find a place to sit but failed, leaving us with no choice but to go find a crowd and get some action. But in that moment, I felt like someone could overhear our discussions.

"I think tonight we should do some damage."

"I think so too."

"Like how?"

"Let's flip the table and run," L suggests.

"I think that would be a bit mean." I cast an eye at the woman in charge.

"Right. We do damage, but we"re not bullies," A says.

"That's right."

"We gotta think carefully about who to bully," he says, putting it another way.

"For sure."

Then we all fall silent for a moment.

"Xiao Ma, did you ever realize that, whenever we used to get like this, it's been because we were bored?" A asks.

"Right."

If we were rich, we would have been players. But none of us had money, so we could only be assholes. It would've been unfortunate if you were to fall in love with any of us, because if you did, you'd become a target. Not because we had any ill will or evil intentions, but just because we were bored. There was only one way to become one of us, and that was to have been one of us from the start. Sometimes I felt like this wasn't fair to other people, and to protect myself, I'd even warned a friend against getting close with A or any of them: "For your own good." I don't know how I could have put it any other way, I really don't. There's just no way around it. It's like Mike Tyson said: "That's just life." Plus, there wouldn't be any way for you to prove yourself—to be as bad, as degenerate, just as bored as us? No way.

With what I've just said, you'd almost think that there really were people who wanted to join us.

Before, at H Tech, every time we wanted to get on the roof of Building Five, we'd just kick open the door. The security guard had no choice but to change the locks again and again. That was also just out of boredom. A was right. It wasn't just that we had nothing to do. We were also really bored. When we were most bored was probably around the time that A and X got their hands on an office space at Wanda Plaza, a prime location in a Development Zone. It didn't cost anything because X's family had money, and aside from being used for a little advertising work, it mostly served as a place for us to play video games. J used to be one of us, and he'd get really worked up while he played, yelling, "Fucking peasants!" Later, he graduated, got a job at a bank, and disappeared for a while. The office also shut down after that, and everyone came to Beijing. I was already living here by then, and every time I went back and stayed up half the night shooting pool with A, he'd self-deprecatingly compare himself to a character in a Hou Hsiao-Hsien film—one of those rural guys. "Look at you, coming all the way from the big city to see us."

But I never once brought any gifts with me.

Afterwards, they all left H, one after another. A and I, we saw each other about once every two weeks, not even close to how much time we had spent together in H. Back then, we were fugitives in the night, busting onto rooftops and—

"You had a motorcycle back then," I said.

"Yeah," A said.

"An electric one," W added. "You and me went and bought it together."

"Why'd you have to bring that up?" A asked.

"Like a scooter," I said.

"Yeah. A scooter," A said.

"An electric scooter," W said.

We burst out laughing. A said with a straight face, "Do you remember when we went to buy that bike... and I wasn't earning a single cent?"

"Yeah."

"Back then, there was a girl there, standing by the motorcycles, real fine, super long legs, tits out to here. I just went up to her and said hey, your bike's not bad."

This conversation happened as we were trying and failing to find somewhere to sit, turning back towards the barbecue stand.

"So I asked her, how much for the bike? She said not so much, a hundred thousand or so." A paused for a second, and we all held back our laughter. "I was just dumbstruck, and then I said, oh, that's nothing."

We all laughed like crazy again.

"That's nothing, I said," A repeated. "Then we bought a scooter."

"About five thousand," W added.

Back then, we had three scooters between us, so six people could ride together. Once we even got three people on one. Me, A, and J. It was summer, and J was on vacation. He'd been in grad school, studying finance. Not long before that, he'd wanted to get the Fields Medal, but by then had for sure given up the idea. Eventually he got a job, got hitched, and now he's pretty much completely out of the group. "Fucking peasants!" Even after he left, we still kept that catchphrase of his.

Usually we didn't go out until eight or nine at night, after playing a few games and having something to eat. Sometime after midnight, we'd move out in a squadron of scooters, taking over the empty streets and driving side by side, no faster than walking speed. That was when strange ideas would pop up.

"Let's go smash a TV."

We weren't into stealing or bullying, and we didn't take advantage of people or harass girls. Typically our crimes had no purpose, no meaning at all. And we didn't get in fights, mostly because we didn't have the knack for it. We definitely would've lost.

Smashing TVs was good enough. Our motives were simple, but you could read a lot out of them. Anyway, that sort of thing didn't take much effort. The fact is, smashing TVs, smashing microwaves, smashing washing machines, there's no fundamental difference. Breaking onto a rooftop or breaking into someone's house is also basically the same thing. But people found it hard to believe we really did all that. Afterwards, I wrote some of it into a novel. I don't know why I wanted to write a novel, maybe because there was some competition going on, maybe because I thought it would be fun, and maybe—guilty conscience. I could only pretend to write fiction, but the truth is I'm just too dumb for it. If I didn't really go through something, I've no chance of writing anything decent about it. So I could only write one kind of story—

"You know, recently I've been writing about us," I say.

"What?" W says.

"Did you forget that the first rule is you don't talk about us?" A says.

"No one's going to believe any of it anyway," I say.

That was true. A film company had bought the rights to the story, but they had no idea how to shoot it. I drafted a couple of outlines and thought up plenty of ways to round out the plot, but they all got shot down. "The significance! Themes! Why do they keep smashing TVs?"

To tell the truth, I don't know why. I could never say it back then—that we just weren't thinking much. Besides, I'd practically forgotten how that novel was written in the first place.

Most of our group had something to do with H Tech: some were students, some had gone to the affiliated high school, and there were also those like me who had no connection with H Tech. But every time the security guard asked, I'd pretend A's parents were my parents. "My mom works here in the math department. Her name's XXX." After a while the guards were no longer totally clear on who was XXX's kid, A or me. To be honest, other than A, I've never been able to trade more than a few sentences with anyone. Take tonight, when we bumped into W in the complex on our way to have a proper dinner. A went for a smoke and I could only strike up this sort of conversation with L:

"Did you graduate yet?" I asked.

"Not yet," L said.

"I remember that you were in grad school at the Chinese Academy of Sciences a while back?" I asked.

"I started a doctorate," L said.

"Oh," I said.

See, we really weren't close. As soon as A came back, L and I fell back into a state of apathy regarding one another's daily life.

That's a lot like the situation I have going on at the gym. Maybe that's why I've always loved going there. Other than the necessary interactions at work, I've slowly cut off all of my friends. I know it's not healthy, but who made the rule that people have to lead healthy lives? Besides, most of my friends are idiots, and I guess to them, I'm an idiot too.

There are eight trainers at the gym in total. I've only ever seen five, and each of them has their own style. There's one named Q who's especially energetic, and every time he starts a class, he always shows off by informing everyone of the following: 1. he studied abroad in Europe; 2. his classes are extremely well taught; 3. when it comes to fighting, he's never met his match. Other than that, he's pretty alright. Also, he's particularly interested in me, always trying to get me to open my mouth and say something. "Why are you so shy?" Every time he asks, I just smile politely. I don't want to tell him that the reason I go to the gym is because there, I don't have to talk. Get it?

Obviously, Q is not his real name. He has a name that everyone knows, because for sure anyone would have met one or two people with that name. I've got one. The Q I know was a primary school classmate. He was one of the most mischievous kids in class, but super cute—the two biggest eyes I'd ever seen. A long time after I transferred to that school, I found out his father was dead. A police officer, gone in the line of duty. One time, when he did something wrong, the teacher told him: "Tomorrow have your dad come into school." He stood in the middle of class and said without a single care, "I haven't got a dad." It almost looked like he was smiling.

My memory has always been pretty bad, and it's gotten worse with age. Usually I can't even remember what happened yesterday. Thinking back on that incident now, I can no longer say for sure if I saw it with my own eyes or if it was just a rumor, something that happened before I transferred. In any case, I'd really wanted to be a cop when I was a kid, but after I realized how easy it is to die on the job, I gave up on the idea.

Many years later, I happened to see Q one more time, in front of the high school. By then he had grown up, and so had I. He looked a lot like Chow Yun-Fat as an adult, and I watched him with great curiosity for a long time before I finally recognized him. He was standing with a few people at the gates when a luxurious limo drove onto the grounds. He went up, knocked on the window, and exchanged a few words with the person inside. The whole thing seemed like a Hong Kong movie, a gangster flick. We eventually got back in touch after some back and forth, but I never asked him if the things I'd heard about him were true, like how his mother had become a prostitute, how he'd gone to the hotel where she worked with a bunch of people, trying to make a scene. How he never finished middle school and was sent to a juvenile correction center for fighting, getting locked up for a year. When I saw him that one time, he'd probably just gotten out. How he still liked the same girl he liked in primary school. My guess is that it's all true.

He had the most beautiful mom out of the whole school. If I had a mother like that, and she became a hooker to support the family, I'd also go crazy with sadness.

Most of the time we'd only chat for a bit. I've forgotten all of it by now, and we've lost touch.

I think that might be the fundamental difference between Q and me—between Q and us. We never experienced any real suffering, so when we did our damage, it was more like a game. There was no profound reason behind it. Players in spirit with no money, parasites of society, trash. Maybe trash is a bit overblown. Just bad people with too much time on their hands.

All to say, we deserved a beating.

The last time that my high school form tutor caught me cutting class, he asked me why I needed to be that way. I also found it hard to explain to him. Like how every time he caught me, I'd put my hands behind my back, and quietly shred a tissue into little pieces. There wasn't any reason, I just didn't want to go to class. But not even I quite believed that explanation, because when I skipped class, I didn't do anything meaningful—I didn't play games, go home, watch cartoons, or go on dates. I didn't do anything except walk around the school aimlessly. But that doesn't sound convincing in the least, because our school was pitifully small. For much of the time I did absolutely nothing, and just hung out on the roof alone.

People like me and A, we don't have anything to do on the roof. We just want to be there, up high. We just need to stand at the highest possible place.

In Beijing, we stopped doing much of that. For one, we moved around a lot, and there wasn't anywhere that we knew really well, so we had no idea which buildings had roofs we could get onto. There are too many buildings in Beijing. For another thing, in Beijing, if you stand around on a roof doing nothing, people immediately assume you're going to jump off.

I met someone in that exact situation on a roof once. It was before dawn, probably four in the morning, and we both got a little embarrassed. I suspected he was there to jump off, he suspected I was there to jump off.

"Well, after you?"

It was on the tips of both our tongues.

"No no, I'm not thinking of jumping. I'm not thinking anything, I just like being up high."

See, that's really hard to believe.

After that, I stopped climbing up on roofs so much, and switched to going underground. One sign of growing up is that you learn not to bother other people.

The most handsome trainer at the gym is the most gentle, while the strictest one likes to hit. Every time I train with him, I get hit, and there's been times when he hits so hard that I almost cry, but I just endure it. To tell the truth, it doesn't hurt so much when he hits you, it's more of a symbolic beating. I don't know why I feel so bad when I get hit. Maybe because it's evidence that I haven't done well enough. Most people can do thirty perfect push-ups, but I'm shaking by my tenth. Maybe I should read *Catch-22* again, even though I've never finished it to begin with. Or maybe *The Old Man and the Sea*, *Moby Dick*, whatever. One of those books that makes you feel like shit if you don't persevere.

Piece of shit.

Every time I get hit, it feels like the trainer is saying just that.

"You should put your whole weight behind a punch, not just your arm," he says into my ear.

Piece of shit.

For a long time I didn't do anything at all, and later I realized that I'd been waiting for someone that whole time, like the Cus D'Amato to my Mike Tyson or the Bazin to my Truffaut. When Tyson was brought to D'Amato, they talked for a while and D'Amato said: "I've been waiting for this kid all my life." So many years had already passed before I read that line, and I suddenly felt incredibly sad. Because by then, I'd practically forgotten about all of it. I no longer lazed around, I no longer did any damage. For quite some time, at least, A and I were scrupulously following the rules. Making money, going to work, pretending our lives were on track, making a show of it, as if there was meaning. Unless you count my daily routine of going to an underground gym and fighting with strangers, I think I seemed relatively normal.

I'd already grown up. Still, no one had ever said, I've been waiting for this kid all my life. A kid like you.

The very last time he caught me cutting class, the form tutor made it clear that he wouldn't bother me anymore: "Do what you want." I was a bit disappointed. I'd thought that he and I would play cat and mouse until graduation. But he obviously didn't care about me that much—there were forty-something students in the class, the college entrance exams were coming up, everyone else was more deserving of his attention. At graduation, I wrote a thank you card to every teacher. You know, the super polite, so-grateful-for-your-support bullshit. I really did like them a lot. There was one time I helped a friend raise money for the orphanage—don't think too much of it, I'm definitely not that good of a person. It was just for fun, and I'd never been to the orphanage, I didn't even know where it was. If one of those kids had stopped me on the street and put their grubby hands on me to ask for money, guess what I would have done? Fuck off, you brat, careful I don't beat you. But all in the name of charity, I ran to every single office in the teachers' building, asking for money whenever I saw an adult. It felt amazing, because I finally had a chance to get something from the teachers. The chemistry teacher didn't even think twice before whipping out two hundred yuan. The math teacher went on and on about how he had a kid on the way, and by the end I'd gotten two tins of powdered milk out of him. The form tutor grabbed a ten yuan note right out of his son's hand and gave it to me. I never got to the principal. He was on the third floor, so probably before I even made it up there, he'd sensed what was going on and ran off like a coward. In the end, it proved that the teachers weren't so bad. I've already forgotten what I wrote in my card to the form tutor, but years later, our old class monitor went to see him, and afterwards he came and told me that there was nothing in the teacher's empty drawer, except for the note I'd written. I said, Old H is a real phony.

I've just thought of at least one time when I skipped class and actually did something. I borrowed a cell phone from a classmate and called Q. "Hello?" It took a long time before the call connected. "I'm looking for XX," I said. XX was a name I made up. "Who?" "XX. You're not XX?" "No." "Oh, sorry, wrong number." "Mm." Then I hung up.

I can't say when I stopped waiting, only that when you've been up on a roof for a while, there comes a time when the wind gets stronger and stronger, and you start to understand that no one's coming, that you should get down and do something. Maybe at some point I started to realize that there's a very simple reason why I hadn't met my Cus D'Amato: I'm not Mike Tyson.

One time when we were doing some damage, we got caught completely red-handed—by an old lady. We were prepared to run off, but she actually thanked us for smashing her TV, and even invited us to sit, putting out peanuts and a plate of fruit. We just looked at each other helplessly and sat down. But we didn't dare eat anything. It wasn't that we thought she'd poisoned it, but it looked like no one had touched that stuff for a hundred years.

I know how it would've tasted, because every time I go visit my grandparents, they pull out the same things. Whenever my grandfather sees me, he sees someone barely keeping his head above water. Looking at me with these despairing eyes, trying to be compassionate. The last time I saw him, he didn't ask the same questions. He just suddenly said to me, Are you lonely in Beijing? If you're lonely, just come back home.

I couldn't look at him and answer. For one thing, it's complicated. The other thing is that he'd had a tumor, and after the operation, he got a hernia, so his stomach swelled up a ton, even though it was already pretty big. But I just couldn't look at him, I felt like his life was ticking away second by second, right before my eyes. He had touched on some essential questions, and I couldn't face those kinds of truths. Anyway, was my answer that important? I just pretended like I hadn't heard what he said.

He hasn't died yet, but he's dead to me. I guess that's pretty brutal. But I just can't take any more sadness.

One sign of growing up is: you learn not to bother other people.

Maybe D also felt the same way. That's why he suddenly disappeared for so long. It was only after a bunch of my messages went unanswered that I realized something was a bit off. By then, the situation was already pretty bad. I've never wanted to be a good person, and when I say that you need to learn not to bother other people, I really mean that no one should bother me. That's why before, when D used to call me, I'd reject it most of the time. D was one of those people who seems really cool and interesting when you first meet them, someone who's always coming up with fun ideas, but afterwards they just get more and more annoying. At that time, I would guess that everyone was ignoring him. Everyone just said, D's my friend. But in the end, no one knew what kind of trouble he had gotten into. No one was really that concerned. It wasn't any use to be concerned. After all, it's not like anyone could deal with things better than D himself.

In that way, I—like most people—don't amount to much of anything. My way of justifying it to myself is to say that the majority of people in this world will never decide if they're going to be a bad person or a good person, because in this lifetime, they'll probably never encounter any major moral dilemmas. Even if they do, most will just find some way around it. And with that, they can go on living naturally, under the illusion that they're pretty good people.

But no matter what, I still tried to get in touch with D. Through his friends, with the people he was still in contact with, I made all sorts of attempts. Then, after finding out what kind of trouble D was in, I felt stupid. I saw that D and my grandfather were the same. They'd both become the kind of person whose life was slipping away one bit at a time, right in front of me. Nothing to be done about it.

Are you lonely in Beijing? If you're lonely, just come back home. Because I'm also pretty lonely.

I don't know why I got so angry at D. Maybe I was getting mad at myself, or at something else, like the world. Picturing some vague, vast subject helped me vent that rage a little. I still have plenty of anger about other things, but I don't blame other people and I don't blame myself, I just blame the world.

When I'm not angry, we go and do some damage. When I'm angry, I don't want to do anything. To do anything would make me feel like a bully.

I don't want to bully anyone, I just want to fight.

At the gym, I'm always fighting with myself. Keep it up for ten seconds and you'll hurt like you're getting beat up. Keep it up another ten seconds and the lactic acid will let you experience something called despair. Now get up, don't plant your heels, stand with proper form. Good. One more set.

The only pleasure is when the fat guy at the gym groans like he's having an orgasm, and the whole place bursts out laughing. That's when I'll also let go of my image as some kind of stoic warrior, and I laugh along. Maybe I don't really want to fight, maybe I just want to punish myself, who knows. In the end, I've just done too many stupid things, and maybe I have too many enemies. Who knows if all those people whose TVs I smashed aren't going to show up at my door one day, saying, Let's fight to the death? When they do, I hope I'll be able to answer like a hero: I did it all on my own. I hope in that moment I'll be Mike Tyson, or at least it'll seem that way.

"Coach, I want to learn to fight." After the trainer named Q added my WeChat, that's what I said to him. Brimming with enthusiasm, he then told me which places in Beijing are the best for teaching Brazilian jiu-jitsu and which are best for freestyle sparring, and he even sent me a file with his price list at the top. After that, I never took his class again. Of course, the biggest reason was because he'd opened his own gym, and no longer had time to teach in the basement. So I kept coming every day to take a beating from the demon coach.

"If you want to learn how to hit, first you have to learn how to take a hit."

As summer approached, more and more people came to the gym. Some of them wanted to lose weight, and some wanted to run marathons. The former learned pretty quickly that this was not the place for them, while the latter were busy checking out the gear of other runners to assess their experience, trying to decide if it was worth it to socialize. There were plenty of times that I just wanted them to shut up, but I knew it would be a futile fight—they'd just think of me as a pretentious dick, or ask themselves if this guy is mentally ill. There was an even bigger chance that they wouldn't take anything I said to heart. I also never dared to fight the trainer, as it was obvious that before even getting out a single punch, I'd wind up on the floor. So I just kept going, keeping it up for ten more seconds.

Whenever I didn't return my friends' messages, and it got to the point where I really had to respond, I'd just tell them I've been busy every day, don't bother me unless something's really wrong. If you need to, come find me. As for the thing with D, I rounded up one of my most clever friends for help. We tried to go around and see him—no luck. After that, there was once, when I'd tried everything and failed, and almost out of desperation, I sent him a text:

> "As stars, a fault of vision, or a lamp,
> A pantomime, dew drops, or a bubble,
> A dream, a lightning flash, or cloud,
> So should one view all conditioned things."

Against all expectations, he called me right after. All choked up. My anger suddenly disappeared. I realized that, since I'd never met a Cus D'Amato, maybe it's because I could become Cus D'Amato. One day, when I am very, very old, and my fists are totally useless, I could wait patiently at the sidelines, and I'll say to the kid who's been led to me, "I've been waiting for you a long time."

I've been waiting for you all my life.

"I think we have to do something."

At that point we'd moved from the barbecue stand to a pitiful little playground in the complex. It was really just a strip of grass with a prefab slide in the middle. That's what A says to us, sitting on the slide.

"The way you said that makes me think of someone," I say.

"Who?"

"Murong Fu."

They all laugh like crazy. All except A, because he hasn't read *Demi-Gods and Semi-Devils*.

"But we should do something. Something real, something sensational, earth-shattering, a big deal."

"Yeah," I say.

"What if we shoot a fake documentary?"

"Sounds good to me."

"So what should we shoot?"

"I think we could shoot *The Murder of a TV*."

"You mean we could shoot what you wrote about us?"

"Right."

"Then it's not a fake documentary, it's just a documentary."

"That works too."

"So we should go smash a TV first."

"Right."

"To shoot something sensational, we'd have to do something sensational first," A sighs.

"True."

"Fine then."

A jumps down from the slide. "Well, first let's go see if you can get on the roof of that building."

"Okay."

"Before that we should think about who to bully."

"Right, we definitely don't bully people."

Now I really have something to think about.

江离

Jiang Li

**TRANSLATED BY
SHANGYANG FANG**

诗三首

Deer Flock

Today is not a day worth remembering.
I'm worried about my deer flock.
They've left me. Each time
after the technical demonstrations
they abandon me further.
It's been a week now, rain has paralyzed
the traffic. It's been a week,
and we remain tangled in an argument of rights
and wrongs— Is this the stupid
but necessary way? In the brightly-lit conference room,
I listed a subset of unconquerables
on the back of a cigarette paper
and thought of the deer flock again,
their round black eyes vigilant
of danger, but at the same time bewitched
by the mosaic of pale yellow and crimson,
forgetting to cross the autumn mountain.
Their antlers grown out of a deep
nostalgia for the ancient sound of wind
ensnaring a slice of memory
no thicker than the frost on a fallen leaf,
no thinner than the vast loneliness after the snow.
O, deer flock, another track of hoof prints appearing
in the flotsam of my sleep,
letting me pluck the void from a nihilist,
offering you a safe passage through the winter.

Miniature Landscape

I hardly noticed this potted bonsai.
In twilight, enveloped in a layer of mist, modest and self-sufficient,
as if it had been here since the dawn of time.

One corner of it has seen some damage.
A few ancient pines, two steep cliffs, clearly, it's dried up
in this rainless November.
A toy boat docked at the sandbar.

This miniature landscape once occupied a place
in the history of private life, though more often, people considered it
an accessory to leisure, an art of simulation.

When peddlers and carriers are troubled by labor,
and disheartened intellectuals seek solace in retreat—landscapes,
gardens, poetry, and paintings,
all constitute a bitter prelude towards nature.

Perhaps this is what art is about:
relating to sadness and vexation, not just amusement.

Even the most decadent poem about the wind
and the moon must always be linked with resistance.

Personal joy and sorrow have shaped the landscape before me
in its pine tips, in the texture of rocks,
stirring an ancient echo. A sparrow must have arrived here
before me, listening to the darkening rain.

A Peach Blossom

After Chen Xianfa

The sky is grey.
I walk within a greyness that seems whole.
Only one peach blossom
lonely, barely opening at its edges.
For a moment,
I thought I was that peach blossom
in the poem of Liu Yuxi,
witnessing the travelers' disappearing faces,
the flames pulsating in their eyes.
When they say, the blossom
is an externalized movement of the heart,
or its existence is an apotheosis
of your looking, the end
of your looking… Traveler, are you prepared
to reconstruct its petals
as they wither—the flower emerging
in language neither real
nor unreal—in the seeing of its name—
the utopia of nomenclature torments you—
perhaps it might just be an early cherry blossom,
or a pendulous crabapple.

三三

SanSan

TRANSLATED BY
MICHAEL DAY

韦氏

LADY WEI'S DREAM

More than ten years prior to that most unusual evening, I had resigned my post in the imperial government and, on a friend's introduction, entered a new line of work, gold trading. I soon discovered that business and officialdom were little different: it remained necessary for me to lay painstaking plans and constantly seek out slight advantages. With the passage of the years, the burden became unbearable. In addition to that, persistent border incursions by Turkish tribes sent shockwaves through the economy, and business was steadily worsening. I was weighed down with worry, troubled by doubt over the workings of fate. Truly at the end of my rope, I had no other option but to seek help from an old friend. My plan that day was to cross the Han River to the south, find this friend, and beg him to lend me money.

When I reached the riverbank, it was deep in the night, and the reflections of clouds flitted over the misted river. I was told the next ferry would not be departing until dawn, so I sought refuge nearby in a dreary, dilapidated inn that befit my meager budget. Upon unburdening myself of my luggage, I realized that I was not in the least tired, so I decided to go downstairs and have a drink in the tavern. I was halfway down the stairs when I saw shadows flickering upon the door curtain, cast by candlelight, and heard the hubbub of laughter and conversation. I paid for my drink and seated myself amongst the other patrons.

We were five. The oldest man wore priest's garb, two resembled scholars, and one wore a black robe, with a long, straight nose and cheeks marred by measle scars. The latter said little, and when he did speak, his tone was as frigid as his expression. The windows on all sides were open, and to the south, faint light glinted on the peaks of the rapids. The mist was heavier than I remembered, and the wind carried the damp, raw odor of spring. Our conversation that night encompassed a wide range of topics, from Chang'an's most popular magic acts to Japanese envoy Awato no Mahito, who had visited China the previous autumn. Shortly, our conversation had meandered to the subject of the trouble along the border, Empress Wu Zhao's consolidation of power, and, finally, Xu Jingye's uprising eighteen years earlier. The man in black gradually became more talkative, letting slip that he was crossing the river to visit the grave of an old friend who had been executed for colluding against the empire with Xu.

At this, everyone's interest was aroused. We all sank into our own silent thoughts. I could not help but recall a friend of my own who had died many years earlier, Zhang Chujin. He had entered officialdom in the Xianheng era of the reign of Emperor Gaozong. At the time of the uprising, he was high minister of the state of Guangling, and he too was put to death for colluding with Xu. The night air seemed to exert a calming effect, and the knots of my memory loosened. I recounted Zhang's story, telling everyone how honest and generous he had been when we were serving side by side. After deciding to follow Xu, he had deliberately distanced himself from me, I imagine to avoid implicating me in the plot. For years, I had harbored resentment against him, but when the Shenlong Rebellion was put down, the scales fell from my eyes. I had met Zhang's wife, a woman gifted with special insight into the Mandate of Heaven, on several occasions. On the eve of the uprising, she wore mourning clothes, and she was seen crying as she saw her husband off.

"She set out to do what couldn't be done. She was a heroine," said one of the scholars.

"She set out to do what shouldn't be done, acting in defiance of heaven's will. A heroine? I have another word for her," said the priest in a tone of venomous scorn.

The scholar appeared to be readying a retort, but at the priest's knowing smirk, held his tongue. The priest looked to me, lowered his head, and said, "This story of yours has been circulating in Chang'an for thirty years. I have heard it before. But there is more to tell." The priest was mistaken. Zhang had passed away just eighteen years before—this was no thirty-year-old tall tale. But I could never have expected the incredible story he proceeded to tell.

⚮

Thirty years ago, during the reign of Emperor Taizong, there was peace in Chang'an and throughout the empire. The men gathered in the gardens to drink liquor and recite poetry, and everywhere the women danced and sang. In those days there were seven or eight dragons in Chang'an, and when they were in good spirits, they would emerge from the clouds, raining golden pills of immortality down upon the city. In this dreamlike atmosphere of intoxication, even eighty-year-old men held out hope of finding love. Beautiful women and gifted scholars and trysts between the two were the people's favorite conversation topics. It was because of her outstanding looks that people first took note of the youngest daughter of the Wei family, whom we will call Lady Wei.

Lady Wei's beauty enthralled all. Quite a few poets had heard of her and composed odes in her honor, but all those who actually laid eyes on her ripped their fancy writing paper to shreds and admitted the futility of words. It was said that Lady Wei once crossed paths with a peacock from the Western realms—it had spread its tail and kept it open for three days, until finally all the feathers had fallen out. A steady stream of suitors proposed marriage to her, some accompanied by large cheerleading contingents, and others slipped gifts such as tobacco to Lady Wei's servants, but none won so much as a second glance.

At first, Lady Wei's mother went so far as to encourage her daughter's aloofness. But when it became clear that Lady Wei truly did not intend to marry, she was unable to hold back some anxiety. Madame Wei did everything she could to urge her daughter to take action. On the night of a full moon, she brought a bowl of stewed chicken feet to her daughter's room and sat down for a serious discussion. However, they only talked circles around each other, with Lady Wei finally refusing to commit. Enraged, Madame Wei tipped over the teapot, and scalding water spilled over the table. Madame Wei said, How could you be so stupid? There are only a few golden years in a woman's life, and you're wasting them. Lady Wei said, The problem is the antiquated ideas that fill your brain. The times have changed. Madame Wei said, Do as you wish, then. I'm simply worried about you. Lady Wei said, There is no need for concern. Two years from now, I will marry a man named Zhang Chujin. At this, Madame Wei started. Lady Wei went on, When I was fifteen, I had a prophetic dream. In the dream, I lived my entire life to the end, and I've realized that in reality, I'm simply reliving that dream in slow motion. Madame Wei reached out and stroked her daughter's forehead, asking, Do you have a fever? Lady Wei shook her head and went on telling her mother about the dream.

In the beginning, all was wonderful. Chujin and I had a son. After the wedding, his career as an official went smoothly, and in less than ten years, he was appointed minister of Guangling. But in his seventh year as minister, Chujin was dragged into a rebellion plot, which led to a death sentence for him and nearly all his relatives. Only our daughter-in-law and I were spared. We were imprisoned in the side quarters of the palace, sentenced to penal servitude, given only scant servings of vegetables to eat. These years of atonement without redemption stretched on. How could I have guessed that eighteen years later, a general pardon would be declared, and I would be set free?

Madame Wei found herself on the edge of her seat, as if listening to a storyteller's entrancing tale rather than the story of her real daughter's life. Despite listening quietly thus far, Madame Wei now broke in: Would it not be better to die in the palace than to be freed and have nowhere to go? Lady Wei replied, Yes, but I had no say in the matter. At twilight we left the palace, driving our horses hard until we reached the Han River. When we came to the riverbank, it was nearly the break of dawn. Frost crusted the tips of our hair, and the nip in the spring air seemed to deepen the cold in our hearts. The last ferry had long since departed—we would be forced to wait until the following day. The more we pondered our predicament, the deeper our grief grew, and we sat by the river, heads buried in our hands, and wept. It was then that we spied a grand mansion in the distance. Though gnawed upon by foreboding, we had no choice but to go beg for a bed. The wide gate to the estate yawned open. We passed through it, then several more wooden gates, seeing no sign of another living soul. At the base of the steps to the great hall, which was locked, a grove of cherry trees grew. Deep in the black night, the blossoms were in riotous bloom. A shaft of clear white light spilled over the courtyard—was it a moon ray, or a mist of radiant white petals? Just moments ago, we had been wandering by the secluded black riverbank, and now we were in what felt like a fairy tale. We swooned, disoriented. Together we reclined upon the steps, and in moments my daughter-in-law was asleep. There I lay, breathing the moist air that filtered down through the branches, gazing at the round, rice cake-like moon. Suddenly, without knowing why, I was weeping. In the palace, despite enduring years of toil and torment, I had never cried once, but beneath the beautiful flowers and the moon, my control had slipped. Just then, I spied a young man in a white robe, accompanied by an old servant, charging toward us, and my daughter-in-law woke with a start. When we explained who we were and where we had come from, the youth sank to his knees and wailed. It was an extraordinary coincidence: he was Zhang Chujin's grandson, and we were presently in the late Zhang's estate. Pointing to the locked room behind us, he informed us that Zhang's belongings were inside, and we went together to unlock the door. We recognized nearly everything inside, including many items of which Zhang had previously told me. My daughter-in-law and I moved onto the estate. Fifteen years passed, and I died.

Madame Wei listened wordlessly, eyes wide. She thought of inquiring as to her own fate, but hesitated and in the end said nothing. Dawn was breaking, and the edges of the churning grey clouds had begun to glow white. Madame Wei stood and prepared to leave, thinking that perhaps our paths through life truly were determined by destiny. Madame Wei never forgot her daughter's words, and went on to implore numerous Buddhists and Daoists for explanation. Not only was Lady Wei beautiful, she told a fantastic story—needless to say, word spread like wildfire. Recall that this was a time when people believed in dreams. With a few days, Lady Wei's dream was a legend throughout Chang'an.

By the time the priest finished, the red candle had burned down to a nub. The bartender switched the candle for a fresh one and topped up our cups. We all downed our liquor in one gulp, as if to wash down the extraordinary tale. Zhang and I had been close, but it was the first time I had ever heard the complete story of Lady Wei, and it stirred emotions of all sorts.

The bartender, who had been listening in the entire time, now posed a question. "A tumultuous life that took extraordinary turns. If it were you, would you live your life in accordance with a dream?"

We glanced at each other briefly before giving our answers, one by one. We had in our midst one determined realist: dreams, he insisted, are illusion, with no bearing on the workings of fate as we experience it, yet the "secondary" experience of a dream turned real can deepen our understanding of fate. Two others, naturally inclined to faith in a power greater than humanity, compared heaven doling out destinies to a mother giving pastries to hungry children; we had no choice but to accept our lot in life. Then it was my turn to speak, and I mumbled something to the effect that it was good to live in accordance with the Mandate of Heaven. Only the man in the black robe remained hesitant. After a long moment, he spoke.

"If you become aware that your current course of action is mistaken, why would you not choose a different one?" asked the man in black.

"No matter what you may do, fate is the same," said the priest, smiling.

"I cannot believe that. Do you mean to say all we can do in life is drift with the current?"

That, however, was as far as the argument went. It was a beautiful spring evening, and we had been sitting for so long—the consensus was that a breath of fresh night air was called for. And so we set out for a walk along the river. The water had recently receded from a high point, and the sandy soil was soft and wet beneath our feet. We were strolling along, talking and laughing, when we spotted two small figures hobbling in our direction. We saw at a glance that they wore women's clothes. They walked very, very slowly, as if extremely fatigued.

"Quickly, what year is this?" asked the priest with a look of alarm, counting on his fingers.

"Chang'an Year 2 of the reign of the sacred empress, and the thirty-ninth year—the year of the tiger—in the sexagenary cycle," I said.

"I might have guessed," exclaimed the priest, but before he could explain further, the women had staggered over and were standing before us. They wore matching dresses. One was a bit younger, with light skin the hue of rice paper. The other was older, perhaps in her early fifties. She looked familiar. We must have met somewhere, but where? I was pondering that when I suddenly realized why the priest had inquired about the year. The imperial court had proclaimed a general amnesty in Chang'an 2, just as it had in the year Lady Wei was set free. It occurred to me that I was face to face with Lady Wei herself. The ravages of life had weathered her legendary beauty, and before me in the spring mist stood an absolutely ordinary middle-aged woman. Face now creased by deep lines, she exuded an air of solemn composure.

"Milady, do you remember me?" Fearing perhaps she didn't, I added, "I served in the imperial government by Chujin's side."

Lady Wei nodded, but it was readily apparent that she had yet to come to her senses. My companions all wore startled looks. Having heard my words, they were now recognizing, one by one, the woman before us. Then somebody said, "Milady, the home and the family you seek are here on the banks of the Han River."

Moments ago, we had been in the tavern, talking about Lady Wei's dream. Now, by the riverbank, we had become part of Lady Wei's destiny. A series of walls had crumbled. I couldn't help wondering, why did Lady Wei not know us? Had she not seen us in the dream?

"Allow me to hazard a guess: you have come here from Chang'an." She let out a sigh. "A place full of old dreams better left in dust."

"You can relax now, Milady. Good fortune awaits, just as the dream foretold," said one of the scholars.

Lady Wei lowered her head and said nothing for a long while. Presently, the hint of a sad smile appeared on her face. She said, "Look—do you see anything out there but darkened ruins? No mansion stands on the banks of this river."

At this, we were all stunned into silence. Even the priest, previously so levelheaded, wore a quizzical expression. Then I noticed that impenetrable clouds cloaked the moon—no ray would shine down upon the courtyard this evening. When we remained silent, Lady Wei went on, "The dream came to an end here by the banks of the river. I invented everything after that."

"Why?" someone asked softly.

"Perhaps I didn't wish to worry my mother. Perhaps enthusiasm got the better of me. Perhaps it was... something I am incapable of describing in words. Once, when I was a girl, I got lost in the woods. It was springtime, and the cherry trees were in full bloom. I lay down on the ground, cried myself to sleep, and when I woke, I was in my bed. The butler had waited until I fell asleep, then scooped me up and carried me home. When I was older, I realized the cherry grove was in fact quite small. I had almost found my way out on my own, but I didn't know it then." Lady Wei spoke haltingly, as if slowly emerging from a daze. "The grand mansion with the cherry grove, that was mere fantasy, but as time went on, I found myself beginning to believe. So many years have passed. Had I not clung to that illusion, I would never have survived so long."

None of us could find the right reply, and after a few final pleasantries, we turned and headed back to the tavern. Before we left, Lady Wei said to us, the whole world is a hallucination, and in the face of heaven's implacable will, all our suffering is hollow. Still pondering what she meant, I turned to take one last parting glance. Just then, I saw her leave her daughter-in-law's side and cast herself into the Han River. There was a small splash and a splatter of spray, and Lady Wei swirled away on the surging current, clutching her old dream like a tiny, glowing jewel.

毛尖

Mao Jian

TRANSLATED BY
YIQIAO MAO

没有人看见草生长

NO ONE SEES THE GRASSES GROWING

Often I wonder if those years, ranging from the late eighties to the nineties, should be treated as treasures or traumas. It was the summer of 1988 that I arrived in Shanghai, and aside from the three years of doctoral studies in Hong Kong, that part of my life was set entirely within the East China Normal University campus. I've walked every single inch along the Liwa River.

My bachelor's degree was in Foreign Languages, which saw about five men to every woman, while the male-to-female ratio of the Chinese Department was much more well-balanced—unlike now. Whenever we had classes in the Humanities Building, we would peek into the rooms where the Chinese Language students sat, envious at that perfect gender equilibrium. Later, I became determined to enter the Chinese Department for my postgraduate studies, and my roommates made fun of me for it, teasing that I was switching camps for the sake of my health. But jokes aside, the time I spent in that department were among the most unforgettable years of my time as a student.

The truth is, in the eighties, it was impossible to resist the passions of the Chinese Department. The notice boards were plastered with adverts promoting literary lectures, and all sorts of clubs and societies adopted the grandiose affectations of *belles-lettres*, prancing about the center of campus. If someone were to ask you about going corporate after graduation, you'd have to self-reflect on the unrefined impression you must have been giving off. Those years were the golden age of Casanovas, who made names for themselves by proclaiming their undying love for poetry, and any girl who could be moved by Rilke would inevitably enter into a spontaneous fling with one of these campus poets.

There was a great many of them, these campus poets, and half weren't even registered students. Back then, they didn't monitor the dormitories so strictly. Each room had eight beds, but hosting a ninth guest for a sustained period of time was quite normal.

To this day I still find it strange, these chaotic relationships that somehow never became obscene—how we kept them up, how they've since disappeared. During my second year as an undergraduate, I lived in a dorm room that was home to fourteen people. After supper, the unattached would head off to study, while the coupled would stay in. At night, when we returned, we'd see the mosquito nets ruffling, quiet murmurs bubbling beneath. In the famous words of our composition professor, the modernist poet Song Lin: "The more one drinks, the thirstier one becomes." We were compassionate to even those who drank poison to satiate that thirst. Once, a roommate's hometown friend ran over to tell us that her university had just caught a dorm in action: an eight-person room with thirteen residents—both male and female!

We didn't have a very strong reaction to her news, but she went on and on: "Depravity, what depravity!" I still remember the sight of her, lamenting and wringing her wrists, then pausing to inhale a plate of stir-fried river snails. But in those days, the word "depravity" almost had a positive connotation. Girls were not fully aware of the many methodologies circulating their bodies, and boys did not understand that carnal pleasure has its price. As such, every romance that started out with the physical often ended in the physical as well: tears, blood. At six in the morning, a classmate would return from a morning run with some news: a Japanese Department student on the fifth floor has just committed suicide, she hung herself!

Everyone's response was the same: her heart had been broken. At that age, save for love, what else could tear the body to pieces?

What could there be? Exams didn't count for shit. The experimental writers Ge Fei and Song Lin co-taught our writing seminars, and I have zero recollection of the literary theories they expounded. However, their attitudes towards grading gave us an instant understanding of what higher education was all about. I can't remember if it was Ge Fei or Song Lin who said: "Let me know if you're someone who really cares about marks." There was always some simpleminded kid who would stand up and ask how essays are graded. "Graded? Easy. We just toss the exam papers in front of us, and whichever goes the furthest gets full marks, and so on."

Twenty years have gone by, and sometimes I question if those words were actually said—and if so, whether it was by Ge Fei, or Song Lin. But really, what does it matter? In those study halls where the lights never went out, the ones who sat at the desks scribbling furiously were never doing it for the grades, but simply to compose the most epic poetry for whomever they kept in their hearts.

The study halls were always flowing with campus poets. Some were graduates who were evading their job assignments back home, some were artsy flâneurs long integrat-ed into the scenery, some had day jobs, some had been feeding off of the university for seven or eight years. A good girlfriend of mine had taken it upon herself to sponsor a well-known campus poet, right up until he eventually found another benefactor. To be fair, sponsoring was quite a clean venture at that time—you just had to divide your meal tickets in two, simple as that.

When the poet left her, my friend treated me to a meal. It was my first time eating at KFC—a location in the Bund. We entered timidly, as if trespassing into foreign territory, intimidated to the extent that for a long time afterwards, I'd continue to think of KFC as a glamorous establishment. Half dejected and half relieved, my friend said, From now on, I won't need to lie to my mom anymore. For the past year I've used every excuse to get money from her, and she's been cursing out the school day and night for its crazy fees. Then we ended up cursing out the poet. As we walked from the Bund back to campus, she recited lines that the poet had written for her. Every time she finished, she'd spit out: "Damn, what a load of bullshit!" Bullshit, of course, was its own praise.

It's a shame that my memory isn't great. Those lines that had felt like Rimbaud's—I can't remember a single one. My only impression comes from the letters that the renowned poet sent to my friend, every single one beginning with "Child" or "Dear Child." Actually, I have to admit that, on those summer afternoons, when my friend would open the red envelopes and show us the letters and poems, I was enraptured, and even one of my roommates couldn't stop herself from saying, Oh, if I weren't so fond of the pork chops at the cafeteria, I'd find a poet to write for me too.

Were those the golden years of poets? Perhaps. Professor Song Lin still thinks that the very definition of paradise is teaching at ECNU. During a conference of the Summer Rain Poetry Society, he recited his own work at the university auditorium, throwing sheets of his manuscript off the stage as he read, and one of the most head-turning beauties on campus had almost flashed everyone while fighting over one of the pages. It's rumored that when Song Lin returned to ECNU after twenty years, he was so disappointed that it only took him ten minutes to walk from the front entrance to the back. Before, the same journey used to take him an entire morning, what with all the young girls and poets he met along the way, all the times when objectives had to change or be postponed! As soon as he stepped out of campus housing, the old security guard would alert him: The two young ladies by the door have come through three times already!

Now all the way up north, the poet Song Lin would certainly be thinking longingly of the rainy southern springtime, the girls folded into those seasons. It's somewhat depressing that these days, when I'm standing up at the front of the classroom, talking about Song Lin to my own students, their eyes no longer light up—like I'm just going on about somebody from a bygone era. In reality, it's not just Song Lin, but so many celebrities from the glory days of ECNU have faded into history. In the library dance hall of twenty years ago, Song Lin danced a four-step in his tall rain boots with the most gorgeous Hangzhou girl of our year. Fast forward and look, the beauties don't even notice him anymore.

But at the same time, in the aftermath of the glorious eighties and their slow decline, the poets and their *exeunt omnes*, I feel that those days should not be seen through nostalgia alone. In fact, the people of that era should be held somewhat accountable; after all, poets of Song Lin's moral character were few and far between. For instance, that benefactress girlfriend of mine had once said to me with great composure, years after the fact: Although I don't regret it—buying him the nicest manuscript papers while never even getting myself a t-shirt on Huating Road—I have to admit that really, he was always selfish. And this selfishness came from the fact that he put himself on a pedestal, as if I should be thinking of him every minute, should be spending every penny to make him happy. And even when he was paid for his pieces, he'd waste it all on imported cigarettes or going to cafés. And what's worse, he never hid that he was interested in other girls, like it was what poets were born to do, but whenever I dated someone my own age, he'd always mock them for being way too sensible, for having no dreams.

Perhaps this is just the way it is. Poets themselves are not materialistic, but tend to propel the materialism of those around them. In order to stay with her poet, my friend began moonlighting as a tutor, and even came up with the idea of working at some big company. In order to stay with her poet, she neglected her coursework, bursting out of her classrooms like some kind of rebel, and ended up studying business English because she couldn't keep up with Shakespeare. In order to stay with her poet, she treated his aspirations and ambitions as her own, and eventually traded in her own dreams. As Yue Fei once wrote, *thirty years of victories all dirt and dust, thousands of miles all moon and clouds*. Looking back, even the poets were surrounded by savagery and slaughter, and once the eighties came to an end, they found out that they too had become King Lears.

Every era leaves its own King Lear, and the eighties just happened to produce more than usual. Of course, one should also say that today, we don't even have a single King Lear.

In the early nineties, I began my postgraduate studies in the Chinese Department. As I recall, the scholars, writers, and poets who lectured to us in the Humanities Building all had a grandiosity to them. Ma Yuan walked into the halls like Chairman Mao, and the packed crowd of Room 301 would immediately split in two, making way for him, and once Ma Yuan walked past, the horde would quickly close back in on itself. After the lecture, Ge Fei and Ma Yuan would leave together with a throng of literary groupies following closely behind, heading to the back entrance for late-night snacks. When they caught Ma Yuan in a good mood, they would ask him all sorts of strange questions. For instance, "When did you first jerk off?" The now-lauded writer Li Er likely scored his high praises from Ma Yuan just for this peculiar inquiry, as, according to Freudian thought, writing is masturbatory. Of course, Li Er's career cannot be solely attributed to Ma Yuan's approval, but at the time, there was definitely a feeling in the air that gave our homegrown selves the sense that this world had a password, one that even lowly people could access, and as long as they called out *open sesame*, they too could get past the cultural elites who stood guard at the gates of literature. But in accordance to the mythical traditions of ECNU, that command of *open sesame* had always been revealed through efforts outside of the poetic realm, and as such, nobody paid much attention to their curriculum. Instead, we devoting our passions to unconventional artforms, with the goal of shocking the world. Li Jie's departure from standardized practice perfectly fulfilled such requirements.

There was a time when Li Jie used to tout the concept of holographic culture, speaking on everything from *Dream of the Red Chamber* all the way to WWII, so sometimes he was Jia Baoyu and sometimes Hitler, until one day, he suddenly showed up at our dorms, said *good afternoon* in English, then proceeded to announce—still in English—that from now on, he would be lecturing on holographic culture, in English. Despite being shocked at the news, we all pretended to be calm, as back then, everyone was collectively engaged in the martial art of "unflappability." For example, if someone argued "*The Plum in the Golden Vase* is actually a detective novel," someone else would bring up "the queer framework of Kafka's *Metamorphosis*." We were terrible at listening to each other, but at a time when the creative forces were flourishing, when *carpe diem* still came with such fervent meaning, who had the patience to take "an hundred years to praise thy forehead gaze," and when Yuan Kejia's translation of Yeats's "When You Are Old" became popular, it wasn't because we were chasing immortality, as no one was interested in immortality, but because "at my back I always hear / Time's wingèd chariot hurrying near." So, when the academic term ended and my supervisor Wang Xiaoming went around collecting term papers, both Li Nian and I said shamelessly: "Didn't do it." Out of the five of us, Luo Gang might have been the only one who wrote the thing. Perhaps, going off of Ma Yuan's thinking, any potential of academic success was already determined by that very first paper.

That was the first time I was ever reprimanded, but I muttered to myself—Are assignments honestly that important? Because of this incident, I even went to Room 625 in Dormitory 9 to complain to Xu Lin. Room 625 was the most important cultural landmark at ECNU during that time, and this had a lot to do with Xu Lin's personality. He had a booming voice and a bulky build, and sometimes when we gossiped in his presence, he would ask at an extreme volume, What's going on with Zhang Hong and Wu Yan? With the utmost persistence, he'd eventually find out that they got married. It seemed that there was this exceptionally brilliant quality to Xu Lin, and this luminosity permeated those around him. I still remember going to the postgraduates' building to meet a good friend, and because the security guard knew me, I was immediately told that my friend had just gone up moments ago with a "tall guy." After climbing up to the sixth floor, I knocked—no answer—but wouldn't give up—and knocked much harder, until the door opened with a squeal. My god, I had thought that such a scene could only happen in alternate universes, but this illicit couple whom I liked so much actually greeted me while wrapped together in a duvet. Freezing cold as it was, they even suggested that I put my feet in there with them. And just like that, we talked until dawn. As I left, the "tall guy" cursed: "Hell, knocking on the door that loud, I thought it was the big fat monk." "Big fat monk" was Xu Lin's nickname. Sadly, he moved to Hunan not long afterwards, and now lives in Suzhou. As for those on-and-off lovers, they eventually broke up, and whenever I think of them, I take out an old photo of us, standing together on the sports field with the "tall guy" using his broad shoulders and wide palms to block the wind. Was that humanity in its infant state? We could've almost asked god for the light, the wind, the rain.

Still, the infant state in my eyes—in the eyes of my teacher Wang Xiaoming—was closer to something like dusk. If the walls of Room 625 could talk, they would shout: I too contributed to the Great Discussion on the Humanistic Spirit! The people in that room, Wang Xiaoming, Xu Lin, Zhang Hong, Zhang Ning, Cui Yimin, always started the discussion seated, but in the end even Professor Wang would be on his feet. Without any recording devices present, we could only take notes in the moment, and while on one side "falsehood" was still holding sway, "absurdism" was taking stage on the other. Zhang Hong and Zhang Ning, who were like twins, even sounded the same, so I'd turn and ask: "Who was it that said this world was pure suffering?" But they were busy debating Yimin, and only Professor Wang was kind enough to answer: "That's not important."

What was "not important" is actually very important, especially as time passes. More and more often, one sees somebody jumping out with a claim: this concept was my invention back then, or, that question was my discovery, and I would think, if they're clawing at the bottoms of their drawers like this, they must be short of money. During those youthful years of endlessly bubbling thought, when no one had the time to listen, when we were all too lazy to even claim the rights to our own ideas, who had the time to help somebody else keep track of their sources and references?

Oh, compared to today, that era of campus life, even the writing and criticism, was too wonderful. There were no base periodicals, no cliques, novels could be written like essays, essays could be written like novels, Song Lin and Ge Fei could take up teaching with only bachelor's degrees, poets could transport the most beautiful girls to Delingha with just a glance. Although Li Jie thought that he had suffered plenty of injustices, the legend of him living in a girls' dormitory for an entire academic term made him the envy of so many men. Like some kind of fairy tale, he had used a piece of blackboard to change the women's lavatory on the second-floor's west end to a men's room, and when the fat housekeeping lady downstairs came to take down the blackboard in a huff, Li Jie just hung it back up again…

But there is no thief like time. Twenty years later, I saw that even the once-peerlessly handsome Song Lin had begun losing his hair. He was walking into the metro station at Xujiahui, and I had such a burst of sorrow, I didn't even call after him. As for me, every time I think back to Xu Lin's last words before he left for Hunan, to "listen to your teachers and make the most out of your studies," I'm filled with guilt and shame. Of course, in those days, to compose "a thousand poems" was not necessarily inferior to "a thousand term papers," and even "a thousand dumplings" would have been a point of pride. Yet whenever I step onto the podium alongside my fellow teachers to discuss "the eighties" or "the nineties," I always feel uneasy. What if I had spent those seven years in the library? What if I just attended my lectures and seminars faithfully from the start?

For quite some time, several of us would take a nightly walk from the east bank to the west bank, and from afar, we could see a figure playing basketball by himself. His moves were incredibly elaborate, as if there were many others on the court blocking his steps. A spin, a glide, followed by a fake-out, then a turnaround jump shot—and the ball doesn't go in.

Reflecting on the days of my youth, I often thought about that missed shot, and sometimes I'd have regrets—how great it would've been if, when Professor Wang asked us for our papers, I had at least aimed at the basket. But at the time, I was young, I felt like there was all the time in the world, so much time left to do my fake-outs, so much time to seek out sorrow and find my regrets, to experience for myself every chapter of *Dream of the Red Chamber*. But finally a gust of wind goes by, and the ball doesn't go in.

Still, I eventually allowed myself this comfort: even the missed shot—it still has meaning. A tremendous meaning, especially from here. After all, no one sees the grasses growing.

杜绿绿

DU LULU

**TRANSLATED BY
DAVE HAYSOM**

诗三首

A Modern Hermit's Day Out

The recluse has emerged at last.

All dapper and thrumming with thoughts—
fastidiousness is a virtue,
worries tremble within.
He extends a greeting or a steady hand,
and notes that the fleeing cat is turning white.

Scurrying inside, as he once had,
to ignore day and night? Or
preferring the quiet scrub of moonlight
—that blue, audacious brightness
driving right through his pupils,
hardening into crystal shards, pricking him,
intoxicating him. He likes the pain.

He dislikes yesterday.
The mountain greys, the soaring birds,
the tumult of beating wings
in formation outside his window.
With every fluctuation the squadron
distorts, sharpening into a lance,
piercing the clouds, and ends up
somewhere out of sight.

He finds his clothes, puts them on,
buttons his shirt to the top.
An outdated cut, dependable for now,
tight against his stiffened spine—
it has its own charm.

No moon,
tonight. Just as he expected.

Introspection on a Cloud

1

Grey cloud grasping light,
unrolling the softness of another world
towards the wobbling plane wing; its folds ripple,
someone has scattered seeds in each furrow.

Who's thinking, underneath the clouds,
how hard it is to restore the life of a flower,
when rain never coincides with favorable winds.

But we have a shred of light.
Today, passing through a mid-air gate
as if remembering.

2

A dim yellow road built up to the sky,
pale cement, your anxious face
like time elapsing, like fleecy clouds emerging.

Motes of light envelop me: I'm reading a novel.
I shoulder it into the crowd,
into recoiling space, its internal vastness expanding.

There's no end, no methodology, sometimes we're in one world,
sometimes another. Most likely,
this one up here.

If imagination is blurry, the clouds have gods to point the way.
If the sky dyes our hair blue,
we won't need our lips shackled by the colors of civilization.

3

Language is a test.
Like turbulence, like diving into the complimentary apple juice—
greenish liquid, drowning me.

Bitterness has a bass pitch.
Listen, the elongated language of clouds
falls on our bended knees
where minuscule joys are being suppressed.

I rush to analyze my thirst, as if
in the clouds, I've seen a second self.

A Peach Blossom

They tumble into a maze.
Heart of the city just ahead, mountain heights right behind.
The stars, river, forest,
they show the way, and they mislead.

The owl sheds a few dun feathers.
They drift in soundless flight,
taking their time,
outlined in darkness.

His breath arrives on the wind,
she trembles with doubt.
A star studs the tip of each brow,
reminding her of life's brevity.

What made her wash her eyes in this dismal stream?
What made her rush, dripping wet,
from her final home?
In immaculate silence, she follows the sly gleam
towards the lantern, him standing beneath it.

As still as bronze.
Running through the crowd, they take shape. Flowing ink.
She thinks: that scholar is painting another scroll.
Two strokes of his brush placing them on a street corner.

But who is it keeping these games spinning?
Who has the order and method
to try and bury them
in this bottomless soil.

The circling brush tip disorientates them.
She senses something of this
but the force of the wind stops her.

They flow into the night
never to return.

霍香结

TRANSLATED BY
BERNIE FENG

Huo
Xiangjie

日冕

STELLAR CORONA

Mo Yuanliang, your grandfather and the last divinely appointed Scion of the Mo family, had a vision on his deathbed: through his mother's memories, he saw his father explaining the skipping-stone theory in the research laboratory beside the cattle pens and horse stables of their ancestral home in Shenhou, while the river cave beneath Goulou Mountain laid as still as a piece of silverware. Fifteen hundred years ago, the Mo family's ancestors had escaped to this place, becoming outsiders among the remote region's ethnic minorities. In their eastward flight, they had traversed several provinces before deciding to head south, avoiding the prominent passes and exceptionally narrow gorges, inadvertently following a river upstream past the empire's perimeter. When the sounds of pursuit gradually faded, when the jungles and rivers grew more peculiar and the spoken languages stranger and more incomprehensible, they finally stopped. Three days and nights were then spent retracing their steps to re-enter the empire's borders, concluding a journey that had taken six years, eight months, and ten days. There, they suddenly found themselves in a wide, primordial river cave, filled with a strong odor of decay. The water's current was laden with glassy ice and heavy metals, and under the moonlight it formed an expansive, silver road, impassable on foot. Pursuing a mournful cry, they captured the Yangtze Alligator of legends and rumors, turned over and held down the labyrinth-patterned backs of turtles with their feet, and looped ropes around the branching antlers of sika deer. Then, after feasting for several days, they loosened their clothes, bared their bellies, and sprawled out on the riverbank.

"It's finally over."

Only then were they able to take account of their numbers and possessions: five families totaling thirty-six people, a copy of the family precepts, and five classic works. Those who believed that they would live—they lived. With the river breeze blowing gently, they stood along the cave's chaotic purple rocks, the ancestors who had chosen this land to settle their kin, surveying the winds and waters. They revised the gene-alogical records to add fifty new generations of descendants, changing their original surnames to implement a new title, one that would continue their bloodline for the next fifteen hundred years, and they began to sow the seeds of a new language in the unfamiliar soil, scorching mountains and cultivating fields with a determination akin to their prehistoric forebears, and there emerged a way of life, separate from that of barbarians who ate raw food, occupied caves, and lived in nests among the trees. Ah, if they could see us today, it would not be with astonishment—the hands of humanity have already stretched to the very edges of the solar system. By the mid to late nineteenth century, in the era of the third-to-last Scion, Master Wenji, the exact location of this place was finally determined on the maps, and Cheng Yingning, an official from Jiangsu who had been banished to Li-Miao Prefecture, entered it into the local records while compiling a gazetteer.

"It's called Shenhou."

He found it similar to the anthills he had seen in the *Haiguo Tuzhi*—the roads hanging along cliffs, tall enclosures concealed among bamboo groves, the sycamores and towering wingnut trees, their bulging black bark coiling upwards like serpents, white pheasants building enormous nests with the branches, owls nesting in the crevices worn away by age. The ravines flowed with clear waters, shared by humans and animals alike. Across the Fuyi River lay a street built in the local style, extending for miles along the valley. It was there, by a cave quiet as silverware, not far from the headwaters, that they chose to live. In a span of five generations, they applied northern architectural techniques to eventually construct something that resembled an impregnable fortress. Each individual residence connected in a circular formation, rounding out along the outside with a rectangular enclosure on the inside. The towering walls held secret passages, with horizontal fences at the entrances and additional doors installed with copper nails. The final instrument of defense was a militaristic gate, as heavy as an elephant. The wells were dug inside, the family shrines and academies were housed inside, the insides were out of sight from the entryways, and those on the inside could, from the upper floors, shoot their guns through small holes to fend off bandits, marauders, and invaders. There, they worked the land, studied, and passed everything down the family line, eschewing the imperial examination system, remaining indifferent to the world beyond. Generation after generation, they applied themselves to the philosophy of change and the mastering of deterministic principles; they learned to interpret omens based on the movements of branches and the calls of birds, and could even predict what would rise to the river's surface during its surges—whether the shadows were creatures or people bearing arms. As for more profound matters, the ancestors were able to instill their foundations in the classics. They determined that the world's creation happened exactly as the classics described. Because they were located at the headwaters, some of the descendants believed that if they were to follow the river downstream, they could reach the sea, but their rafts simply sailed into an endless lake. Surrounding the lake were people much like themselves, with only slight phonetic differences in speech. That's when they knew that they had departed from the central heartlands. On the way back, they planned to avoid the river, instead traversing the rainforests and mountains in another direction, aiming to reach the southernmost tip of the mainland, and this trip would take them three years. Along the way, they encountered the largest animals they had ever seen, with statures rivaling cliffsides. The roar of tigers in the forests diverted them from their escape routes, and the apples hanging from towering vines were as large as bull testicles. They hunted pythons for their bile, which was used to treat malaria as well as various wounds, and used machetes to split open the durians and jackfruits ripe with tropical stench. After a year and several months, the raging sea appeared before them. At its center was an enormous fish that spouted water columns far into the sky from its backside, along with ships like bombardier beetles that sailed the receding tide. Finally, they reached the land's end, and they stood before the foaming, snowy waves, the coastline stretching endlessly from either side of their bodies, the waters before them sliding down like a mountain slope, the great sailboats that ploughed the seas disappearing with an air of desperation. The same path home took them twice as long, and they eventually recounted everything to the people waiting at home. In the end, the explorers presented their descendants with a conch shell the size of a helmet.

"Listen—it's the breath of the sea."

It was just as the classics had depicted in one of its ancient illustrations, and the descendants listened attentively while examining the conch in their hands, saying, Every continent is an island—an island like a conch. We're merely living on one of these shells. As they finally realized that they were destined to be mountain people for their entire lives, despair gushed from their hearts like a black spring. In the centuries that followed, the descendants would once again set out on expeditions, only to reach the same conclusions. Who's to say otherwise? The globe we're living on is just like a conch. They then made a new inference, that each person is their own center. This held until recently, when their father—leaving them with the last words of his generation—spoke of what he had dreamed the previous night. All of the prior descendants, now dead, were warning him of an astonishing revelation: the world has changed.

As the new Scion, awakening from the grief of his father's death, opened his eyes to survey this world, countless unfamiliar things were pouring into the town of Shenhou. An Indian man with a charred beard appeared along the streets, leaning on his cane with one arm and shoulder exposed, spreading to the dried fish peddlers and the local tribesmen a philosophy of spiritual silence that led them to abandon their families for the mountains, where they ate pine nuts and wild fruits, burnt their fingertips one by one, and never returned home. From the distant north, Russians arrived with horses, monkeys, tigers, and blonde women who smelled of livestock, their skin so pale it could split at the slightest gust of wind. They settled on the riverbanks in their enormous tents, drawing everyone in with their commotion. The local tribesmen came with yellow pelts of weasels, duck feathers, grains, and a bundle of vegetables—just enough to raise the floral cloth at the entrance of the tents and snatch a peek at the treasures within. The hunters of Shenhou Cave came bearing arms, intending to capture the golden tiger to distill their medicines. Still, the animals that they hoped to see—those recorded by the ancestors—never arrived. Instead, from Jiaozhi, Cambodia, Siam, Chenla, Annam, and Sumatra came Malaysians and Persians, people who had sailed across the distant oceans with tobacco, firearms, and silver Mexican dollars to trade for spices. No matter if they were Folangji, Castilian, Italian, Moor, British, French, or Hungarian, they appeared on this piece of land south of the border, speaking languages that even the wisest men found difficult to understand. Lingxi's provincial officials made sparse recordings in their ledgers about the various miraculous, dazzling trinkets that were brought along—plants, animals, books, maps, instruments.

The last to come was John Thomas, the blue-eyed missionary. He explained to the Scion, Lord Mo Wenxian, how God created the heavens and the earth and mankind, about their distant ancestors Adam and Eve, about all the hardships their predecessors had endured before reaching the promised land through the parting of the seas. Finally, he spoke of the coming of a Messiah who sought to bring hope of redemption, but was crucified at a young age on two intersecting pieces of wood. Lord Mo was unmoved. At several crucial points in the story, he changed out his long, gold-threaded pipe. As he listened, he juxtaposed those tales with the philosophies of his own heritage—the missionary's divinities had led his ancestors to abandon sorcery during the Roman era and instead embrace faith in God, but by then, our ancestors had long rid themselves of occultism and its interferences, instead choosing the path of the classics. Questions of whether a persimmon should enter heaven or fall into hell did not interest the Scion in the least. After hearing the story, the women felt great pity for the man who was nailed to death. Having been rejected by his homeland, he still harbored love for the world, and yet he had died so tragically. They wiped away their bitter tears that would not stop flowing, weeping and cursing the executioners, "What terrible people."

But the Scion took a liking to the other ideas brought along by the missionary: arithmetic and geometry, their calculations. He believed that for humans, this was the only language by which they could all communicate. The idea that the world was composed of these shapes and numbers coincided with the views of his ancestors. The missionary wanted the Scion to understand the more mysterious and decisive powers behind these shapes, to which the Scion replied, Then there are no differences between us. With that, early next morning, when the fog over the river had not yet dissolved, the missionary boarded a boat and left the cave. His dark silhouette, gradually melting into a tunnel among the river's white mist, did not disappear for a long time. Soon after, the philosophies of the missionary were weaponized, sparking a rebellion in a village no one had ever heard of on the other side of the mountains. The leader there had raised his arms and rallied charcoal burners, farmers, and herders to join him in establishing the promised land of God. In this earthly paradise they sought to build, there would be no oppression, no tenancy, no landlords, no despots or villains. Everyone would have their own land to cultivate. Across the region, this movement to sell the experience of heaven resonated deeply with the inhabitants along two out of the Four Great Rivers. The Scion sighed. The allure of worldly philosophies could only amount to so much; true doctrines must be capable of establishing nationhood. When the Scion returned to his chambers to examine the papers that held the studies and expositions of his ancestors over the centuries, he discovered that same truth reflected in the texts, and also saw that the thoughts behind these heretofore undiscovered writings were flowing through each and every one of the descendants. From then on, he began to organize the works, establishing private schools of thought to extract their essence. Talented descendants of the Mo family worked to transcribe the elaborate manuscripts, organizing them into volumes. The Thirteen Classics were once again read through and summarized, all to show that any rest must only reluctantly follow the gaining of tremendous knowledge. In between these efforts, any mention of nation-building in the works were slightly concealed, replaced with existential arguments to avoid attracting violence or disaster. Those who studied the Mo doctrines all regarded themselves as adherents of the Shenhou School, while those who learnt the principles of the Shenhou School through hearsay and rumors were deemed students of the School of Gradual Influence. The fact that a School had emerged from the Mo family was a form of rebellion against the various contemporaneous Gongyang principles, and a challenge to the two-hundred-year-old academic traditions of the Celestial Empire, all of which held different views of how a new national philosophy should be established. But the Mo Scion paid no attention to what anyone said—he knew very well that actions speak louder than words.

"You've never known the sea," the Scion said, "so you do not know how to wage war upon its boundlessness."

Thus, using the entirety of the Mo estate as collateral, he hired teachers of the Dutch, Spanish, German, and English languages. They were invited to teach the Western natural sciences—how rulers, compasses, and blueprints could be used to make steam engines, how to turn stone into iron, and, in turn, how to turn iron into warships. The Scion was tremendously impressed by the marvel of the steam engine, and when he mentioned his desire to use the iron-like wood of the south to make a frame, fitted with a steam engine, that could take one soaring like a bird through the skies, his wife Lady Wang mentioned that, for her father's birthday, they had the obligation to build and contribute a ceremonial manor for her sisters' dowries, and thus an overwhelming portion of the Mo estate was used to purchase that land. But the Scion was not someone who gave up easily. He called upon everyone to first learn the various dialects of Great Britain, Germany, and Italy, and then to study the fields of arithmetic, physics, astronomy, oceanography, mechanics, radio, and shipbuilding. Truthfully, he somewhat regretted his rash dismissal of the missionary, who could've aided him in learning many more things about the world beyond the continent. He was mesmerized by the elegance of Euclidean theories, and implemented everything he learned from them into the works of the Shenhou School. It was as if he had discovered a new world. Before long, he once again dismantled the works and recompiled them anew, like a bird instantly switching its feathers. He lamented that his ancestors had never once repented for the arrogance that entrapped them; having continually explored the mysteries of the universe with intuition alone, they were unable to invent even a simple steam engine. With the children, he skimmed the waters at the river's edge, the pebbles skipping forward like a string of coins and eventually dropping, like an extinguished flame, into the water. He said, If we had great strength, what would happen if we skipped stones on the ocean. The children replied, If we had great strength, the pebble would fly out of the ocean and into the sky, shooting into the depths of the universe.

"No," the Scion said, stroking the child's head. "If we had great enough strength, this pebble would orbit us like a moon."

Without any evidence, the children refused to believe him. The Scion began quoting complex formulas to prove his idea, but it only served to confuse everyone. He could only splay out his hands and say, "Right, but that's how it is." He then drew two concentric rings on the ground, with an arc flying from the inner to the outer circle—mimicking how stones, when thrown, will always land somewhere in the direction of its trajectory. However, there is a centripetal force at work on Earth, affecting everything on its surface. Without it, our stone would fly away. We don't soar from the earth when we run, and that's because of this force. With this explanation of the skipping stone's trajectory, the doctrines of the Shenhou School reached an unprecedented depth. The people of Shenhou Cave were still puzzled, but the Scion's explorations never ceased, and nor did his willingness to explain. The next deduction from the principle of skipping stones was regarding the operations of the stars and the galaxies—it was so obvious to him. Although the moon is very far away, it is still bound by Earth's mysterious force, circling, tirelessly rising in the east and setting in the west, rising in the west and setting in the east. By this logic, the sun behaves similarly—or in other words, if its force were slightly stronger, it would fly into a larger rotational orbit, just like the other celestial bodies. A picture of the universe with its many rotating stars unfolded in his mind, its intelligibility encompassing everything as small as a speck of dust or a wave, as every tide, heartbeat, and thought, to everything as large as Venus, Mars, Jupiter, Saturn, and even Uranus and Neptune. The comets too. Carrying this cosmic vision within him, he spoke it to others and mumbled it to himself, mixing profound cosmological stone-skipping theories into everyday conversations. He was like a leaky bucket, splashing his excess contents onto every unsuspecting passer-by. It pained him that he had no kindred spirit to share these thoughts with. Profoundly frustrated, he was often found hanging his head in dejection.

One early morning, the blue-eyed missionary John Thomas emerged from the night with mist and dew still clinging to his collar, reappearing before the Scion. After failing to send shockwaves throughout the entire world, Father John Thomas had returned to Shenhou, and the Scion explained to him this new theory. Your research aligns remarkably with that of Sir Isaac Newton, the missionary said in the complex tonal accent of the southern continent, adding: However, I believe it is all simply of God's will. The Scion felt fortunate that a like-minded individual could be found on the other side of the world. After listening to John Thomas's account of Newton, he said, There are some differences between him and I. Our theory holds that everything is in motion and interconnected—such is the wisdom of our ancestors. When their conversation shifted to the brilliances of their respective ancestors, it abruptly ended. To break the awkward silence, Father Thomas could only ask how the Scion had discovered this theory—one profound enough to change people's understanding of the universe, to rage into a storm.

"Sit here on the swing."

He relayed the story to Father John Thomas simply and elegantly. Under this very tree that held the swing, he had once drawn many circles, small and large, with a piece of limestone, and it was within these circles that his swing gradually came to a stop. At that moment, a divine inspiration struck him, and he suddenly understood the mysteries of the universe and everything within it. Even a river must follow the same motions, high to low, moving forward or backward like the swing. The Scion was not someone who indulged in small talk or mystifications, so after that, he began setting up telescopes on the watchtowers of the surrounding ancestral residences, using them to observe the meteors, comets, and celestial movements in the skies of the summer nights. He also opened up several utility rooms near the old cattle pens and horse stables to use as laboratories. He started drawing plans for cannons and flying machines, aiming to improve the Four Great Inventions. It was time: the five elements of metal, wood, water, fire, and earth were on the verge of unification. The peacocks strolling leisurely in the courtyard slowly spread their feathers toward him, and children sped past his eyes riding broomsticks. Just when his experiments had met certain insurmountable difficulties, missionaries brought something new to Shenhou Cave: the telephone. Faced with such a miraculous object, the Scion was immediately moved to say, The spirit of material is omnipresent. The thing he was searching for all his life had finally appeared before him. It would change everything, heralding another revolution in the wake of the steam engine. So it was that the Scion then incorporated concepts of materialism and auditory perception into his teachings, and further developed theories related to vision, touch, and smell. He continuously bemoaned that his ancestors had not been fortunate enough to witness such marvels—to exchange greetings with someone in the distance as if they were standing face-to-face, like a ghostly rendezvous in the dark, where there was no telling if the voice on the other end even belonged to a living being. Following that, photography entered Shenhou Cave, and from it, the thoughts of the people became frenetic. Everyone lived in a maze of buzzing electric currents, unable to find the once-straight and now-winding paths home. They could only exchange photographs to remember one another, the dead commingling with the living in the space of the picture frame. For the Scion of the Mo family, the universe was meticulously ordered in his heart—there was no room for the slightest bit of chaos. He rejected the view of the universe as a frenzied vortex, as well as all mythological interpretations. He even scrutinized the teachings of Huang-Lao and the techniques of alchemy, just to see if they could align with his new theories.

Soon after, the Scion delved into the studies of optics and anatomy. The former was a common yet perplexing phenomenon. What is its smallest component; could it be severed into pieces as tiny as that by which we think of atoms? We can block a beam of light with our hand, and it does not accumulate like water; when we release our hold, the light continues to pass. Without light, we cannot see. The distant stars appear to us, but it is because they're guiding our vision, they're sending their light. Neither we nor the earth can emit enough light to reach them, but given such vast distances, we can imagine how intensely those stars must be burning for their light to reach us. Before reaching us, they've already traveled a long way through the universe. How far exactly—no one knows. If the distance is extraordinary, it could bring us great harm, for ten thousand years is a profoundly destructive force for anything on our planet. Another significant goal of studying light is to understand its particular properties of neither increasing nor decreasing to cross immense distances, and that knowledge could be used to create better telescopes, or more superior optical instruments for magnifying and reducing objects. All this fascinated him. As for the latter, anatomy, his observations stemmed from the hunters who used poisoned arrows to incapacitate their prey—it was unclear why the animals lost their capacity to flee, whether the poison served to block the nervous system, or if it paralyzed the muscles. It was even more puzzling that the internal structures of animals were fundamentally the same as that of humans, yet their functions remained a mystery. Despite this, he continued to develop the existential theories of his ancestors until they formed the kind of concise statement required in academia: the universe is the work of a supreme architect. Order stems from its own divine nature. Any existence beyond the human body is the large universe, and human beings are its replicas—each a small universe. Therefore, we can understand its drive. The cosmic nature that continually wakes within us will ultimately cohere our selves with the universe, and will establish for us a similar will. We communicate, interact, and obey the universe. From it, we gain everything that we need to build our inner sanctum. This is the essence of shendu—the lone cultivation of heart and mind, and therein lie the mysteries of *Great Learning* and *Doctrine of the Mean*. Without such prophetic teachings, humanity would have been struck down by nihilism and torn apart by loneliness long ago—for we were once only aware of our own insignificance.

John Thomas was horrified by the Scion's teachings, but the Scion explained that this was simply something he inherited from his ancestors, and there was nothing shocking about it. He had merely reiterated the knowledge in the language of Shenhou Cave. Isn't this why your God enters your body and soul?

Back when the uprising was suppressed and all the rebel leaders were wiped out, Thomas had escaped, claiming that he was just a missionary spreading the gospel. The Scion wanted to investigate the true purpose of Thomas's return to Shenhou Cave, and so he said, Our philosophies serve the national temple. But, Father Thomas replied, the sacred temples of the East have already taken on a different hue. Oh? The Scion looked at him with one eye and continued his inquiry with the other: Will your doctrine lead to an upheaval amongst my people? If so, Thomas irresponsibly replied, isn't that the charm of such a doctrine? In that case—the Scion's two eyes converged in a radiance, and he said—my entire clan will be annihilated. It was as if he was once again seeing the exodus of his ancestors, who were all designated as mere barbarians by the curious naturalists of the history books and the writers banished to the south. Nevertheless, the Scion offered John Thomas sustenance, and allowed him to stay in a spacious room on the second floor of the old enclosure. He was permitted to teach languages and mnemonics, but the Scion forbade him from preaching his beliefs to anyone.

One autumn afternoon, the young chief of Shenhou, Gao Xiaorong, came by on horseback, appearing along the bridge with a group of attendants. That moment marked his arrival from the depths of history, as he dismounted far from the gates and walked towards the Mo family estate. You had not yet arrived in this world, and you could not know that he would become, within the fissures of time, one of the most essential components of your pedigree in that labyrinthine genealogy: your maternal great-grandfather. It's a pity that back then, your great-grandfather Lord Mo had not yet realized the extent of his own arrogance. The greeter of the Mo estate informed the Scion. The Scion entered the reception hall, where Chief Gao crooned the proper salutations before saying: My lord, I heard that a priest has arrived on the Mo family estate. The Scion replied that while the Chief does indeed possess profound insight, there are only foreign teachers of various specialties on the grounds, and he extended an invitation for the Chief to examine them in person. With a gentle and humble smile, Chief Gao said that he had been ordered to carry out an inspection. The Scion complied: Please look around at your will. Then, he tapped his shining, brass opium pipe on the ground, knocking out the excess ashes. That echo, as well as the intentions behind it, were so obvious that Chief Gao felt his insides tighten. This is the Mo estate, after all. Chief Gao didn't dare to carry out the inspection, and as such, on that autumn afternoon, he stepped out of the reception room and walked up to a peacock, giving it a few strokes and stealing some extra glances at the neatly woven eyes of its feathers. It was his first time entering this circular, fortress-like building, and each time he swept his gaze across, it returned to his own body like a boomerang. Finally, he decided to go to the Scion's laboratory and assess the situation. There, a beam of sticky, vibrant sunlight was refracting through the window's glass onto the workbench in the center of the room, filling the stable-like laboratory with ethereal color. The room was ripe with a thick, animal smell, and a blue-eyed foreigner stood dissecting a rabbit. Chief Gao fanned his hand in front of his nose and asked if the man was killing rabbits for Moism. The Scion said: My American research assistant wants to understand why the urine of carnivorous wild rabbits is as clear as that of pigs, horses, cattle, and sheep, as well as the how the vascular nervous system affects blood supply. Chief Gao was at a temporary loss for words. The Scion continued: Because the digestive fluid secreted by the rabbit's pancreas can break down fat into acids and glycerol. Chief Gao stepped out of the room filled with colorful light, and bowed repeatedly as he bid farewell. The Scion was extremely satisfied. Before the fortress of an intellect formed by language, the Chief had admitted his inferiority, and retreated. This was not a matter of knowledge, but clearly a mentality—a way of understanding and explaining novelties through naming. We rename the aspects that had once escaped our notice, thus forming new systems of knowledge. After many years of being ensnared in the field of anatomy, it took the last words of his wife, Lady Wang, to suddenly jolt him awake.

"You are a piece of trash."

At that moment, he suddenly became aware that he was nearing eighty. Immersed in scientific experiments, he had long distanced himself from his relatives and neglected the family's affairs. His wife, Lady Wang, died holding on to her sorrow and her despair, and there would never be any forgiveness, even if her existence were to evaporate entirely from his memory. Her final sentence made him understand with the utmost intensity that language could be a kind of poison. Determined to restructure the family line, he decided to infuse the energy he had gained from the universe into the feminine divine, so that the women around him may blossom and bear fruit. In the second spring after his wife's death, on the occasion of his eightieth birthday, he decided to take a second bride. He had no offspring, and this filled him with melancholy. The priest asked him if old seeds could still sprout, and the Scion replied that the eggs of aged fish may lie dormant for a thousand years, but once released, they cannot be contained. He dismissed the foreign tutors of various dialects, the great engineers of skill and materialism, and with their departure, the beautiful languages and wisdom too receded from the minds of the children. The Mo estate returned to its previous rhythms, pragmatic and productive. The steward was sent across the river to bring back a matchmaker, who arrived with a prominent beak-like nose and an assumption that she was to arrange marriages for the Mo family's children. Immediately, she announced: The eminent Hao family has a son. Impeccable social pairing. I've long had this arrangement in mind. The blush that spread over the Scion's dark face drowned his face in humiliation. It's me—I want to take another wife, he declared. The matchmaker's eyes rolled back, bulging out, and her jaw hung slack for a long time. It was only when the Scion lifted the red veil over a platter of silver that she finally recovered. Closing her mouth with her hand, a deformed smile came over her face.

"Women are more full-bodied in youth."

The scion walked away, leaving the matchmaker with only these words. The seven lively sons that later arrived to the Mo family would be born by Pang Bai, a young, sturdy, voluptuous woman. Built like a tower, there was a shy, sensitive heart hidden beneath that edifice of a body, and her beauty was undeniable from any angle. The Scion was overjoyed. Soon after their meeting, children sprouted from Madam Pang's womb, dropping out startlingly one by one, like gourds.

"I've brought home a big, strong wife."

What remains indelible in the bustling, splendid river of memories are Mo Yuanliang, the eldest son of the Mo family and the scion of the Scion, the second son Mo Danliang, the third son Mo Zuoliang, the fourth son Mo Yòuliang, the fifth son Mo Yongliang, the sixth son Mo Youliang, and the seventh son Mo Yuliang. The youngest two resided with the Scion and Mo Yuanliang in the old estate, while the other four moved into newly charted areas. The second son's residence was the House of the Azure Dragon, the third son's the House of the White Tiger, the fourth son's the House of the Vermilion Bird, and the fifth son's the House of the Black Tortoise—all in perfect order. The Mo estate held eight or nine hundred residences, filled with countless people. Has anyone ever counted the number of ants in an anthill? Father John Thomas was always curious about the grounds, which during the day seemed like a huge beehive, glinting with flowing glass and the transparent buzzing of something akin to newly molted butterflies. How could a household of this scale run so smoothly?

Mo Yuanliang and Mo Danliang soon reached the age of instruction. Along with the other children on the estate, they knelt before the memorial tablets, adorned with pig heads wrapped in red cloth and other offerings, to make the formal announcement to their ancestors, receiving scriptures and writing materials amidst the sound of fire-crackers. The Mo family tutor would enlighten them on the matters of life, officially inducting them into the ranks of those who have studied the sacred texts. The ceremony was solemn, decorous, and despite the children's general unawareness, that serious atmosphere and the deafening pops of firecrackers permeated their minds, and they left something like a promise before the tablets. Mo Yuanliang and Mo Danliang were ushered into the estate's academy, and reverently set out to explore this place that was considered sacred by their peers. With their chests adorned with red silk flowers, the students followed ten private instructors, led by the Host, into a spacious room. The portrait of a sage hung on the north wall, accompanied by a couplet: *Were the world untouched by Confucius, history would be an endless night*. After kneeling in greeting, one of the tutors called on them to enter the Palace of Learning. The ceiling opened up, and through the meter-wide hole came a melodious recitation of scripture. A wheeled wooden ladder was promptly pushed up to the opening by the school's steward. Mo Yuanliang and Mo Danliang, along with the family tutor, scaled the almost perfectly vertical ladder, and entered the classroom. The others remained below.

"What the Great Learning teaches is the demonstration of illustrious virtue; to exercise it amongst the people; and to rest in the highest excellence."

Standing before the image of the sage, the Scion soon heard the voices of his own descendants mingling with the sounds trickling down. At this moment, the thought of having a hearty meal randomly occurred to him, and at the same time, he heard the floorboards being laid down, cutting off the stream of sound as crisply as celery stems by a knife. From then on, the brothers and students Mo Yuanliang and Mo Danliang spent their days reciting scriptures and writing characters one by one in large empty grids printed along papered boards. They were forbidden to go downstairs during the day, their lunches were hoisted up in baskets, and they were only allowed to return home once lessons ended. In the classroom, the family tutor wore a pair of tortoiseshell glasses and sat up front with a book, glancing at everyone out of the corner of his eye, a long bamboo rod laid across his desk. For the students who failed to recite the daily lessons or caused trouble, he would set them in his spectacled sights, and send over a smack to the head with the rod that reached as far as a fishing pole. His charge was a garden of fruits and vegetables, with each plant at a different stage of ripeness—some were just beginning to mature, some were familiar enough with the scriptures to begin their own compositions, and some were even ready to start teaching. The family tutors gave their own distinct forms of guidance, determining the academic advancement of their students, and the Mo children who had passed through this instructional period soon began to express their views on the world, seeking out their own places within this vast organization. The Scion had long cultivated and solidified his views on this pedagogical method.

"The first mouthful of milk determines one's future."

Holding on to the summaries of his own experiences, he set aside his scientific experiments and writings, instead bringing his two sons—along with several other children who could walk and sit still—into his laboratory for lessons in astrophysics, biology, electromagnetism, mathematics, history, and geography. He let all of it spread like a single seed on this land of hope. It didn't matter to him whether they understood or not; he knew that understanding was of no importance, and what mattered was that the seed would take root and sprout in these young minds, initiating a curiosity and imagination about unknown territories, ultimately growing into a forest. Although it would be a long time before they bore fruit, he had already crystallized his own curiosity and imagination into something called determination, and just as he had cleared all the obstacles to knowledge with the principle of skipping stones, he was not trying to pass on any specific intelligence, but simply the need to find one's own singular form of skipping stones. Their young mother, Madam Pang, also sat beside them, listening to these strange insights while nursing their newborn son, first turning rigid from all the unfamiliarity, and then exhausted from all the rigidity. The little ones dozed in all directions. The Scion persisted for twelve months, but in the end, seeing no improvement, he had no choice but to send them back, one after another, to the classroom of the family tutor.

It's just me now, Madam Pang said affectionately to her husband, you can keep going. The Scion was stunned by his wife's curiosity, which was exactly what he had been looking for. Still, she was already an adult, and had no use for such things. The children were the priority. He looked at his wife's hips, broader and more gracious by the day, and though a sense of relief came to him at seeing her chest swollen with milk, there was also a kind of loneliness that he had never felt before. Go on, he said, back to your chambers. But Madam Pang insisted, The baby in my belly wants to listen.

Just then, he seemed to hear the rumble of cannons, and a sour sensation welled up in his eyes. It brought him one step closer to reality, and he was once again flooded with the understanding that progeny is a kind of force, connecting him with everything far and wide. Mo Danliang in the House of Azure Dragons would later recall those mornings and afternoons spent under the eaves, forgetting everything else except the lasting scene of the family, listening to their father's lectures in that laboratory where the strangeness of amphibian odors mingled with the scent of mother's milk. The brothers were sprawled about, some sitting on the ground gnawing their toes, some chewing on the debris collected from the cracks in the ground, some falling asleep while holding onto their stools, each as sturdy as a sea otter. Their mother, a white-feathered hen guarding her chicks, lounged in a sand bath while rising clear-eyed among them. He longed for the world described by his father, a map unfolding before his eyes with the mainland clearly imprinted in his mind, Africa and Latin America like the pointed, drooping peaks of his mother's breasts, Australia drifting like a crab, the two island nations of Japan and Great Britain like the ectopic pregnancies of the Eurasian continent.

"Ah," their father said, "the blue sea pours into the heart of the continent along the riverbeds, it does not rush towards the ocean. Those places that have fallen away are lakes."

Then he inverts the map, and their mental worlds would turn upside-down accordingly. Rivers were always flowing in reverse like octopus tentacles, and not even the Pacific and the Atlantic Oceans combined could outsize the Mo estates. He made them understand that there were many other countries like theirs in the world, that beings like them lived in Iceland and Cyprus, that the West's Napoleon had invaded the northern wildernesses of Catherine the Great, that on the Greek peninsula off of the Mediterranean, there lived creatures who loved wisdom enough to risk their lives, and that in the time of Ashoka, the nearby bordering jungles had been home to many ascetics who lived without food or water. The holy child that the priest spoke of was still roaming a desolate forest somewhere on the map, and his fate was not unlike that of the princes in various epics. As for the stars and galaxies beyond, they were interconnected like blood brothers, or like family. When the children all fell into a daze at this jumble of information, their father would take them into the yard to see the well—a passage connected to the world's other places—and in all of this he was following the ancestral tradition of the Mo family, in which each scion would pass down a silk-bound diagram of the well to his successor. The image showed a well, a tree, and a person, with a long rope attaching his waist to the tree's trunk, observing the well from above. What did it mean? The descendants of each generation must ponder this question. The diagram was hung in the inner chambers, and they would often sit in front of it in silent meditation. Mo Yuanliang and Mo Danliang felt nothing when playing by the well alone, but when everyone leaned over it together, a magical, electrifying sensation would come over them. Their father offered no explanation, merely encouraging them to look again and again, and among the brothers, one developed a lingering fascination with the well, sensing that it inspired a boundlessness in their imaginations. Eventually, the well became a mantra, became the mentor of their lives. Only then was the Scion completely freed from his teaching responsibilities, and he confided his expectations to Father John Thomas.

"That will become the skipping stone of the future."

Father Thomas advised that he should send the children to the provincial capital for their education. Looking at the unfinished steam engines and the rusted iron knots, eroded by the rain along the riverbank, he told the Scion that, after all, everything here is still in its infancy, and not all grand ideas can be realized. The Scion immediately adopted his suggestion. He began strategizing and called for his deputy. To the members of the Mo family's Assisting Commission, this Scion has not handled the affairs properly for the last fifty years. He had failed the provincial imperial examination four times, and during the low periods of his life, he would entrust all the familial affairs to Master Mo Wenshu, and turn to some new object of study. He had always attributed his consecutive failures to the degeneration of the Sacred Empire, and now, this newfound desire to sell off family properties would surely be seen as a great betrayal. The Scion was forced to consult Master Mo in figuring out the most opportune moment to make his announcement in the ancestral hall. Though it troubled him, he felt it to be his only choice—that the future destiny of the Mo family was at stake. Master Mo was in opposition, but had to obey the Scion's decision.

"Tomorrow, say the same," the Scion said. "Speak up and make your case. If you do, my decision will sound all the more genuine, and it'll be more convincing."

Early in the morning, as the sky brightened, the Scion arrived at the ancestral hall of the family temple, and walked up to the center position. After twenty-four drum beats and the singing of greetings, he addressed the ancestors, recited the family rules, and everyone took their seats, left and right. They all cast their clear and curious glances upon him. This was all new to the Scion—all the leaders of the Houses and the duty-bearing clansmen had gathered. Having avoided his responsibilities for many years, the Scion did not recognize certain new faces. Master Mo instructed the Host to introduce the current serving members of the family, and the Host, Mo Zhengze, asked the newly introduced to stand up and acknowledge the Scion. They included the clerk in charge of records, logistical plans, and compilations; the attendant in charge of overseeing surveillance, rewards, and punishments; the official in charge of speaking the family rules and assisting the rural leaders in the promotion of benevolence; the chief accountant in charge of managing keys and payments; the new administrator handling cashflow and leases as well as the old administrator handling weddings, funerals, and sacrifices—both of whom oversaw the ledgers of rental payments, rental debts, and taxes; the head of sustenance and clothing who took care of sericulture, weaving, and seasonal wear; the officer of shops and commercial activities; the greeter who took care of welcoming and entertaining guests; the planner who managed wedding ceremonies; the various individuals responsible for livestock and agricultural cultivation; the woman assigned to oversee the kitchens; those in charge of inheritances, school properties, medicine distribution, homeschools, group exercises; and various family elders. A total of sixty-two people.

The Scion wanted to sell two thousand mu of land at once, relocating the industries to the provincial capital. It was unprecedented, but he had thought everything over. This was the correct interpretation of the last scion's dying wishes. The world has changed, and the Mo clan had to adapt with the times. Still, this suggestion had not once been brought up in the last fifteen hundred years, and it burst over them all like a bolt from the blue.

"The ancestral grounds must be preserved throughout the generations," objected the Scion's deputy. "This is something that can never change. We must only scale up, not scale down."

The Host Mo Zhengze seconded this opening, supporting Master Mo, which led the others in voicing their agreement. The Scion said that the words of Master Mo and the Host were not unreasonable, that their heritage must be preserved for eternity, but the method of preservation is what must be determined on this day, and it was no simple matter of increasing or decreasing the family properties. The essence of preservation. The method of preservation. With the fifteen hundred mu of land reserved for dowries and the five hundred mu deducted from school properties, there would be a total of two thousand mu going towards the establishment of a trial residence in the provincial capital, allowing our children to enter the city for education. This is true preservation. Our era has changed, and the world is getting bigger. We must adopt new methods of preservation. The old ways no longer suffice, and it is uncertain whether or not we can hold on to even our old estate. The Scion's words resonated with some, but not all. At this point, Master Mo took his opportunity to speak, saying that the reduction of school properties is not an actual reduction, as any expenses incurred upon the children's enrollment in the city must come out of the family's resources—it would effectively be a kind of transfer. The Scion said that Master Mo was speaking sensibly, and as for the organization of wedding ceremonies, dowries must from now on be frugal, and so must the celebrations. One does not choose on looks alone, and one should not marry for money alone.

The Host continued to oppose, but the Scion's proposal had gained the majority's approval. Thus, the Mo family's ancestral register was brought out and unsealed. The two thousand mu of land were earmarked, and the book was sealed again. Those present were not to question the Scion's decision any further. In the East-West lane of Lingxi's provincial capital, a manor was built and fitted with a plaque reading "Trial Residence of the Mo Clan." Out of two family stewards, he selected Mo Xiaolian, who had passed the imperial examination, to manage the new property, and appointed a new steward in his place. The Trial Residence was only open to children who had studied at the Scion's residence or intended to write the imperial examinations—anyone else wishing to stay overnight had to receive approval from the Scion personally. Mo Xiaolian, along with his wife Lady Zhou, their young son Mo Xiliang, and a cage of snow-white pigeons, went to guard the new residence. In addition to the four sons of the Scion's family, other children who had been taught by the family tutor also went along. Under the big maple tree not far from the waterwheel, Madam Pang watched the departing boats. Unable to bear the pain of farewells, she began sobbing loudly, making no attempt to hold back her tears. Mo Youliang was in her arms. Mo Yongliang pinched the bloated belly of a urinating frog with one hand, and the other held tightly onto his mother's thigh. Seized by the sudden crying, he too began to wail loudly, and even the unborn Mo Yuliang began to kick in his mother's belly. When the adults stopped crying, the children stopped as well, as if they naturally understood what it means to weep. Silence and noise are both forms of intense combustion, and in that moment, they occurred at once. The Scion appeared even more emaciated next to his statuesque wife. In the springtime frost, his once-rounded figure had already been eaten away by thought. He seemed to see a vision of himself, many years ago, when his father had suddenly passed away. He had left the caves to take the imperial examination, and found himself returning as a failure to take over as the Scion. He has not left Shenhou since.

The season back then was one of warming weather. The currents surged and returned, stirring up white swirls of turbid sand, turning with a clap into waves of lettuce leaf, swaying back to the riverbed. The boat could only come to a stop once docked at the river's lip, and a flock of black-winged waterfowl, their feathers and claws shimmering jade green, rushed to peck at the shrimp and small whitefish stirred up by its arrival.

He descended from the boat with a slight tremble, and his servants were already at the pier to greet him, with the women and other family members waiting in formation at the Mo estate. The characters "Shenhou Ancestral Residence" were embedded above the gate, and the rounded forms of the lintel and the dragon-shaped structure looked somewhat twisted and deformed. My Lord, please enter. He made a sweep of his cloak and sat on the palanquin, rising up with the shouts of four men. The palanquin bent and dipped, and he sank into that seat like a sandbag. After the bearers had stabilized the weight along their shoulders, they began moving across the flat ground, heading towards the sloping path along the cliffs. The four of them formed a rhombus, constantly changing positions as they traversed the fields, slopes, steps, mud, and uneven terrain, while the person atop their shoulders remained unaware of the ground's complex changes. A white dog waited by the door, its tail erect as an arrow, howling at the palanquin with a fierce expression on its face. After they entered, the dog turned and followed. The welcoming group at the door kept pace with the palanquin, forming a pair of trailing parentheses around it, and as it disappeared through the gate, they also straightened into a line and entered the confines. The last in the long line were armed imperial guards who had also descended from the boat, and when they too entered, the spectating children dispersed at once. The Scion in the palanquin took stock of the so-called homeland before him, and walked into the largest building in all of Shenhou, the other surrounding houses resembling overturned jars in the distance. The low wooden houses of the farmers were scattered between the family residences, hidden behind the phoenix tails of spiny bamboo, banana trees leaning against their walls. All around lay the bright black of rice fields and the yellow-red sand of farmlands. The distant ranges of the Xiongguo Mountains appeared dark blue in the twilight, with the further peaks in pale blue. The face of the homeland retreated into a yellow-white dusk as warm as an orange, stirring up bubbles that looked like the eyes of fish passing through algae. And that heaviness never disappeared.

"Time is always boiling," the Scion said.

付炜

Fu Wei

TRANSLATED BY
AUSTIN WOERNER

诗三首

Blossom Song

Spring colors flow away, night rain crescendos
What fades, besides nesting birds and lingering voices, are
the gazes of things, a glancing of petals
holding us at the tip of the tongue, then letting us go
as the Shu River laps against its banks
we pretend we're just passing through this garden

Yes, the scenery is a never-ending meal—suddenly
you are sated, and a bounty that eludes the mind
is reborn in words, the way stories passed
from mouth to mouth grow confused in the retelling
We are wreathed in the weighty glory of blossoms
and yet, in this moment—we have nothing

Only we know whether to speak or stay silent
The only thing brewing in our silence
is the mutiny of the blossoms
If we break a branch, are we saving ourselves?
And if we don't break it, perhaps it will save us,
the wordless and the uncertain, traveling together

Reading Man Seeks Crane

If there is a crane wheeling through the air
there must also be a crane with a heavy burden
a crane that was once a man
and a man with the mind of a crane
Immemorial waters have flowed from my eyes
ages of hidden bitterness
I too must face this—
the weight of destiny in every stroke
I stand between the calligrapher and his crane
I write, and something flies free
like the cry of a crane in a cloudless sky

Lines on Ripped Silk

> *My guest has gone. The pool laps against the railing*
> *and the cicadas have fallen silent. The branches are heavy with dew.*
> *— Li Shangyin*

The water is dazzling; it is midnight and you gaze
at the moribund moon, imagining it struck down
by a fallen leaf, alighting right at this moment
to accent your loneliness, or perhaps to measure you—
your shadow's returning journey

The south wind departing in the mirror, you lick
the salt off the night, as lamplit lovers
grow old in one another's arms
Your missing answers, your last remaining gifts
are fogged over by emptiness

Don't worry, better to know you've taken a wrong turn
To be a contemporary of the sleepless, you must let
the late tide soak the pages, carve unsent letters
onto the shore rocks, for who will ever
pore over fantasies you've never put into words

Like a perilous ambush: with a crack
an old garden crumbles to pieces
Time alone drinks up the bitter dew
while the rest of the world says nothing
like a silent onlooker, never moving an inch

陆源

Lu Yuan

TRANSLATED BY
ANA PADILLA
FORNIELES

大月亮及其他

THE LARGE MOON AND OTHER AFFAIRS

What do you do there, moon, in the sky?
—*Giacomo Leopardi, 1798-1837*

1

The moon is getting larger and larger, its rounded silhouette gradually bending the dome of sky, taking over nearly one-ninth of the expanse. Brazen stars exalt amidst these newly captured territories, competing to unfurl their limpid, distant secrets. This autumn night is a sapphire rose, then a ripe amethyst grape, metamorphosing like Athanasius Kircher's magic lantern, recklessly parading its ever-changing shapes and shifting sentiments, all through the night. Still, it won't be long until the soaring moon splits in two. They say it happens because of the strong attraction between the earth and the bearded wheatgrass.

Dimmed down, the earth is majestic—a blazing book of infinite pages! Brimming with the most bizarre words, the most obscure and complex syntaxes, the most splendidly glittering sentences and sequences. But let's look back up to the moon, strange moon, that disc of glistening amber. After humans lent themselves to polish its exterior, it's come to resemble a dice without corners, a glowing Montgolfier hot air balloon, the gloomy face or the buttock cheek of a cherub. The broad, barren surface can be seen as clearly as if projected through an enormous funhouse mirror—the upper half filled with crater-like birthmarks, and the remaining half blemished by scabies, warts, acne scars. Some believe the moon to be the soul of Kuafu, that ill-fated giant who decided to chase the sun. Running a hand over the ridged top of his head, Mr. Lu let out a long sigh, wondering—why is this unlucky, darling moon of ours getting larger and larger?

This misshapen giant orange, this lonely super satellite, this widespread, trademarked Danish fairy tale, outgrowing itself before our eyes. Undoubtedly a bitter consequence of excessive anthropogenic activity. If you were to stare unblinking at this self-satisfied moon, it would slowly change from pomelo green to deep emerald, the same shade as the elusive five-point star at the center of Morocco's red, rectangular flag. Ruminating on this strange phenomenon, Mr. Lu walked along a sparsely populated road in his old jacket, a Filipino cigarette dangling from his mouth. In the last few days, his hands have been experiencing occasional tremors, and when he sank them into his frayed trouser pockets, the action triggered a shiver throughout his entire nervous system. The intermittent sound of barking dogs traveled in from the distance. The darkness of the night lingered in the long streets and alleys, hiding from the rich, viscous moonlight. The evening sky emptied away, quieting.

When the moon started to grow, Mr. Lu began losing sleep. Having accustomed himself to the nocturnal roar of construction sites, he soon learned to sleep peacefully amidst all the clamor of the urban network—the rock band rehearsing the music of Brazilian lumberyards, the incredible rhythms of lustful newlyweds swimming in currents of love, the naughty children who never tired of screaming. An overwhelming, withering exhaustion always knocked him down—a strange force like that of a nimble lightweight boxer, or an illusory kangaroo, bouncing left and right to take aim. Mr. Lu could hardly even stay awake to drink his laxative tea, brewed according to a secret ancestral recipe. Made from cassia, radish seeds, mulberry seeds, and hemp seeds, the concoction unfailingly cleared his longstanding constipation, night after night.

Mr. Lu laid down and spread out his limbs, letting the heavy sound of his snoring diffuse into everything else. In the very early hours, the sky looked as if someone had gone over it with a plough, tossing it haphazard like a trampled woolen blanket into a corner of the heavens, unexpectedly revealing a storage rack brimming with precious treasures, pilfered from the perpetually ragged bottoms of divine trouser pockets and the thick, unrelenting slurry of time. Drunks straying across the streets. Cats in heat. Mr. Lu rose from the valley of dreams and rowed out the window, picturing himself as an unthinking mycoplankton or a sea cow, heading back to the Amazon River Delta. Riding upon the clouds and the wind with neither a northeastern wife nor a Vietnamese mistress at his side, the invoices seeking his death had yet to arrive, and the murderous plots working their shapeless, invisible night shifts had been temporarily put on hold. There were no cold, mechanical alarms, no greasy company breakfasts, and definitely no covetous relatives, neighbors, acquaintances, or colleagues. The naked Mr. Lu, wearing only a heavy pair of hard plastic slippers, flew over the sparse suburban streetlights, bounding towards the corridors of stars spiraling in a snail-shell pattern along the horizon's towers. A thin sheet of fresh air gently caressed his bulging beer belly, and the city was as far away as a firefly, succumbing to the hallucinatory bird's eye view of inebriated men. From east to west he drifted, free and at ease. Above the oceanic depths of boundless night, a densely packed colony of starry mitochondria teemed, and a thick cloud of water vapor skulked along the sky's edges. Great quantities of fantastical spores rubbed against Mr. Lu's shoulders—having awoken from a hibernation of a billion years, they were filled with the breath of volcanic rocks from Iceland, carrying with them Parmenides' fragments and Zhuang Zhou's cyclical reveries, they drifted with the sea monsters and the Persian demon kings of *One Thousand and One Nights*, silently, aimlessly. Even the royal albatross could not possibly attain such heights, where the state of matter is so thin you can almost see the Great Red Spot of Jupiter, and the entire bead of earth is reverberating so slightly that it could be mistaken for the air passing through an infant's nose, or the incomprehensible, rambling murmurs of scarab beetles.

Now, it was precisely on this majestic night, which streamed towards the final deliverance of mystery, which opened onto endless, dazzling celestial phenomena—it was on this cruel, rowdy night, with its hundreds of ghosts roaming the streets, that a silent army, led by the moon deity, made its sudden entrance. The populace, ravaged by noise, panicked, as if they were suddenly able to hear the moonlight's annihilating roar. How magnificent—the aria springing from the depths of the universe! The immense moon was like an apostle wielding a birch, seeking to instill piety, scaring off the vermin, tuning the blasphemous commotion into the gentle hum of a Nordic forest, into the melody of a nine-stringed guqin, harmonizing all the hormonal fluids of every living being, and even the unstoppable frenzy of loneliness...

2

The giant moon's edges flare with a pale blue incandescence—the indelible imprint of oxygen atoms, filling it to overflow. Particles have rushed from South America to the poles of the moon, and there, they've quietly ionized. At this very moment, nebulae are whirlpooling across the sky, like the octopi of prehistoric myths. A torrent of cold Siberian air pours itself over the colossal, malignant growth that belongs to the sadness of the night. As the moon comes closer and closer to our planet, it throws all those lithe surrounding gasses into panic, forcing them to madly circulate the two celestial bodies, incubating the atmosphere into a double-yolk egg. The aurora lights spread towards the tropics, and the magnetic lines at their apex are no longer elongating themselves outwards and away from the sun—instead, scholars are comparing them to lemur tails, coiling around the moon in invisible loops, drawing countless springing coils of exquisite shimmer along the sky's canvas (sadly they do not comply with Hooke's Law).

Soon, a gravitational void emerges: somewhere between the moon and the earth, at a Lagrange point to be exact, the opposing forces cancel out, leaving behind an array of dust and stray debris floating in that vacant arena, drifting aimlessly like unwilled limbs before finally gathering into an icy sheet, which then streaks across the evenings to a reception of tremendous fanfare. The residents in the southern hemisphere can see the reflections of that motion without even looking up, and the best viewing point was surmised to be in the outskirts of Buenos Aires. Slowly, the debris changes formation, shining brightly against the backdrop of the pale, orange disk. With it, the night sky brightens, like a grand amusement park where the strangest colors alternately appear, and peoples' dreams come faintly into view. It's still an autumn night by name, but in truth, the four seasons have already been entered as rare relics into the Museum of Illusions: summer has to be found within a picture frame, winter is an ancient site, and spring is filled with cracks, wounded all over. Eventually, the moonlight will usher in the collapse of the great blue dome that lies over us all, bringing down its immense vault of mirages. The brilliant constellations shall be given boundless range, and all of its shapes and conformations will ring out, as light and delicate as a bell on the clearest of nights.

The sponge-cake moon hung precariously overhead, the districts were lulled to silence, the ground of white light rolled and boiled, and it suddenly struck Mr. Lu that he was in an excellent mood. A long-lost sense of invigoration surged within him, once again inciting a wild fantasy: the longing to get away from the dust and shackles of this world, to go on an extraordinary journey—to drive his tugboat to the moon.

Walking through a large night market, once bustling and now deserted, Mr. Lu was glad to see that a single building remained lit, spilling its brightness outward. Whenever the glass page of a window was opened or closed, it would sweep a rhombus shape of light across the roads, the telephone poles, the frozen structures, the hanging loads of colorful laundry upon the balconies. Paired with the neons, the scene looked like it had been taken from a slide show, or like a deity of the night was flipping the pages of a huge, half-full album of Impressionist gouaches, silently reading through a particularly long and dry essay. The makeshift stalls that had once dotted the market were nowhere to be seen. Not only did they use to sell shoes, socks, and dresses, they also offered—for both retail and wholesale—gold-plated busts of Chairman Mao, replica Order of Blue Sky and White Sun medals, and all kinds of odd and mysterious documents. In the past, Mr. Lu had spent decades driving tugboats and pulling barges, had liked watching the rows of 人-shaped waves streaking from their tails. He has since decided to let it all go, to explore instead the sky's expanses, to carry out that ridiculous dream of landing on the moon, to be heroic and unwavering, to be someone who wins. There are moments in life that call for recklessness in the face of danger, that urge you to move forward, spear in hand! Time is of the essence! Soon it'll fall from its heights and fill the entire basin of the Pacific. Later, when Mr. Lu is aboard the local bar owner's flying bathtub, heading towards the moon with a brisk uptake of wind tossing away the sounds of his laughter, he'll forget everything about himself, everything about the world, and the worries that had burned through him would be swiftly eased away.

The wind was blowing in all directions, and the solemn lid of clouds pulsed with electricity. The entirety of the autumn season had been compressed and fermented into a cloyingly rich, sweet syrup. The universally intoxicating fragrance of leavening wheat during a golden harvest. The great night of August 15 stretching infinitely into the future. The whole world was about to witness the full moon taking over the daytime sky in its hegemonic rule, like an arrogant, chubby infant sprawling across the distant mountain ranges. No patch of cloud could possibly obscure that desolate, intricate, and mysterious facade, sketched unmistakably with hundreds of thousands of radial streaks. It wouldn't be too far-fetched to speculate that Chang'e had long been exiled, and that Wu Gang, sentenced by the heavenly courts to the eternal task of cutting down a self-healing osmanthus tree, had succumbed to illness. The moonlight was striking, the temperatures plummeting, and Mr. Lu longed for a strong drink. The forces of unusual tidal pattern had enlivened the Earth's soft upper mantle, triggering a greater frequency of tsunamis, and vast floods of terrestrial runoff were racing unrestrained across the seven oceans, crossing them in broad sweeps, sending earthquakes ripping violently across the Eurasian Plate, the North American plate, the African Plate, and across the world the flatlands were bulging and wrinkling, invading dykes and laccoliths swarming beneath them. The old man had the delusion that he had become a stone, a piece of ordinary silicon caught in the thundering sand washer of a mineral processing plant... According to the news reports, Kavir Desert, south of Isfahan, is about to transform into a vast swamp, and Lake Titicaca, Peru's "Pearl of the Plateau," had somehow evaporated over the course of a single sunny afternoon. Its dry beds are now filling with dung beetles, led there by the moonlight's polarization patterns. Later, in the evening, a glistening silver storm would envelop an area near Machu Picchu whole, filling the steep ravines with bright, warm rainwater. At the bottom of the cordillera, the footpaths between rice fields are due to become subaquatic ruins.

How should this cancerous autumn night be forgotten? It's a stage of miracles, the intersecting point of three worlds. The moonlight has made the city boundless, and the moonquakes have brought in fierce winds, rolling all sorts of objects into the clouds. Not far from here, a girl tenaciously chases the fluttering lace of her nightgown, panting with every step, not quite understanding how the fabric had managed to escape her body. Other objects that joined this tremendous parade were poplar branches, posters of famous singers, dinosaur fossils, constitutional documents, open-crotch trousers, inflatable life rafts, sexy skirts of black tulle floating like stingrays, counterfeit banknotes, feigned diplomas, fake account books, tumbling pet pigs, jade pillows adorned with seven-colored mountain patterns, well-known poetry professors rife with shame and outrage, and little boys as rebellious as they are malnourished. A Ukrainian sex worker floated mid-air, teasingly wriggling her eyebrows at Mr. Lu, but her drowsy breasts seemed uncooperatively listless. The old man raised his head and saw a large pair of white legs, attached to tight buttocks glazing with a leather-like sheen. The foreign hooker was wearing a pair of extremely gaudy stilettos, her toenails painted with cheap nail polish, her lips burning with rouge, and a fragrance, at once pedestrian and alluring, flowed from her body in an onslaught. Ever since the people—driven by ignorance, helplessness, fear, and a childlike excitement—had fled to the suburbs to live in simple shacks and build earthquake-proof Japanese-style paper houses, the urban prostitutes and their flesh trade have gone into decline. They hate the enormous moon and its power to imbue local men with morality, which deals a heavy blow to the business of vices. As a result, these fearless sex workers, both veterans and newcomers alike, had begun desperately applying lipstick and eyeshadow, completely disregarding regular fares to offer discounts and promotions. They hand out coupons, perform stripteases, pole dances, belly dances, even Indian folk dances, they treat their pimps to drinks and meals, pulling out an incredible variety of flashy marketing tactics. When a great wave washes away the sand, gold is left behind! As for those hard-knocked women with few talents and only a vestige of past beauty, they have no choice but to adopt kindness. Just yesterday afternoon, Mr. Lu had personally witnessed a fight between two of these streetwalkers competing for customers, rushing with admirable, tireless strength towards the patrons seeking to part their petals. Pushing and pulling, neither giving in. So it was with an expression of concern and sadness that Mr. Lu lifted his head to look at the brazenly coquettish prostitute, and he spread his hands silently. That pure, saintly gaze told her everything. She tapped the man on the forehead lightly with the tip of her heel, and flew away.

Under the vast galaxies speckling luminous with color, the once prosperous city lay riddled and scabbed, the open-air markets reduced to a shell. Leaving Xiaoyao Street and turning into a side alley crowded with ghosts, Mr. Lu arrived at the door of a bar he frequents, and happened to see the two infamous xiangqi players. Having long abandoned any world beyond their game, they sat in the middle of the road wearing tattered cotton robes that have been mended a hundred times over, deep in their long and difficult thoughts, as the starlight of a trillion years poured over their heads. A heavily balding pug with only half an ear and a stub of a tail came running in from somewhere and circled the elderly pair, sniffing here and there, frantically awaiting the leftovers it would never receive. The gossip and criticism around this odd couple have gone on for many years without ever dying down. Still, at the moment, Mr. Lu had no time to react to the old players—a fresh rye brew was calling him, teasing out his alcohol dependence. The man spread his craving, bounding strides, that urgent thirst already having claimed total victory over his body.

3

A fugitive shadow had strayed from Liu Yiqing's *Records of the Hidden and the Visible* to cover the entire city. With its crystal, limpid silence, the night clears the scattered impurities of all earthly objects layer by layer, unfolding in its place a swelling, dark nebula, gradually thickening like duck feathers drying in the sun. The bell tower releases its wide palette of muddled colors in plumes of steam, blurring and merging everything into one of those anonymous masterworks of the Song Dynasty south—a dim, yellow sheen transporting the flourishing capital of the Chunxi era from history, through millenniums, to the present. But the brilliant, sparkling mirage disappears in an instant. From where the road ends, a large group of birds and beasts can be seen swarming in—hippos, Indian elephants, Arctic foxes, capuchin monkeys, magpies, giraffes, barn owls, red-fronted gazelles—with many long-extinct species following as specimens stuffed with sawdust—Javanese tigers, dwarf emus, laughing owls, southern pig-footed bandicoots, Choiseul pigeons, Atlas bears, painted vultures. They wield their stiff limbs, following the cries and roars of their immense transversal advance—a stubborn, never-ending stream. This army of living and undead creatures are afflicted with selenophobia, which had immediately activated their instincts to flee, and their stampede stirs the congealed aspic of silence into minced meat porridge, each of them bounding towards the holy land that has been passed down their many generations, all to pay tribute to the King of Beasts.

In any dilapidated old bar, there's always a crowd of drunkards hanging around, greedy and loving towards their half-full cups, heavy-headed and light-footed, with a penchant for yelling in veering tones and a tendency to aim a bottle at their companions' heads. The waiter, his face hanging with exhaustion, is busy pouring barrel after barrel of a thick, bright, fragrant nectar into a dozen foul mouths, lined in a row, foaming white at their corners. One guy has already lost track of his tongue, not to mention his hands and feet. By the corner, another small herd of men are sprawled upon a small round table like ailing pigs, successively muttering eloquences in their repose, as if having entered themselves in a competition of who could sleep more deeply. They huddle against one another, they embrace, struggle, and fight, using their legs, arms, elbows to fend each other off. Like Sun Wukong trapped in an invisible athanor, left with no choice but to grab hold of that heavy golden handlebar, this group of men must catch their breaths between each tussle, and are now devoted to their deep slumber. As to why they are at once so attracted and so repelled by one another, that is a real mystery. To seek the dignity of the alcoholic? For Dionysus or Bacchus? Or was it for the sake of some extra-pure Er Guo Tou? Mr. Lu saw himself fighting with this group of unconscious drunks, sweat pouring from their bodies in great floods, until he too reaches the point of exhaustion, floating towards the honeyed lake of sleep, entering ever deeper into its most mythical, prismatic layers.

The drab, monotonous lighting was like the sleepy eye of a bull, rubbing one's vision to a dull point. Amongst the display of glass bottles, the cabinet also holds a plump, pear-shaped jar made of calcite, its surface engraved with the emblem of the Egyptian pharaoh Ramses II. The bluish-greenish tartan wallpaper has grown a rosary of swollen pustules, swimming silently along the walls. In the bathroom, there hangs a crude reproduction of a Persian miniature, its complex patterns gracing the drunken patron with a distant vision of heaven. Entering the bar, Mr. Lu was immediately taken by a strange, remote force that teetered him, robbing him of balance and nearly sending him to the floor on his ass. But the familiar scene in front of him put his mind at ease; the owner was curled up in an English-style chaise, wearing a wide-sleeved robe, hiding amongst the meat and seafood marinades, floating over the stark clarity of dead fish and rotting shrimp, reminiscing on his magical adventures to the haggard regulars drooling at his side. He was born with a pair of exceptionally high eyebrows, and had long maintained a somewhat outmoded mustache, neatly trimmed. Mr. Lu has known him for many years, and was aware of his lifelong enthusiasm for seeking out new objects of intrigue—but with the faintly rotten smell of his body, his clumsy way of moving, and his old-fashioned smile, it all coalesced in an impression of unbearable agedness, bringing to mind the growth rings of ancient, fossilized trees. This is a man who had authored a monograph of supernatural tales, formed a spiritual choir, opened a sanatorium, and even subsequently transformed that institution into a lover's den for elderly people to indulge their carnal fantasies. Despite the high rates of cerebral aneurysms making business difficult, old men came in great numbers to seek that dangerous mixture of pleasure and death. The owner was always careful with the investments procured from his numerous generous sponsors, and eventually, the venue grew into a fully functional exhibition hall of sex. But truthfully, this entrepreneur who had thrown himself into the pleasure industry on behalf of his elders was always himself free of desires or wants, sorrows or joys, and did not even shed a tear at the most intimate betrayals. When someone asks him the secret behind his stoicism, he quotes the polite answer of a gourmet from the last century:

"Without engaging in trivialities, how can one possibly endure the finitude of life?"

Mr. Lu sat and felt as though he had sunk into a turbid fog—his head spinning. Better raise a glass, dip your lips into the foam! ... Men have always felt that the bar owner was a time traveler, an actualization bounding outward from the depths of some famous painting in the Qing Dynasty collections, always outpacing the pursuant tombs of time. The way he looked was so difficult to describe, more incomprehensible than the oracle bones of Yinxu...

"Ah Moon, your bitter, leprosy-stricken visage, you golden plate of corn cake, lump of rancid dough!"

Out of a roar of laughter in the other room came a burly and careless young poet, briskly walking forward. A defiled Ganymede, he was built like a large wild taro root with a head full of long, shiny hair, bloodshot eyes under a set of swollen eyelids, purple veins bursting at his temples, and at that moment he was emitting the voluminous roar of a sudden epileptic fit, shamelessly peddling his poetry collection to everyone around him. His expression was rife with obstinacy, and he was so moved by the golden spangle of pure poetics that he trembled all over, as if the fever was intolerable, as if he had been forced to admit defeat in its wake. Having long been a strong advocate of Blanquism, he likes the idea of an autocratic regime, plotted by a small gang of revolutionaries, facilitating an overnight transition into an unrestrained communist society. The young man firmly believes that creative output could allow him to offset decay—that his fate, rubbed as soft as toilet paper, would eventually smooth out. Rumor has it that this poet is a lark, is composed of a special fire-resistant material, is the sacrificial lamb of an absurd moon filled with inspiration—all of which could explain his emaciation, his unbearable piteousness, his excessive, ghostly cries. He believes poetry to be a receipt issued by god after having received the emotional and spiritual payments expected from humanity, that poetry hides in the darkness of the utility room upstairs, and its creaking footsteps can be heard after midnight. He declares himself to be the omniscient, omnipotent champion of new language from the ancient Greek dramas, a master of the Yun Jian School of Poetry, and an acolyte of French symbolism, German expressionism, and English metaphysics. Between his young thighs a mottled rash of psoriasis has spread considerably, and the veins on his back seemed ready to burst, to unleash that dark concoction of blood and tar in a jubilant flow. At that moment he was extremely impatient, darting back and forth, his throat cracking from the recitation of his own majestic words, inhibiting everyone's drinking.

"Leopoldo Lugones, the illegitimate son of a silk-cotton tree and the moon!"

The young poet bumped into Mr. Lu and roared with all his might, revealing two rows of large yellow teeth in his gaping mouth. Outside the window, the moon was rapidly following a death spiral towards the main star. The old man mistakenly thought that the young man was greeting him, and he feigned a dry smile in return. The tall young man became overjoyed at this, believing that he had finally been rewarded for his sacrifice and determination. He burst into wild tears, grabbed Mr. Lu's arm, and invited him to partake in the sacred figs, shouting once more:

"Diana, you plump old cow!"

In fact, few readers could appreciate the young poet's refined sentiments and elegance. His hatred of secular morality was so deep it could've been written in his bones, and at the same time, he was well aware of his freakish nature, and never harbored any hopes of being loved. But—in truly knowing oneself, even death brings no fear! Profusely excited at the illusion of turning from cocoon to butterfly, his tongue and uvula overlappingly darted, and his saliva gathered into beads, splashing out in beautiful parabolas with varying focal radii and eccentricities.

In front of the poet's matador-esque recitation, the bar owner turned a deaf ear, continuing his own mysterious story. His well-fed body leaned forward slightly, forcing the proximal crowd of dazed and silent drunks to stay upright, and even to glance over once every so often. Among the listeners was an overweight Mongolian man, completely sober and keeping himself amused by flipping through a volume of Ishihara Gōhin's yōkai artwork. At first, the bar owner had been simply blathering some nonsense about past sailing adventures. However, there was no containing his penchant for absurdity, and his narration jumped here and there like a little marmoset. In Ushuaia, the southernmost city in the world, he had been a volunteer postal worker, stamping postmarks everyday for tourists from all over the world, and people even said that this stamp was god-given, holding the fire seal that leaves deep marks on time itself. In New Zealand, the bar owner caught some of the largest, ugliest giant wētā and personally experienced the hunting patterns of orca whales, those sea-predators that use terrifying bellows to drive away panicking swarms of mackerel. In Baffin Bay, near the Arctic, he was trapped on an ice floe, surviving only by feeding on huge mantis shrimps. In Madagascar, he followed the trail of some old baboon to the beach at low tide, where he plundered the eggs of tiger sharks—luckily this was during the brief rainy season, and he could see the baobab trees opening with plump, azure flowers amidst its leaves and branches, thousands of them blooming before his eyes. He had also seen the angelic, noble grey-crowned crane in East Africa, a three-meter rock monitor lizard known for its shyness, and greedy chameleons that never let go of their prey, the pitiful digger wasps. What's more, the bar owner once rode a camel across the Sahara and partook in the strange late-night funerals of the Yao people. In Xishuangbanna, he tracked the vestiges of the Ancient Tea Horse Road and investigated the white-browed monkeys, the wild dragon bamboo, and the konjac flower known as the Jungle Witch. He'd had a near-death encounter after coming across a Tailiang knobby newt, a disgusting creature that grew fleshy sacs along its back, filled with a potent poison. In western Sichuan, he once accidentally wandered into the Ice Mountains, and it was only thanks to an elderly Yi man and a walnut as big as a fist that he made it out alive. In his recollection, the old man had been wrapped in a smelly woolen turban, his face was a spiderweb of dense wrinkles, his skin was dark as charcoal, and his hair was growing sparsely on a head like a large nut. In a nameless village at the foot of these snow-capped mountains, the bar owner had engaged in a drinking contest with the red-horned leaders of the local tribe, smoked hookah with the hunters, and became enamored with their rough songs and fierce way of speaking, the local wolfdogs and the golden glow of early mornings. The women in that region were all extremely beautiful, and the men extremely ugly. To endure the harsh blade of winter, they would suffer the chill together with their cattle and horses, drinking a thick, roiling soup brewed from bricks of tea, breaking off the icicles hanging from the bellies of their pitiful livestock, and finally falling to sleep in large wooden boxes filled with wool, one by one like corpses laid to rest in their own dark coffins…

"Oh, young man, dedicate your youth to the garter of Princess Kaguya and the great harmony of the world!"

The poet with wide, dewy-eyes next to Mr. Lu was sickly thin. Recently, he had fallen head over heels for his landlord's only daughter, and every night his desires were set aflame by the young woman who screamed in fits of self-induced ecstasy upstairs. He was also obsessed with the slender wrists of the bar's waitress, the waists of dancers, and the two female middle school students who walked by his window everyday—their ankles, their deep, dark navels. But even with a heart restrained in a thousand knots, the young poet continued to look for the Finnish poet Edith Södergran. He had met her once in a dream and now longed to be at her side, gazing up at the autumn night's star-studded, deep-flung cosmos, rocking in the broken cradle of summer, becoming the youngest failures of a dead springtime. Oh, the string of never-ending worries! Oh, to indulge is to suffer, to abstain is to suffer as well! There was no end to the tall, burly young poet's troubles—not only was he a titan lamenting the past, but he also claimed an inability to comprehend the geometries of love and its causal relationship with poetry, just as he couldn't understand why mediocre people had smooth bowel movements, and valiant heroes were inevitably struck with the shameful predicament of constipation. Mr. Lu sat beside him in complete silence, taking one large swig after another, stopping occasionally to suck on a cigarette butt that has lasted forever.

Outside was the uncanny moonlight and the humid air. Frost drifted and glittered, and the last train swung its whimpering loop past the city borders. Cumulonimbus clouds, looking like a swarming colony of enormous black tadpoles, shook gradually closer. Twenty-eight thousand post boxes slowly ascended, shaking and dragging, flipping over the rooftops and soaring towards their long-desired destination. These omens and harbingers led Mr. Lu to sense that tonight, all of these empty and inferior lives will surely be swept away by that imperceptible force.

4

The skies of another town display a different kind of colorful rhythm. Many of the citizens have slowly come to realize that their whole bodies are being overlaid with layers and layers of a three-dimensional mirage. Sooner or later, this bright hologram is certain to submerge reality in its entirety. A thousand years ago, the Gnostic sect that had advocated for the commercialization of the clergy saw the truth for what it is: our world was created by the devil. As such, they had aspired to use the treasures of hell to build a temple of darkness on earth, to spread the annihilating gospel of the *Black Bible*.

"Small turtles for sale… painted wooden turtles… red-eared sliders… three-keeled turtles…"

The mindless peddling is accompanied by the wails of a huqin, stirring up tracks and ripples in the moonlight, shooting the multiple trajectories of its halo in rapid expansions towards the broken-open void of night. The kaleidoscope stars dazzle every single eye. The old xiangqi players have shifted their battlefield to the sidewalk, devoting every last ounce of energy to a match that would never end.

Outside, a quiet drizzle is falling. The very first droplet had carried a reflection of the universe's every dimension, descending towards the fleeting depths of eternity. The drunks unsteadily wandered out of the bar, as if towards a surreal, beautiful, imaginary world. The lightbulb ran dim; its dark, motionless dome seemed to cohere a thousand inscriptions into a single night, and Mr. Lu's consciousness—elated, joyous—has already retreated into the underworld of sleep. The puzzle-board of constellations was still arranged in an extraordinary order, forming the closed ring that represents infinity.

The witnesses to that magnificent astronomical event all liked to say that the story told afterwards by the bar owner was pure nonsense. Nevertheless, until he flew to the moon in a bathtub, the stern expression on that old face—which had suddenly seemed young again—still convinced everyone that in our existence, anything is possible.

Moonlight poured into the room in a huge splash. Recently, researchers have been releasing occasional articles to broadcast their findings, and according to them, when the moon enters the earth's synchronous orbit of thirty-six thousand kilometers, it will come no closer. But Mr. Lu thought that if the moon wants to get even bigger, insistent on giving us the kiss of death, these lying prophets will have nothing to say. The old man wondered what the residents of the larger planets felt when facing those thousands of moons every night. Moons big and small all crowding the open air, gathering, competing, rotating, colliding in the arena of a silver-grey sky, stirring the darkness into chaos. People are even able to see the biggest moon's skyscrapers. And how did the residents of the smaller planets pass the long nights? They don't have moons, so they can only stare upwards at a dark, miserable expanse, spending all those wretched hours with the languid stars.

5

At this moment, dense, wavelet shadows are expanding in circles, and the countless flickering transmission towers are being overloaded by the growing influx of dark energy, standing erect amidst the electromagnetic storm, trembling in the dark-blue and lucent-purple arcs of light, gushing golden flames, flashing in the vortex. The bar owner goes on and on in his low-frequency chest tones and high-frequency head tones, speaking continuously of that time, many years ago, when he had ducked into a mountain cave to escape a snowstorm. On the street, a steel stream of motorcycles slug through the city, the rumbling of their engines forcing the fog into condensation. The drizzling rain is still dancing, but the droplets descend much slower now. A careful observer of the scene would've found the line of rainfall to be falling at a slight slant, that the plummets are wriggling, and passers-by are holding their umbrellas at oblique angles, walking all crooked. So it was that everyone became aware that maintaining a particular, persistently stable angle with the moon could elevate moods, animate bodies, and beautify women. In fact, all amateur poets have the same reasons behind their passionate songs of the wind and compositions of the moon. They're weeping for their own wrongdoings, treating the city like a big wine cellar, gathering in groups to cause mayhem, to flaunt their debauchery, causing damage to public property, hunting down old women, pissing and shitting all over the place. After their virulent roaming, they'll lie in the corners, letting the rising sun decide if they should live or die.

The rain is gradually intensifying, turning streets into riverbeds. In the blink of an eye, a vast, blue layer of water spreads over the night, completely covering the glittering eddies of the Cone Nebula and the Azure Dragon's seven mansions, shaking, undulating, discharging a brilliant light in shades of smoky quartz and jade. Pedestrians seem to be under water, and the city is glinted through with gold and splendor. Countless marine animals are falling with the rain. These pitiful shrimp soldiers and crab generals compete against one another, slamming against the roofs, tumbling into the squares, eventually falling into the ruins, a few of them returning to the ocean.

"That day, the avalanche blocked the opening to the cave," he opened both arms wide, as if embracing a clear, crystal sphere, "but who would guess that the cave itself would get wider and wider, and warmer even..."

Actually, no one could guess that the entire story, like some kind of legendary saga, was meant to demonstrate, at its core, the supernatural masterwork of the Creator. Mr. Lu absent-mindedly relished one beer after another. Golden flecks of foam gathered all over his seven-foot frame, materializing in another kind of vitality—one that seeks to gain strength, that covertly attempts to seize control. All of a sudden, he thought of the two old men, playing xiangqi just outside the bar. These taciturn Messiahs, incarnations of the sacred dragon, are they still just as obstinate, continuing on in a match that only they could understand? Has the rainfall destroyed their board? Their decaying bodies, occasionally twitching, will vanish, dissipate, under the seabed of this enormous moon. As they always have, the two of them are looking down at the joyfully bathing subjects of this world. This turbid, foam-filled world, still humming a happy tune as if alone in the showers, not realizing that the layers of wind have already opened up a gaping, inviting road of clouds to carry them away, to set reality back to zero, to let the era begin again.

黑陶

Hei Tao

TRANSLATED BY
SIMON SHIEH
& IRENE CHEN

散文三篇

吴 *(Wú)*

The Ming-dynasty magnolia, within reach, standing before me—I can't make up my mind about what to call it: monument or tree? Judging from its shape, it's simply a thick, withered piece of ancient bark, porous in places, the support of steel scaffolding keeping it from collapsing under its own weight. But it is still a tree. The new branches, growing near the base and crown, are almost large enough to wrap one's hand around, sprouting blossoms of snow, of silk, of a thousand thinly sliced pieces of jade, dancing in the early spring breeze. The simultaneity of a cracking, warped decline and a pearly, flourishing brilliance—a breathtaking contrast. The original circumference of this sagging, deciduous magnolia is impossible to trace (perhaps due to centuries of gentle rain and wind?), yet it lives. With light seeping through that thick, withered bark, it still draws nourishment from deep within the earth, sending it to the billowing flowers at its crown. In such ancient, dying figures along the southern Yangtze River, I see the surging, boiling blood of youth with a striking clarity.

⇌

"Rich tea is mother's milk to the people of Hui Quan Mountain." Flowing from darkness, gliding over the lively roots of flourishing mountain trees, a singing of spring water travels across black, sandy rocks into a deep, tranquil lake, colored with the hue of moonlight in spring. These waters—I study the traces they've left along the archives of Wu-language literature, of tea and its practices. In the Tang dynasty, the nomadic poet Li Kun had yearned for home: "In front of the Hui Mountain academy, under the pines and bamboo, was a sweet spring, an earthly elixir, purifying the body, cleansing the mind. Any tea made from this water shall be graced with fragrance." Then in the Song dynasty, a Sichuan poet known for his worldliness and transcendence had traversed the green mountains of Jiangnan, "carrying heaven's little round moon, to taste the waters of the second-best spring on earth." The spring here is an elixir; a tea of the rarest kind. That "little round moon" in Su Dongpo's poem is explained by Ouyang Xiu in *Diary of My Return to the Country*: "this tea, in which dried leaves are shaped into cakes known as 团茶, is more valuable than dragons and phoenixes, with eight pieces weighing five hundred grams… At its highest quality, the smaller cakes, which weigh five hundred grams at twenty pieces, are worth two hundred grams in gold. But gold is easy to come by, whereas the tea nearly impossible." The gurgling spring, brushed by piney winds and pooling in stone wells, comes rippling in from history, saturating the lands of a southeastern city. But the tea, originally brewed in the small bamboo stoves associated with poetic meditation, has long since been relegated to the ordinary bronze pots of earthenware fires. Nevertheless, "the first drink washes away idle dreams, the second clears the mind, the third brings one to enlightenment." Through the fragrance of rural teas and the people who know their true value, the spirit of local tradition has been continuously actualized, tirelessly kept alive.

≈

The soil too is unique: ebony, robust, and loamy, characteristic of the region. "Under Hui Quan Mountain, the soil is moist." Even if rolled into finger-long strips, this dark earth could still stand upright, whereas soil from other regions would inevitably bend. The soil here has a spirit, and the people are skilled at bringing it to life. In the hands of the slender Wu people, a lump of ordinary black mud transforms into a dynamic cast of characters right before one's eyes: fat Ah Fu, the god of longevity, a flowery maiden, cats, dogs, chickens, cows, lions, tigers, all vividly life-like. From them, Ah Fu is a classic character among mud figurines: those big, bulbous ears and round face radiating Buddhist mercy and good fortune, a peony on his head and a longevity pendant around his neck, wearing regal boots while embracing a green-maned lion—all items symbolizing wealth, longevity, academic achievement, and protection against evil spirit (the ideal aspirations of common folk). As for the origin of mud figurines, one legend traces it back to the Northern and Southern dynasties' "Shan Ye mud." After an enlightened monk in the Yangtze River region achieved Parinirvana in death, his ashes were mixed with the mud to build statues, and this material was given the term *shan ye*—the "mud of good deeds." The technique was then passed down through generations, forming a legacy of artisanship. Another explanation relates to local working life. During the season of silkworm farming, each household would make small cats and lions out of the mud to ward off rats, and the practice slowly developed into a distinct craft. The fertile soil in this region is also perfect for growing broad beans. At the beginning of summer, tender, plump broad beans are popular among both country and city folk, who call them "Hui Mountain beans."

☙

As the gods say, gouge out your own eyes, fated sons of the people. As such, a night never before seen quietly spreads across the sky, and the heart of the Yangtze comes into focus: darkened snow, a cold moon, a threadbare bamboo basket, paulownia blossoms imbued with dusk's lonesome scent, the alleyways of blue-green cobblestone, boats, black tiles, soy sauce soup noodles, the wooden house that fades into the night, the slanted, crumbling pink wall, the canals, the faces, the polished eaves of houses... The villagers returning from town saying: Greetings, these ears of mine. In the senses and the hues of the heart, these phantasmal, determined ears are brewing sounds. Ears. A blind man walking with a stick carries an erhu on his back—those vagrant, attentive ears of the people, recording everything they hear. "Song of the Cool Spring Breeze," what beautiful words! The distillation of sacred ears has finally been exhibited through that instrument of lonely fates—the erhu, its melancholic voice, which itself originates in the melancholy of the southern Yangtze, an unfathomable sound...

PASTORAL FORMS

At the threshold of the courtyard, a sliver of open air is swept up in the elaborate exchanges between the southern night sky, the snow and frost, the rhythms of domestic life, the scorching sun, the livestock, and even fate. A mud path, trampled by generations of footsteps and the slow march of time, is paved haphazardly with rough-hewn stones (to stop the flow of mud from going indoors after a spell of rain), with the cracks in-between hosting tenacious, delicate blades of grass. During the turbid rural summers of quietly running streams, a whole world can be found in these dense, narrow shadows, cast between the stones. Legions of ants trekking through what they believe to be vast, shaded canyons, terrifying centipedes occasionally scurrying into the open, waxy-yellow critters with countless microscopic feet (giving off the fetid stench of cigarettes) shuffling absent-mindedly by like miniature train cars. At the start of autumn, black, crystalline crickets emit tiny droplets of dew at daybreak, chirping until the courtyard becomes one resounding instrument. Clusters of cockscomb flowers begin to bloom with roosters wandering freely amongst them, making it difficult to distinguish between the fiery blossoms and the flaming crests. The branches of an empress tree (planted by a grandfather or great-grandfather) stretch across the roof, shedding their foliage to the wind. These brittle, unbroken leaves cover the rooftiles in yellow and green, and when blown onto the mud path, they pile before the locked door of the empty house in an array of patterns and colors, as if by heavenly design. A brilliant white chrysanthemum sits beneath snow in its broken pot, the blazing tallow tree leans against the house (a peaceful conflagration), and the sunset's warm, red reflection casts the entire scene in its haze, before throwing its slanted light ardently at the wooden door and its pile of leaves... And winter is quiet, pristine. Amidst morning frost shrouding the grass in fine mist, one or two sparrows flit between the stones, searching in the mud and the crevices for seeds dropped during autumn's harvest. The air, delicate as a sheet of ice, cracks into an exquisite labyrinth of fissures with the first jubilant note of birdsong. Winter nights are always so long. In the dreams of children, a shimmering constellation whirls through the clean blue of the night sky, gathers into a sparkling milky way, flows onto the naked earth before the doorstep. This inscrutable courtyard, like a bottomless abyss, soaks up the billions of stars glittering above the village. Finally, spring arrives, squeezing green out of even the darkest corners. Lured by a sea of rapeseed flowers, low-flying bees dance across the swelling river in golden clouds, throwing the village into turbulence overnight—in the blink of an eye, the muddy courtyard and the sunken village houses are filled with fragrant echoes, like smoked wine pouring down from the boundless fields.

Dark grey. Along the house's outer walls, the fluid markers of time—rainwater, sunlight, moonlight, wind currents, the air—reveal their shared essence: a dark grey. Exposed to the elements, the large, mottled slabs of paper-speckled mortar form a sanctuary for the remnants of spirits. Along its surface come whirling clouds of smoke, jet-black night skies, aged forests, luxuriant flora… Those inky hues, capable of the strangest and most bewildering transformations, could have emerged from the heavens, though their ingenious design puts even the gods to shame. The supernatural wall unfurls like a scroll, in which any careful observer would be able to discern the ink-blot fly of Cao Buxing, the immortals of Gu Kaizhi, the cicadas and sparrows of Lu Tanwei, the Buddhas of Zhang Sengyou, the helpless fish of Bada Shanren, or the sunken cheeks of Munch, the long necks of Modigliani, the supple clocks of Dalí, and even the undulating canvas of Picasso, pulsing as if to music. Time paints without inhibition in crisscrossing, ungovernable lines. Yes, lines. What accumulates most of all upon the illegible wall are lines, in the strange shapes of flight, unbroken and elliptical, in rainstorms and whirlwinds, billowing and circling (I see a grand Han ideograph being born, dancing drunkenly; I also see the very first wellspring of Chinese calligraphy, along with Zhang Xu and Huai Su's meticulous markings). The limestone has been chipped away in places, revealing grey blocks (covered in flourishes of green moss) still shining with the delicate craftsmanship of ancient bricklayers. To me, this diagram—its complexity rivaling the eight trigrams—is the vague, enigmatic face of time itself. Its figures, alternating abstract and concrete, are like omens, full of the south's own symbolism, laying quiet and still, awaiting an exegesis. But ultimately, how many among us are actually capable of understanding them, of exhausting their hidden meanings? The contiguous, lonely walls stand naked in the earth, whittled away year after year by the hands of time. From their formations, a book of southern sculpture emerges, bearing countless secrets of our world, of nature.

Tiles: green-black. Glazed in flames. Holding a gentle curve. These tiny, countless structural components in the shape of butterfly-wings, layered one by one in fish-scale pattern, form the roof. Their delicacy, order, and compactness finally metamorphosing into a marvelous whole, a grand simplicity, a vigor and strength sufficient to withstand downpours, lightning, the scorching sun. Perhaps an embodiment of the southern soul. The roof folded with dusty tiles is the blue-black ridge of a fish's back. Bobbing up and down, the houses of the south are swimming, from the dawn of one era to the dusk of another.

In the living room, the wooden door is something special. Split horizontally into two parts, the upper half can be opened separately; when it's lifted, the closed door doubles as a window. The dark yellow wood has loosened, and with all the knocks and abrasions, the door seems to be covered in scars, wounds (on its tortured mix of colors and textures, one can still make out a trace of *Quotations From Chairman Mao Tse-tung*: "To investigate is akin to the gestation of pregnancy, and solving the problem is the day of birth. To investigate a problem is therefore to solve it."). Through the door, beneath a shelf strewn with electrical wires, a scroll hangs from the limestone wall. A kind deity, white-bearded and luminously bald, is standing amongst the bright, wispy clouds enwreathing the Mountain of Immortals. One hand is holding a dragon-head cane, the other an enormous peach, a sprightly deer flitting at his elbow. On either side of the scroll are two slightly altered lines of a traditional couplet: "May blessings be as boundless as the cerulean East Sea, and life as long as the red clouds of the Zhongnan Mountains." Below the scroll is a long ceremonial table, unique to the rural households south of the Yangtze River. At its center, water trickles from the reverent form of a porcelain Guanyin Buddha, and scattered along the sides are bottles: plastic thermoses, medicine bottles, empty and half-drunk bottles of Tanggou wine, vases filled with dusty plastic flowers—with several types of outmoded semiconductors littered amongst them. Right up against the ceremonial is a traditional Eight Immortals Table (surrounded by three benches), occupying the middle of the room. Its surface shines with an old coat of lacquer, with the passage of many years, the grease of daily use, and many passes with various cloths—one can almost make out the smiling reflection of that peach-wielding deity. To the right of the scroll is a door leading to the kitchen, where an enamel washbasin, embellished with a scene of splashing mandarin ducks, sits atop a rickety, three-legged stand. Against it, the wall is not a wall at all, but only a bare wooden panel. Two thick, rusty nails are hammered into it, a blue wire connecting the great distance between them. Hanging along the wire are an abundance of objects, including a towel, an apron, a pair of sleeve covers, wire coat hangers wrapped in plastic. Below them are two bamboo chairs, and as the sunlight shines through the top half of the wooden door, the reddened, dilapidated chairs glisten with an oily shine at their edges, as if giving testimony to the long years endured in silence.

The most fiercely scorching place is also, for the better part of the day, the most desolate and lonely: the kitchen. A single incandescent lightbulb drifts from a slanted wooden rafter, mid-air and unmoving. Most of the southern wall is made of low, latticed windows that no longer shut, and in the tiny squares of light, fine particles of dust are dancing. Iron hooks dangle from the supporting beams, and from the hooks hang bamboo baskets—some empty, some full. Where the flames have been temporarily put to rest, a cracked pillar stands, seemingly capable of holding up the skies. Nails have been hammered into it, angling upward to hold two or three blackened pots, trailing down the pillar like snails on the stones of a country river. Opposite the windows, cooking fumes are streaked broadly across the north wall, resembling certain famous Song dynasty artworks that have been eaten through by rust and humidity. Against the wall, a cupboard holds dishes gone cold, a half-scooped pot of lard, secret rations of hardened sugar, tall piles of glossy, brittle plates, and porcelain bowls. At its foot lies an abandoned grinding stone, upon which sits a long-extinguished charcoal burner. As for the sturdy, reliable, clever stove—the central feature of the kitchen—it's on the east side, between the north wall and the south-facing windows, the color of white limestone and smoke. Two huge, majestic pot lids rest like upturned wooden basins along the smooth, curved surface, and a dazzling copper spoon is balancing casually on top. Beneath the lids, the steel woks have been left callous and cold (inside are small puddles of water slowly forming a chimeric, yellow rust), and a tiny square cavity between them is the only eye that has been open all along. Above it is a niche, pasted with a woodcut of the Kitchen God ("When heaven speaks of auspicious things, peace is maintained on the earth below")—one of its corners is stained yellow and dragging down, while before it the incense burner is overflowing with ashes left from the long days. On the edge of the niche, bamboo steaming racks dangle silently like decorations. They are the sacred objects of village households, motionless in their self-contained familiarity. The east wall against the stove has been dug out with two shelfs, crowded with the essentials: oil, salt, soy sauce, vinegar. Even in broad daylight, the small area in front of the stove is shrouded in darkness. Branches of willow and mulberry, wheat and straw pile into that gloomy corner, concealing their incendiary secret. They are waiting—in a single day they shall blaze at three different times, finally calling the room's sleeping objects to wake.

A white mosquito net has been rolled out onto exquisitely designed hooks, pinned left and right. The bed is empty, neatly made. Where did they go—the one who had slept so peacefully through the night? A footstool by the bed. Flowers carved into the headboard. An old wardrobe (on the door one can almost make out the traces of a sunflower design, pasted and torn away in a previous era). A lamp, its iron shade shaped like a bamboo hat. The lower end of its nylon cord tied to the bed. A round wooden stool. A table with drawers and copper handles (its slightly dented surface, two wooden strips propping up one of its legs). A brown rattan chair. The toilet tucked away behind a curtain, between the wardrobe and the bed. An aged new year's painting on the wall. Under the bed, a chamber pot; above it, a mess of trunks and cages, filled with miscellaneous objects. Parallel rafters and beams strewn with silky cobwebs. Meshed brickwork. A skylight. Outside, the ground is littered with the tattered red remains of firecrackers, and a newlywed couple sits at the foot of the bed... A newborn baby screams for its life... The sleep of a middle-aged couple on a cold winter's night... The interminable, unbearable dawn of old age...Death... A face walks into the mirror on the wall.

A somber beam of moonlight pours down from the skylight, gathering on the tiled floor like water from a village well—ancient, cold.

THE TOWN, OR THE DESTRUCTION OF THE SOUTHERN YANGTZE

First there was the pale light of freshly made tofu in wooden boxes (like the color of new snow at the end of the lunar year). With a shake, it brightens the deepest darkness that precedes dawn. Dreams and the rolling pavilions of stone and wood, all struggling to shake off the fishy dampness. Still quiet, the river changes from jet black to deep blue under the dripping eaves, the rocky embankment. Along the waters, the tofu shop is busiest at midnight. Steaming in their wooden grids, the snow-white blocks are irresistible. A drop of soy sauce poured on a square of tofu is like a dark red nail piercing into the softest skin, color diffusing slowly on that white surface like a blooming rose. A quiet boy from town had once inscribed these memories on paper, of tofu during the Lunar New Year.

The teahouse, which also sits by the river, wakes up after the tofu shop. Flanked by two wooden pillars, its rooms are filled with tables and stools, flickering with the lit heads of cigarettes, and a pale mist is always hanging in the air, like that of winter bathhouses. Water boils at all hours on the earthenware stove, parked in a dimly lit corner, and the kettle, its iron neck wrapped in cotton, maneuvers like a nimble duck among the guests—elderly farmers, each bearing the weight of a journey. The tea, strong and piping hot, one by one revives those frigid hearts, exposed to the elements through their many years of labor. Rid of its wooden door, the teahouse stands open to the world: the river's shimmering fragrance, the aroma of fried dough, baskets of fresh vegetables balancing on shoulder poles, all of it mingling with the guests and their coughs, their chronic illnesses, their lack of sleep, like layers of clouds, gathering and rolling within the walls.

The ghostly-blue, waterlogged alley writhes, stretches with a yawn. A baby lets out a splendid howl from the top floor of a nearby house. The red morning sun that looks like a bronze incense burner, slowly revealing its face. A green passenger ship sailing in from town ploughs open the river's smooth skin, pulls into the tattered port between the barber shop and the shop selling southern goods. The farmers scramble ashore with their piglets in tow. From tightly bound sacks, the animals' childlike screeches draw out the sun's entire crimson body. The still-sodden alleyway opens onto a path through a nearby field, where the rapeseed, rice, wheat crops, and moonlit frost are rippling and swaying, as far as the eye can see. Down the narrow alleyway, the smell of the farms comes in waves, enveloping the town in an earthy aroma, from the small closet to the darkest kitchen corner.

Ah, these towns. Today, when looking at a map of the southern Yangtze, anyone can see that the elements which unite and define these traditional towns are slowly disappearing. Thus, in the annals of time, I am living and witnessing a slow death: the death of the south.

檀林

Tan Lin

**TRANSLATED BY
AIDEN HEUNG**

诗三首

Autumn in the Capital

Through past letters, important names,
I feel the autumn of this northern land.

A cup of tea rich in poetry.
A traveler saddened by rain.

It's good to watch the moon above Yu'quan,
The clanging bells of Tan'zhe.

Life be worthless were it not for such splendor.
An aged city of history tracing its grandeur.

On Reading Eight Courses of Poetry: Erotica from Jiang Ruoshui

In small steps Lady Luo comes flowing.
The night is care-free. Dust, rain.

Pistils touch, timidly intuiting perfume.
I undo the satin. Her body jade.

Graceful the trembling flower,
Lightest butterfly caress.

In the afterlife, we're a painting.
A whisper renews our vows.

Response to a Friend

After endless storms and thunder-strikes,
it's all suddenly dust left behind.

The moon above an empty city, the barking dogs.
Furtive laughter and curses through palace walls.

When the royal house demands an ode,
I want a brave man's most striking words.

The world happens, as illusive as dreams.
How much of the chimera was once true?

李宏伟

TRANSLATED BY
DAVID HUNTINGTON

*Li
Hongwei*

引雷

PULLING THUNDER

Not long after starting up the mountain, the sky changed. Clouds gathered from far and wide as if for worship. As fast as the clouds moved, what changed faster was their color. The most delicate and therefore languid bonds of white, in their rushing, descended into heaviness, into portent, first swelling and bruising, and once beyond relief or recovery, into carbon black, ink black, abrading, colliding, twisting, bundling up into a rich and miserable purple even more fathomless than black, awaiting only some senseless prick and spark, at the point of bursting, on the verge of conflagration.

Turning a bend in the mountain road, Jian Ke stopped, looked up and down. The clouds below were still piling together, while the clouds above pressed ever closer. They were arraying themselves for war, their aura one of siege—a battlefield of brewing tempests. Though the impending storm might be incapable of tearing this meager hill from the earth and tossing it into the ocean, it would still scour the grasses and trees, the sands and boulders, one by one, until all was cleansed anew. Should he seize this slim opening before the rain fell to hurry down the mountain? A Huo and the others had probably already slaughtered the sheep they'd picked, and just now they must be skinning it, preparing a stew or a roast... A flash of lightning interrupted the thought. A silver light burst out through the cloud-folds, slicing north to south through the sky in a broad vertical streak, teeth and talons in all directions, stretching and coiling, hanging one root-like tendril around the mountain's waist as if seeking out the point where he'd set his eyes, before swiftly disappearing. In the midst of this flash, right where the lightning disappeared, Jian Ke glimpsed the curve of a roof's flying eave.

It was hard to keep moving. The trail along the backside of the mountain was narrow and steep, and rocks buried in the earth would occasionally ambush his feet, sending him staggering. Moreover, the reaching branches above and slanting grasses below looked unaccountably fiendish in the darkness, like countless hands, endlessly clawing.

Fortunately, lightning would occasionally drag across the sky in stray shapes and directions, permitting glimpses at the path. Albeit too weak to light the way, it was enough to dispel the dread. So Jian Ke never once lit the copper lighter in his hand.

Amid the flashes, in steps long and shallow, Jian Ke made his way beneath the thickening clouds, the rain still withholding. He was lucky. But also, he sensed that something wasn't right. What was it? After turning another bend, with the corner of the upturned roof a few dozen meters ahead, the vague shape of an answer began to take shape. Just then another flash of lightning redirected his attention, revealing the pavilion to which the flying eave was attached and, in the pavilion, a human silhouette. The answer slipped away.

The so-called flying eave was no more than an upturned corner, reaching out about ten centimeters from the roof's edge. Getting closer, he could see that it was just a few wooden boards pieced together at a sharp angle, their paint peeling. They were lined up badly, with years of exposure leaving them swaying, but the layered top of the hexagonal pavilion was built following the suspended style of the imperial roofs, so despite the unrefined appearance, the height lent it an impressive stature, and it could be seen from even the bottom of the mountain. Jian Ke wanted a closer look at the figure inside, but the lightning, like a candle flame stirred by breath, shook only once more before vanishing. A vestige of silvery light hung in his retinas for a moment longer, and he realized that the surprisingly gentle flash had lingered for an unnaturally long time—he was even able to study it closely. A sense of awe and fear seized him, and when curiosity finally won out, Jian Ke composed himself. He waited for the silver to fade, letting his eyes adjust to the darkening light before sending his feet, one after the other, towards the pavilion. The answer that had escaped him resurfaced briefly—only for a moment—but he had no mind to chase after it.

The person inside seemed to be illuminated from within. It stopped Jian Ke in his tracks, ten meters away. His hair and beard were completely white, though this whiteness itself was a kind of light, illuminating the man's features. It was difficult to determine his age, as the face amidst the hair betrayed a childishness, and the contrast of his two braids—one gathered at the back of his head and the other jutting from his chin—gave him an odd look, simultaneously vulgar and refined. For a long time, Jian Ke waited outside the pavilion, but the man never so much as glanced over, which eventually compelled Jian Ke to follow his line of sight, settling not far beyond on a sapling growing in the seam of an enormous boulder. It was just an ordinary red pine, no thicker than a baby's arm and just over a meter in height. Trunk, branches, needles—all new. Unable to bear the pressure of the dual gaze, the little pine tree began to tremble and shake, as if trying to evade the vastness and frigidity of something inevitable. What? Jian Ke looked up. After their initial phase of blending and devouring, the dark clouds had conjoined into slow, enormous blocks, and their collisions were less frequent but far more forceful. From the jostling fringe between two clouds escaped a thread—white, fine, and fast—leaping straight for the pine.

Do not end its life. This was not a prayer, but a fleeting thought. At the same time, Jian Ke's gaze shifted, landing on the sharp horns of the boulder. The white thread was like a needle, piercing straight down until, when only meters away from the tip of the pine, it suddenly bent at the slightest of angles, diverting itself toward the stone. A tremendous noise was followed by smoke and dust, as the needles on one side of the young pine caught fire. Whether out of anger or tenderness, Jian Ke bolted over, opened his hands, and clapped out the flame. Where the lightning fell, the corner of the rock had been violently cleaved open and the fractured area left exquisitely clean, far beyond what could be attained by any craftsman. Just then, something stirred in Jian Ke, and the idea from before returned to him, carrying a half-formed suspicion. As if in response, an explosion sounded out. It was impossible to discern where it came from, but it couldn't have been far. It drove straight into his skull, speeding through every limb and every bone and his heart and liver and spleen and lung, and only passed through his ears after reorganizing everything inside him. With its emergence came a command, and four more explosions detonated simultaneously, equally distant, equally forceful. They struck Jian Ke in the same fraction of an instant, and thereby the four sounds became one, one sound with four parts—the sorcery of stereophonic audio.

If the man in the pavilion hadn't looked this way, if his expression hadn't somehow been transmitted immaculately through the darkness, Jian Ke would have been driven by the thunderbolt to cover his ears. The look on his face was indescribable. One might say that it was a mixture of emotions—agitation or fear or peace or restlessness… It vacillated, but at its base was a simultaneity of incredulity and vacancy. An expression not directed at people but at things, like a child looking at an ant. Jian Ke had a little more dignity than an ant—at the very least a dignity registering on the human level—and so he felt that he shouldn't be so easily overwhelmed by loud sounds or the fears they incite. He gathered himself, purged the sound reverberating in his head, took control of his softened limbs, and walked towards the pavilion. With each footfall, in rhythm with his steps, a succession of weaker rumbles broke out from above, seven in total, from slightly higher above and slightly farther away. It was as if they belonged to the five sounds before, an echo or a coda.

As he entered the pavilion, the white-haired, double-braided man glanced towards him. Suddenly, Jian Ke felt as though a blade had slid into him, gouging wherever it pleased, and when the pain stopped, he let out a small gasp amid the iciness. Not knowing what to say, he walked over to the stone table at the center of the pavilion, took a seat on the bench, and let his eyes wander the structure, looking at the pillars, the beams, the roof, then returning to that man, his snow-white hair standing up then hanging down, like flaring nostrils.

"You've studied the art of pulling thunder?" The man spoke in a clear voice contrary to his appearance, with the steadiness of an elder. A moment passed before Jian Ke realized the question was directed at him, but he still didn't understand.

"You must have studied the art of pulling thunder!" the man said, with growing seriousness. "Otherwise, with all my practice, how else could I have been so easily overtaken? Unless—" He looked at Jian Ke and let loose a grin. "Don't feel too good about yourself. I was just careless, letting you knock out that one. Everything's still within my control."

"So you're saying... the lightning just now was your doing?" The words were unbelievable, but Jian Ke couldn't help himself from asking: "In that case, all the lightning around the pavilion has been under your control? And just now, that roll of thunder—even and in rhythm—all of that was under your control?"

The man gave Jian Ke another look. This time, instead of a knife-edge, his eyes were filled with a pure, unrestrained curiosity. After the once-over, he fell silent for a while before saying, "You don't believe me? Could it be that you've really never studied the art of pulling thunder? Impossible. Even if you've never studied, you certainly know it. You can guide, or at the very least intercept the bolts. Otherwise, how else could you have done that so easily?"

The man's calm certainty sent Jian Ke into his thoughts, racking his memory, but no particular instance came to mind. Unless... He recalled a time when he was five—an overcast day and a large yellow dog blocking the way home, flashing its teeth, emitting a guttural growl, ready to pounce at any moment. As the adults had instructed, he had squatted down slowly and made to gather stones, searching left and right in his periphery... After much effort he felt upon a suitable rock, and prepared to rise with it in his hand... But at just that moment, a burst of thunder rolled overhead. If this thunder... Before he could make up his mind, it opened like a floodgate. Without lightning, it was only a pent-up sound that came down on the dog's head. Startled by the explosion, the dog let out an anguished shriek as it scampered off at full speed, tripping on its hind legs and tumbling into the gutter. For years, that shriek had reverberated in Jian Ke's memory, but the thunder bound up with it had gradually faded.

"You remember?" The man perceived Jian Ke's hesitation and saw through to its source.

But… *Wait*—Jian Ke halted the revision of his memories. Because only a few minutes later, who would appear in the frame but A Huo. A Huo, only a half year older than him, was holding his father's copper lighter in his right hand while his left drew a firecracker from his pocket—the ones that come in a roll of fifty. Assuming the posture, he lit the firecracker, preparing to toss it at the dog in the ditch… And maybe there's more… Jian Ke looked at the man, but couldn't stop the flow of his thoughts… About eight years ago, on a similarly overcast day at the office, he and A Huo had stood up at the same time and faced each other in silence, until outside the storm clouds pressed everything into blackness, and the streetlamps started up their timid glow. "If I get involved," A Huo spoke quietly, pausing after each word, "let Heaven punish me with the Five Thunders." When his voice fell off, a string of thunder exploded, seemingly right outside the window. Watching A Huo's swaying figure, the thought of *no* arose, even though Jian Ke wasn't even sure what he wanted to stop, and he couldn't bring himself to look at the face before him. Are certain memories in need of correction? He was sure of the thunder and A Huo's distress. But there was something he could add: as the thunder churned, he had smoked a cigarette in the silence, and said nothing when A Huo walked away.

Something else he could add is that after A Huo left, he turned on all the lights in the office, and under that reddish-white glow—fixed as if in the moment of a lightning flash—he pulled that anonymous document from its drawer and read it again, beginning to end, A Huo's actions playing out once more before his eyes. Afterwards, he stopped trying to guess the intentions of whoever had sent him the document, and under the watchful eyes of the sheep on the paper shredder's logo, he fed it the papers. Then, he printed out the resignation letter that had been prepared long before this incident with A Huo—the letter that had just been waiting for the right opportunity—and signed his name. He called over the secretary, handed it to her, and instructed her on what to say when submitting it on Monday. Then he left the office, took the elevator down to the first floor, and exited the lobby. Outside, as if to send him off for good, another bolt of thunder clapped him in the face… And there, that's the end. There's nothing more, he couldn't say more, nor did he want to. With that, Jian Ke returned to the present. He put the lighter in his pocket and extended his right hand to his interlocutor: "Jian Ke. *Jian* as in *easy*, *Ke* as in *guest*."

This caught the man off guard. He clasped the hand awkwardly. "They call me Old Yin. *Yin* as in *pull*—as in pulling thunder."

"Was it you controlling all that thunder and lightning?"

"Not controlling. Guiding," Old Yin corrected with some seriousness. He stopped, a displeased look spreading across his face. "Of course, at the highest level, control is possible. But it's also not control, it's all in one. It's like... that line from Confucius, follow your heart's desire without transgressing the rules. It certainly doesn't mean leaping outside the Three Realms, exceeding the Five Elements, doing whatever you please and completely disregarding all the established principles. Rather, we're talking about following a strict ascetic practice until you reach a certain level, where the heart's desires are within the rules, when the heart's desire and the rules are one, so following your heart cannot transgress the rules. Ha! Who knows, this is just how I think. I haven't reached that stage, so I can only speculate. In the end mine are the remarks of an outsider."

"You mean, this, this—the art of pulling thunder—is distinguished in stages, as if—like the ranks of academics or government posts?"

"Right! Doesn't every trade have its ranks, its hierarchies?" Old Yin looked at Jian Ke as if he had discovered an alien, holding the gaze until Jian Ke grew embarrassed, at which point he waved a hand and dropped the debate. "It wouldn't hurt to say a little more. That trick you caught me doing just now should give you a clue as to what this practice entails. Who knows, you might become a convert and really get into it—" He gestured to stop Jian Ke from interjecting. "If someday you truly commit to the practice and manage to achieve the point of perfection, then I can claim to have initiated you. Wait a moment—"

Old Yin stopped Jian Ke again, shutting both eyes and returning to his meditative position. No spectacular scene followed, no flying sands and stones, but Jian Ke distinctly felt the world speed up, as if everything was being projected at double speed. He looked to the sky, where the clouds gave proof. They no longer drifted but remained in place, melting like ice cubes cast in hot water. Pitch black withdrew into ink black, ink black withdrew into midnight blue, midnight blue into grey gloom, grey gloom into... The grey gloom just hung there, dispersing in all directions, one flat sheet across the horizon. No peaking sun, no limpidity, but unlike earlier, there came a certain clarity. The narrow field of vision opened wide, and the backside of a mountain—previously obscured by dark clouds and mist—came into view. Its emerging summit, no more than two- or three-hundred meters beyond the pavilion, sloped precipitously. Not imposingly, but with a subtle grace, like the body of a small herbivore.

In this unveiled landscape, Jian Ke saw that their side of the mountain was sparse, decorated only with stones—some bigger than houses, some smaller than millstones. Everything was craggy and rough, with nothing to please the eye, and scattered thinly and lawlessly among the stones were red pines, a few stubbornly protruding from cracks in the rockface. All the stunted trees were thrusting boldly, as if in an angry attempt to elevate the entire landscape. They came off to Jian Ke as uncommonly arrogant and withdrawn, as if they had turned a cold shoulder, unwilling to look anyone in the eye. An illusion brought on by the weather? Between himself and the distant beyond, Jian Ke swept his eyes across the mountain several times before finally realizing: the "cold shoulder" was no misconception—it was real. One side of every pine tree was barren while the other remained lush, looking not unbridled but trimmed, either pruned or chopped off. A few of them had shaven tops, or were split down the middle.

"It's the result of my work." Old Yin had once again anticipated Jian Ke's thoughts. "Come. I'll show you. Though there will be no more practicing today."

After examining a few trees, Jian Ke saw that their distinct profiles had been manufactured. All of the trees were riddled with scars, and the remaining needles were lucky to have survived. Yet, their greenery was oriented toward the pavilion in such a way that, standing there, an observer might not catch on, and could imagine the pines as verdant as ever. The scarring was all charred, time having washed away some of the burnt blackness, leaving only faint wounds as testimony. But other marks were fresh. At the slightest touch, charcoal would fall from the openings in bits and pieces, in grains of dust.

"You did all this by pulling thunder?" Jian Ke stopped and stood still. The scarred sides made him think of a camp of wounded soldiers.

"Progress has been slow." Old Yin became a little bashful. "Before, in the south, I used to practice on live animals. I don't mean chickens, ducks, geese, cats, dogs—I'm not that well off, and I'm not heartless either. And I'm certainly not talking about people, that would be against the law. Bugs, snakes, mice, I used those, and occasionally a stray bird. I practiced for ten years, but all I did was empty out the land. Later, I understood. Living animals are moving, too difficult, and the ones I pursued were so small, they called for extraordinary accuracy. I was disheartened, so I left home and drifted about, and for several years, I hated the thought—and even the sound—of thunder.

After arriving here, while staying at the village below, one day I happened to climb this side of the mountain. Seeing these pine trees, I felt something. A few tests confirmed it—this was a training ground sent from heaven. It has the capacity to take in the power of thunder, and the pine trees are perfect targets. The power of light and electricity manifests so—"

"You just practiced by yourself, with no guide, no reference?"

"You think I've gone full Wild Fox, huh?" Old Yin laughed, unoffended. "The art of pulling thunder isn't so rare, from what I've heard. Legends about the art are plenty, and the practice is quite diverse, crossing many forms of thought, from Daoism and Buddhism to occultism, sorcery, even magic and so on. Some even call it a miracle, the workings of spirits. More recently, some people have attempted it with scientific methods... But anyway, where you place it, what your theories are—that's not important. What's important are the results, and where these results lead. In other words, what is the point of pulling thunder today?"

Taken aback, Jian Ke could only parrot him: "What is the point of pulling thunder today?"

"Good question!" His exaggerated tone made Jian Ke want to laugh, but one look at Old Yin stopped him. The braids on Old Yin's head and chin had begun to lift. The chin braid was especially prominent, jutting straight out, almost horizontal. The unbraided hairs on his head and chin flared up as well, standing on end, silvery white and rigid, as if they could lift him from the ground at any time. But that was nothing, because the real terror was in Old Yin's expression—and beyond terror, there was something deeply concerning there. Old Yin's whole face was empty. Empty like a sheet of paper blank for so long that it could not tolerate a single new mark. The fullness of emptiness, the emptiness of fullness. Even more difficult to grasp was the look in Old Yin's eyes, now directed at the right side of a red pine split in two. Unreconciled, it was the gaze of neither beast nor bird, lighter than a spiderweb, almost as strong as the wind and yet void of the wind's impetus.

Just when Jian Ke's dread grew unbearable, he began to suspect that Old Yin was putting on an act. The old man thrust up his head, throwing his sightline past one of the pines and into the sky. He reached towards the layers of diminishing clouds and yanked them down, as if on kite strings. Then he turned back to the tree. A ball of white-hot light flashed down, enveloping a half-broken branch that still held a bit of foliage along its charred surface, gnawing it down bit by bit like a stick of sugarcane. Puffs of green smoke rose with the popping sound of firecrackers, and it was impossible to tell whether it was coming from the light or the flame. After the round of gnawing, a loud bang ensued, and all at once the sound vanished with the light, leaving only its reverberation.

"If you master the art of pulling thunder, you can mend the world." Old Yin pointed to the pine, and Jian Ke saw that the broken branch had been swallowed by the bolt. "This kind of physical modification is just a secondary effect, the very least important aspect. When I truly succeed, when I have attained a state of spiritual perfection, the art of pulling thunder will be no mere practice but a judgment. It will be how human and superhuman powers converge to influence, to amend this world below..."

"Wait, wait—" Jian Ke called out. "This is too much. Judgment? Influence? Amend? Like some god, reigning over humanity? Shouldn't we, as individuals, aim to fix our own lives first?"

Old Yin flushed red all the way down his neck, a deep embarrassment taking over him. "Who said anything about reigning over humanity! It's no more than—no more than an aid, a supplement. What you speak of is unthinkable to someone like me. My imagining stops at—at simply being a functionary, an attendant, a follower, to put it plainly, a humble servant to the gods. I lack imagination in this regard, and pulling thunder's fundamental meaning, its flawless integration into this life, is beyond me. This is why I'll only ever be a second-rate thunder puller."

"A second-rate thunder puller? According to whom? By what standard?"

"No need for anyone to judge me." Old Yin shook his head, regaining his composure. "When you really get into something, when you approach it through technique—from the inside—you'll get a clear picture of its depths, and you'll know precisely where you stand. It only takes a bit of calm, objective analysis to know what's what. Even if you can't comprehend the ways of a superior practitioner, you'll sense that the difference between the two of you is no mere trifle—that they're on an entirely other level. It could be compared to... Hmm..." Old Yin raised his head and searched among the clouds for a long time. "This storm, its thunder and lightning, the grace of its rainfall— there are different systems to determine its nature, its quantity, and each system will have its own standards. But one thing is clear: an expert, someone who has studied the art of pulling thunder, will know at first glance if someone else has been meddling with the elements, using them to practice their craft."

"But wherever there's someone who interferes, there's someone who takes notice. When things are disturbed, a trace always remains, no matter how much you try to rub it clean." A daze suddenly came over Jian Ke, and when he came to, he was stricken with the same embarrassment that had overwhelmed Old Yin. "I'm saying, it's like... It's like someone crossing a river barefoot, though they arrive on the other side, and though the water washes everything away..."

"No need to explain." Either out of understanding or charity, Old Yin smiled, bringing the topic back around. "In the past few years, this mountain, these pine trees, they've been of great use in my training. They've witnessed my progress and, at the same time... they've stuck with me as I plateaued..."

His words tapered off. Old Yin closed his mouth tightly, and silence resumed. This time, Jian Ke no longer felt awkward. He stood beside Old Yin, unable to find any words of comfort, unsure if he should even make an attempt. It was hard to distinguish the truth of it all. It was believable, but how different could it be from common superstition—those past obsessions that he could never help but bring up with A Huo and the rest of them? Not even the heavens can nullify the natural order of things, right?

Looking to the distance, the sky retained its gloomy hue, but twilight was approaching fast. The zipper of dusk would soon seal everything into night. In the thickening air, each breath had a weight, and the red pines, one by one, drifted into their own isolation. Gradually, the wounds left by manmade thunder became obscure, melding into a blur. If they could speak, would the trees not resent Old Yin and his habits? By what authority could one justify taking trees as targets?

"I don't know how it got this bad..." Old Yin forced his way out of the silence. "Who got me fixated on pulling thunder? After it possessed me, after I'd entered into it, I had to accept that there's a threshold I would probably never cross, that I'll never reach the inner circles. Or at least, it's highly unlikely. But..." Old Yin turned away, the smile on his face growing increasingly beatific, then looked back at Jian Ke, twilight's softness dimming his insistent eyes. "If you want to study, I would certainly—"

"I don't. I don't want to go down this particular path. . ." Jian Ke shook his head. "Even if you're right and I have some kind of talent, I think I'll save it for imagining. Then, whenever I hear thunder, I can have this dream, and it'll bring some joy."

Upon hearing this, Old Yin averted his eyes, and again said nothing for a long time. Finally, his eyes flashed back over Jian Ke before he turned away. "Come. I'll show you my secret chambers."

Onward, the path grew narrower. After only a little ways, they had to walk one after the other. Old Yin led, Jian Ke followed. Other than the scattered, unrehearsed cries of insects and birds, the only sound was their footsteps, heavy and relaxed, jumbling together in a barely discernible four-count rhythm. Weeds and thistles snagged at their shoes and pants, but relented with a tug. The road was not long, and about thirty meters later, they arrived at a massive boulder, rising from the ground like a sail. Old Yin raised a hand in signal, turning to enter it.

The stone's interior was surprisingly smooth, without the pits and pockmarks of its exterior. It enticed the hand to caress, to receive a certain coolness and, within the coolness, a subtle warmth. Following the rock wall while pulling at the few shrubs adhered into the stone, they ventured a few meters farther, and, following another turn, arrived at Old Yin's "secret chambers." Actually, it wasn't at all secret. With one's back against the stone, everything lay open to the world. The interior side was about one meter high, straight as a knife, and a slanted top acted as a shield. The floor was another supporting slab, inclined about ten degrees, and at the point where it joined the wall was a platform, just about large enough for a single person to lay supine. In the dim light, Jian Ke couldn't tell if the platform was the result of human labor.

Needing no one's permission, Old Yin went straight to the platform and sat down, spine erect against the vertical wall, two legs splayed out, steady and at ease. If it weren't for the white hair fluttering in the dusk, or the gentle quiver of the surrounding air as he inhaled and exhaled, one might assume that he'd been sitting there since ancient times, passing in and out of the stone at will.

"This is my master's seat. He's sat here for a long time, meditating, training, and pulling in thunder while pushing out lightning."

"You have a master?" Jian Ke uttered in astonishment, then said apologetically, "Has he attained the highest stage that you talked about? With his guidance, don't you think… It could… You shouldn't lose hope, sooner or later you'll cross that threshold."

"My master…" Old Yin lifted his head, looking at Jian Ke, a slyness rippling across his face, "is myself. Ever since I grasped the joy of pulling thunder, I've decided to immerse myself in it, unafraid of having nothing to show at the end of it all. The joy has already rewarded me, although… as time goes by, the bar for that joy raises more and more quickly, and the only thing that can lead me on in my journey is—finally, ultimately—myself. In this way, I've become my own master. And sometimes, when I imagine the stage that a master could attain, I almost feel like I truly do have what it takes."

"Wait—" Jian Ke had trouble following his logic.

Old Yin did not listen. He dropped his head, passed a moment in silence, and raised it again. He looked not at Jian Ke but into the far distance, into the blue and boundless, dark and dusky horizon, into what lay beyond it. *Perhaps, from his seat, looking out at the space between these two rocks as if through the end of a periscope, Old Yin really is capable of remaking the world with sight alone...* Unable to follow the fragile, weightless spindle of that gaze, Jian Ke lost himself in thought. But suddenly, something stirred in him, and he stood. He took a few large steps sideways before bending down again in a squat, half-leaning on the stone, once again taking in the view through the periscope.

There was soon a response. Initially it was just a small, white flash, as fine as the first awns of ripening wheat, but before one could blink, it had transformed into a grain of rice, then a bowl, then once more into a round plate... But there were no more metaphors to be made after that. There was no time for scrutiny, because it was upon them. A great ball of light filled their shelter within the stone—no, not filled but melted the whole space, leaving a radiance that blinded their eyes, stopped their mouths, and deprived them of all senses, banishing the ground beneath their feet, making it impossible to peel their consciousnesses away from the light, to confirm their presence. There was no separation or distinction, all was melded into one, and they could feel neither the light's heat nor its coolness. The only certainty was one of total immersion, of having been removed from the category of time.

But time must ultimately resume its course. As long as the foundation remains, consciousness will inevitably rise to the surface of any depthless waters. When Jian Ke, steeped in the light, became aware of himself and his place once again, fireworks began to blossom all around, and suddenly the light was bursting open, pouring forth the softest purple, streaming through his body and down the mountain like water snakes dissolving into the immanent night. Or rather, it was only after the light had blossomed and dissolved that Jian Ke regained his senses and took to his feet. The sound came after, soft and intimate, as if those same water snakes were chasing each other, igniting upon contact and cracking open the air, with a sound that couldn't be quite called thunder.

"How did you do that?" Jian Ke asked. Old Yin didn't answer. Looking over his shoulder, he saw that Old Yin had, at some point, retracted his legs into the lotus position. Upon seeing this, he turned away and waited. When he sensed a change, he looked back once more. Something was off. Old Yin was still sitting there, but it was as if a light was shining exclusively upon him, distinguishing his body from the surrounding darkness. No, that's not right, the light didn't shine upon him—it radiated out of him. No, that's still not it. Jian Ke looked more closely. The light was emanating from the stone behind Old Yin's body, but it wasn't that the whole surface was shining, only the part of the rock he leaned against, so that along his silhouette was a glowing line. It's something depicted in both Eastern and Western paintings: a halo around the heads of spirits, bodhisattvas, and saints. Only here, the aureole traced the shape of his body. The shining line was just the circumference of a light that filled his entire torso, radiating faintly through it like a flashlight shining through a palm, letting a slight transparency range out from both sides of Old Yin's spine.

Old Yin sat there, eyes closed, motionless, the light supporting him from behind. It didn't frighten Jian Ke, but he felt confused. What was all this mystery hinting towards? It might've been a simple act of persuasion, but it wasn't convincing him of anything. What's more, this art of pulling thunder, it doesn't really need so many practitioners… And in any case, it was about time he headed down the mountain. But what about Old Yin? Should he just leave the man to himself? He even… At this, a shocking thought passed through him. He walked up to Old Yin, who did not seem to be breathing, and extended his right hand. Leveling his index finger under Old Yin's nose, it was as if…

Old Yin suddenly opened his eyes and stared at Jian Ke, his gaze slowly steadying. When he had fully recovered, his eyes sparkled, and he stood. The light was still radiating from the rock face behind him, shifting from white to rose to purple before fading away entirely, suddenly.

"When I first discovered this place, I couldn't believe it," Old Yin said, looking back at the stone, returning to the surprise and joy of that first discovery. "In the end, pulling thunder, like everything else, is a way of confirming one's own passage through time. To have a place that preserves these impressions, that verifies the arrival at each new stage—any dedicated practitioner would be lucky to have such support. This rock is my preservation, my proof."

"And then? Are you just waiting for the perfect day to come, for you to break down the wall?" Jian Ke was losing patience. Things had taken a turn for the trivial, and some all-too-familiar motifs were recurring with increasing frequency.

"No no, it's not that kind of story." Old Yin shook his head. "It's more complicated. To put it simply, every stage that I've gone through in the art of pulling thunder, I've verified with this wall. I sit here, pull in the thunder, and when it acts on my body, the light that is left on the stone displays my current stage. Compared to last time, about three years ago, I've made some slight progress, but nothing substantial. If I achieve perfection one day, the silhouette on the wall will remain for a long time, as if I've crossed the threshold and left behind my mortal remains. Then I'll be able to ride bolts of lightning far and wide, free from all worldly restraints, sending down thunderbolts to punish evildoers and bless the virtuous. Just think of a freedom like that—it really doesn't move you?"

"This freedom you speak of, it still has existence at its core. It depends on reality.

No, it doesn't move me." Jian Ke shook his head again. "One day, you won't need the gathering and colliding of storm clouds to pull down thunder. You'll be able to call down thunderbolts from blue skies whenever you please. Or to go even further, when you no longer need the thunder, when the pulling becomes unnecessary, that's true ascendance."

Old Yin's knotted brow began to soften, and his two eyes blazed brighter. He made to speak, but Jian Ke raised a finger to his lips. The two of them remained this way in silence. A gust of wind blew past the secret chambers. Suddenly, Jian Ke burst out laughing. This started Old Yin laughing too, and amid their guffaws, Jian Ke addressed a bow towards Old Yin, bidding farewell.

"Wait—!" Old Yin called out. He walked up, grabbed Jian Ke's right hand with his left, spread it open, and with his index finger traced a figure on Jian Ke's palm—a word or a Daoist symbol, or perhaps both. "Thank you for what you said. Everyone has something like thunder to pull. They have their own path to walk, and there's no need to remain on any one road. It looks like there's still something weighing on your mind, so I'll send you off with three thunders. As dazzling as the sun, as hot as fire, and the sound—well, that's so-so. It's just a game, so don't take it too seriously. It won't harm anyone."

On his way down the mountain, the image of Old Yin kept returning to Jian Ke. He thought of the stone wall, the white hair gently fluttering in the evening breeze—that airy grace of an immortal, and yet the pitiful feebleness of old age. Who Old Yin really was, the trueness or falseness of everything that was said and done, and even if the events of this afternoon had actually happened—none of it mattered. What mattered was... Jian Ke stuck his right hand in his pocket and, as was his habit, groped for his lighter. Oddly, it felt different in his hand. Holding it up for examination, it was, unmistakably, only a pebble. He felt around everywhere, but the copper lighter that had belonged to A Huo's father, the lighter that accompanied him for so many years, was gone.

Jian Ke stood there with the intention of identifying the pebble, to deduce something about its origin, when, without warning, it crumbled—no, disintegrated. First it broke into a few pieces, but in a flash, it became a handful of sand. The grains followed the creases in his palm down through the gaps between his fingers, flowing faster and faster, and within the space of a breath, there was nothing but dust, scattering in the evening wind. The only meager consolation was that, as the pebble passed into sand and dust and wind, a low and muted thunder sounded, like the yowl of an infant beast.

A Huo's yard was already in sight. Just then, his phone rang. A Huo asked, "You coming down?"

"Almost there."

"Great. You and I are gonna have a good one tonight, gotta make up for these last few years. Since…" A Huo mumbled something, then let out a string of laughter, his signature, devilish laugh. After it had passed, he said, "I was starting to worry that you'd been kidnapped by Old Yin!"

"You know Old Yin?"

"Neighborhood's not that big. Who doesn't know Old Yin? That guy, I wouldn't say he's all smoke and mirrors, but he sure makes a lot out of nothing."

"Like everything he says is made up?"

"Well it depends on what he said. Flip it, flip it, you have to sprinkle it along this way—" A Huo's attention diverted temporarily to his visitors, and he let out another laugh. "Where are you? This lamb is almost done roasting! Right, right, about Old Yin. Whatever else, if he gave you that spiel about pulling thunder, don't believe a word of it. He was nearly struck dead by lightning a couple years back, and ever since then, he's been telling that story. A few years ago, some people came to the village, maybe artists or some kind of researchers, and after Old Yin spent a couple weeks with them, he really started to believe that he could pull thunder. Might as well go along with it—it's nice to see the old guy happy, if he's happy I'm happy. Some people have even seen him burning those pine trees in the middle of the night, but no one cares. Anyway, the trees are spread far enough apart that it won't lead to any trouble. Besides, so many of them, burnt like that, there's actually a weird appeal. Did you see them? Hello? Hello—?"

Jian Ke hung up. A Huo's voice carried over the wall, and after a couple more "hellos," he gave a defiant shout: "Lamb waits for no one!" It wasn't just in his head. Rising up with A Huo's voice was the delectable aroma of roasting lamb, the meat over the fire cooked till golden and crisp, slow drops of oil sizzling in the flame. It made him unbearably hungry, but somehow anxious at the same time.

How could he not at least try? The thought came to Jian Ke, and he brought himself to a stop. Standing in place, he looked up at the dispersing haze, soon to merge entirely with the night. Extending his right hand, he rubbed at the fissures in the clouds. A thread of white light gradually wound about his hand, twirling and weaving into a ball.

When that round of lightning was as large as a dish and as hot as a forge, Jian Ke flicked his wrist, sending it over the wall to strike the splayed sides of the lamb. Amidst cries of alarm, the fragrance of roasting meat wafted towards him, heavy and rich.

葭苇

Jia Wei

TRANSLATED BY
LIUYU IVY CHEN

诗三首

Me in the World

You are most distant to me
when the low flames of spring reach the highlands.
Distance does not recognize where you are
as north. I mean
in time, all those flocks of sheep
turning up and quieting down, bringing everything
within touch: forbidden lands, the eyes of clouds,
the mutinies of lovers. Were hands of lovers
gentler, another lamb would be born
from the clouds. Before the dowry of spring is delivered,
each peach tree will have borne a serene bride, not quite covering the hills,
and no one teasing her for being too thin.

Empty Things

As we leave, Xishuangbanna is entering monsoon season.
The cigarette case is empty. Curls of smoke
converse on subjects beyond silence.
Before falling asleep, my friend and I exchange our latest dreams.
This lonely camp. The territory of the rainforest
woven by banyan trees with strangling grips of love.
The only survivors are birdsongs from the treetops.
Knees submerged in rainwater. Because of love, I can no longer
speak properly. I'm no stranger to
pulling out the beloved handgun of my mouth
with the voice of children telling stories,
to aim at unpenetrated beauty, and make the kill.

To Ristore

The train did not stop.
Twilight spreading across the prairies.
Twilight small and quiet, and light… I mean
a lake.

At eighteen, soft waters of happiness ran through my fingers.
I learned to rise early, leave home, to turn at a quiet corner.
To boil oatmeal with twisting winds and a slow fire.
One ounce of cloud more than enough.

Later, I fell in love with a castrato.
My love included mountains, rivers, chapels,
and readers. By the Susquehanna River,
a Gregorian chant died out in murmurs.

Such loss is not merely individual
but is what the city walls, the moat, the silver needles of the wall clock endured.
Once, it even plotted a pause.
Then, a deep, vast emptiness. It still is.

Footsteps quicken, pointless for poetry. And a period
added to the night of lost virginity. Commonplace.
Ruins in relation to river stones.

Kind ones, you are what lies in a remote place:
you are snow white, you are expanse, you are tranquil stars.

A sheet of frost, a letter in an envelope, how many stars in water do you carry
to bring me my fortunes? Rehearse, turn,
fail at another forbidden enterprise.

Flash back to 1894, you see the same face
before the loom, mutely drawing out soft threads
to make children's clothes.
How about raincoats? Linen or acrylic?
A mission more futile than fish traps in the arid north?

Now and then I butt heads with a drop of rain: a blind needle from the sky!
What are you dispatching? Come and read my heart:
a cup of light. Glorious whispers, glory always leaving
a lamp of moonlight for whispering.

The only rivet. Clear, bright night sky.
Mud, chain, provisions...
The undiminished tender heart of a mule.
You whisper, I whisper it
—under the starry sky there's no need for literacy.

On the outskirts of Beijing, I read the last lines of Ristore's letter:
"Sometimes you give too much trust to people.
Although I find it laughable, I too once fell under its spell."

索耳

Suo Er

TRANSLATED BY
ZHI HUI HO

伉俪

MAN AND WIFE

I. FRIENDS

I've lost another friend. Honestly, I didn't think I had so many friends in the first place. Every day, I'd take my university's alumni records, put it in my lap, and flip through the pages, running my index finger over rows and rows of delightful, unfamiliar names, asking my wife: Are these my friends? And each time, when she said no, I would realize that I'd lost another friend. No regrets though. In fact, I'm happy about it. The feeling of putting aside a heavy burden. It's like playing the basketball game at the arcade, flinging ball after ball at the machine. But my wife has told me that I'm no longer allowed to go to such places. I'm not allowed to go anywhere, except for the park while accompanying her on an evening stroll, or to buy things for her. "Things" include Lee Kum Kee oyster sauce, kailan at $2.50 per jin, and gacha toys from Kaiyodo. In her eyes, that's all I'm good for. We make love irregularly, sometimes every other day, but sometimes we don't touch for two months at a time. Also, my wife has a quirk. When she climaxes, she likes to bite. Once she almost bit my ear off. I told her: Why don't you find something else to bite instead, and immediately after that, we had a dry spell of more than a month, until she fell in love with the main character from the anime *Genki Electric Dog*. She ordered a big plush version online and told me that she didn't need to bite me anymore. Really. She began biting the toy dog instead. After that, I felt pretty weird every time we did it. I couldn't tell where I was sticking my dick, and it might very well have been in the toy dog. Every evening after dinner, I take a walk with her in the park. Whenever we walk past the ruins of the old gates with their upside-down U-shape, she asks: Where have all those friends of yours gone? And I reply: It's all your fault. Her: My fault? Me: No one wants to be my friend when I'm with you. Her: Don't make me laugh, you've never had any friends. I'm the only person who's ever been willing to get close to you. She thinks

I'm joking, but I'm not. To be honest, before I married her, I still had two or three close friends. We didn't meet often, but we wrote letters to one another. One of them was from the same hometown as me, and after university, he'd chosen to stay in the village. Every time I went home for the Spring Festival, we'd have a drink together. He was passionately in love with fishing. Every letter he sent me was a continuous river of words about all the fish he'd caught: snakehead, hairtail, sand lance, pomfret, silver croaker, grass carp, tilapia, sweetfish, largemouth bass, barramundi, catfish, mackerel, fairy basslet, common rudd, sand whiting, yellow croaker, moray eel, catfish, red gurnard. He also sent us some of his homemade fish jerky. But then came three months of radio silence. When I returned home at the end of that year, they told me that he'd fallen into the river while fishing and drowned. The other two friends are a married couple, also friends from university who had bought a house in Shenzhen. At first, we were all on pretty good terms. In the first year after I got married, they even came over to visit us, and we all went to climb the Great Wall together. But the day after they left, my wife left me a note in the bathroom, proclaiming a "Mute Day." And indeed, she didn't say a single word to me that day. Ridiculous. Later, she told me that she thought I had a thing for that woman. I was at a loss as to how I could defend myself. She also said: I bet the three of you were in a love triangle. Right. I wasn't going to fight her. Her quivering, twitching, convulsing nostrils were a sure sign that if I didn't give in, there'd be hell to pay, so the only option left was to play along and confess that yes—the three of us had indeed been in a situation like that, all those years ago. But the important thing, I em-phasized to her, is that you are my true love, the one I've been waiting for all along. I said that several times, and those passionate avowals were enough to satisfy her. I know my wife's temperament well. She's the kind of woman who forms grievances quickly, but puts them aside just as easily. That said, if she gets it in her head to be angry at you, she could come up with the strangest things. It wasn't just "Mute Day." There was also "Noisy Day," "Naked Day," "Crying Day," and "Pranks Day." Accordingly, she would chatter nonstop from morning until night, walk back and forth in the house without a stitch of clothing on, and cry or tell jokes for twenty-four hours straight. The worst was "Kiddie Day." Just because I'd had a pleasant little conversation with a five-year-old in the courtyard of our complex, a note had been left in the bathroom, and true to form, she'd spent the whole day pouting and being coquettish, throwing tantrums like a five-year-old. Was she insinuating that I was a pedophile? Sometimes she really is too much. But I tolerate it all. I love her. Yes, very much. For her, I'm fine with being friendless. I'm happy to cut ties with everyone and everything. Plus, no one wants to be in touch with me either. She's bound me to her side like a toy dog. She always says that it's good to have no friends, that we've saved a lot of money by not having to give out red packets at weddings. She does have a point. Being friendless helped us make a financial comeback. After we'd lost big on the stock market a few years ago, all our savings basically evaporated, so my wife announced a no-spend plan. For three years, we didn't buy new clothes, didn't shop online, didn't eat Western food, didn't go to amusement parks, and used water and gas sparingly at home. The numbers in our bank account slowly ticked up, and we inched ever closer to our target, the steam of our happiness rising closer to its threshold. Recently, she told me: Just one more year. One more year and I'll lift the austerity order. Nothing could have been more thrilling. Other than the economic impact, I was slowly beginning to realize that the frugality was having another effect on me, which I'll call the "moral effect." That might not be the best turn of phrase, admittedly, but it really exists. You'll only come to know it when you experience such circumstances yourself. In rejecting all communications with the external world, you'd think that all of your ties would be severed, but in truth, new ones gradually form—novel, unprecedented ones. If you look carefully, you might even see their shining beams in primary colors. There's no making without breaking. With these new ties, my relationships with the world and with other people have actually become stronger. Even though I don't say a single thing to another soul, and though I have no idea what's actually happening in the news, I'm closer to people than I've ever been. I'm closer to their essence. I'm crystal clear about the need to express and to be expressed. These new powers of perception have greatly improved my life, and even the insomnia plaguing me since my teenage years has slowly vanished. Thank Athena. Every day, my wife sends me to the supermarket to buy kailan (one of the ways that she shows love), and every time I stand on the moving walkway, kailan in hand, I feel as though I'm slowly inching towards a mysterious, unknown space—in it are all the vegetables we like to eat, pipes flowing with our love fluids, and lots of cute 2D pets scurrying about. That space isn't any different from the space we live in now—that's a good way to think about it—but simply exists as an overlapping of ideas. My wife has a habit of writing in her diary after she's made dinner. She doesn't let me read what she writes, claiming that it's the only secret she keeps from me. According to her, it would be too terrifying to have absolutely no secrets between two people. I don't really agree, and I figured that she only does this out of vengeance (because she suspects me of keeping many secrets). Such actions are threaded throughout human history: betrayals, departures, rebellions. Once, I secretly read her diary and found it filled with the minutiae of daily life. In fact, almost everything was an experience we'd had together. Some examples: "Today I saw a kitteh under the bridge. He had a chocolate-colored spot on his head~ so cuteeee~ but he ignored me." Or, "Today I made shrimp-and-tomato dumplings. I steamed them for longer so that the skins would be softer." And another: "Today in the store I saw the cutest meow-mie but what I actually like is woof ahhhh noooo I'm going to turn moe too but I didn't buy it in the end tho!" These are secrets? I couldn't believe it, so I read her diary cover-to-cover again, but eventually just put it back in its place. How disappointing. I had actually hoped that she was keeping something from me. Instead, it looks as though she has no secrets whatsoever, which is even more difficult to fathom. I don't know. Maybe she just likes the sense of being engaged in a battle of wits. I especially like that she consistently does ridiculous things with utter seriousness. Once, when I was sending her off to work at the bus stop (we'd stopped driving to save money), she said: Bus stops should have beds, so that people can make love while waiting for the bus. Don't you think that would be really interesting? To fuck while you wait. It would relieve anxiety, and you could train yourself to have better self-control during orgasms. Then she really wrote a letter to the city council the very next day. After a few days, the council wrote back. Thank you for your kind suggestion. We anticipate that the timeline for successful implementation will be one hundred years. The reply bot had quite the sense of humor. I'm in charge of our emails, though admittedly, there isn't much to be in charge of. Since I cut off contact with my friends, only ads come to the inbox, and after the cost-cutting edict, even those gradually vanished. However, a week ago, an actual email arrived, addressed to me. The writer claimed that he hadn't seen me in a decade, and wanted to check on how my wife and I were doing. In his last line, he asked: How was your "little reunion"? The letter was signed "A-Li." Did I ever have a friend called "A-Li"? Ten years ago, I was still in university, so it must have been someone from that era, but I didn't remember anyone whose name included "Li." I even went through the alumni records to make sure, but there was no one with a "Li" among my classmates. Maybe it's someone from a different class, or a club I had been in. I searched again. Nothing. For the sake of being thorough, I looked through the university's entire directory of students, and shockingly, there wasn't even a single person with the "Li" character in their name. I found that a little strange. I copied the letter out on paper and deleted the email so my wife wouldn't see it, but in my mind, I kept chewing over the words. Especially that last line. What had the writer meant by my "little reunion"? A few days passed, and I still had no idea. I didn't dare to let my wife know. There wasn't any reason in particular, but I was just scared for her to find out. As I dithered, another email from A-Li arrived. He said: I think things aren't going well for you. I mean, you two. Both of you. You guys should go on a holiday. That's my suggestion. I deleted it the second I finished reading it. His tone unsettled me. Over the next few days, I tried to stay calm, but my wife still noticed something was up. We made love, and as she climaxed, I accidentally put my finger too close to her mouth, and she bit so hard that it dripped blood. After we were done, she helped me bandage the wound, and asked if something was wrong. I said: Nothing at all. She asked: Are you cheating on me? I pointed my injured finger at the heavens and swore that I was doing no such thing. She stared coolly at me and said: You'd better come clean. I'll give you three days. "Three days" is her catchphrase. She knows that typically, I'd cave and confess in half a day. But this time, she miscalculated. We gave each other the silent treatment for three days, until the plane tickets that I'd bought online arrived. Tickets in hand, she couldn't help asking me what I'd meant by them. I told her that a vacation would be the best way to resolve the crisis between us. She nearly flew into a rage hearing that, and I hurriedly added that if she agreed to come with me, I'd give her the whole story while we were away. She considered this for a moment, then asked: But what about our no-spend plan? I said: Forget it.

II. HOLIDAY

My wife jumped onto the little automated train and waved excitedly from the big carriage at the back. It was her fourth time already. The first three times, I'd ridden it with her, going through the tunnel from east to west and back again. But this time I just stood there with my back against the walls of the cave, gazing up at where my wife stood. I didn't want to go again.

"Come on!" she shouted at me. "One last time, please!"

"I'll just watch you!" I shook my head.

She turned away, ignoring me. The cream-colored train started itself up every five minutes, the two great wheels at the front giving off a deafening rumble. Simultaneously, there came an accompanying tremble from the body of the train, gentle but persistent. My wife's silhouette shook as well, dissipating into the surrounding air. Right before she disappeared into the tunnel's darkness, her clothes reflected one last gleam of blue and white back at me, then vanished without a trace. My wife, like a letter that had been ripped open and shoved down a throat.

After approximately ten minutes, the sound of the train rang out again, and the shape of her materialized in the tunnel. She didn't wait for the train to come fully to a halt before slowly descending the ladder. Her face was filled with anger. She glared at me, then turned and stalked off towards the exit. I shouldered our backpacks and followed closely behind.

"Why didn't you join me just now?" she asked loudly.

"Didn't feel like it."

"You went three times already!"

"You were fine on your own, though…" At that point, I saw that there was a swollen lump on her forehead, shaped like a horizontal Y. "Hey, what happened here?"

"Something scratched me, I guess," she said resentfully.

"That last time on the train?"

"Yes! Maybe if you'd been with me, I wouldn't have been scratched!"

I felt a little guilty. "Does it hurt?" I asked.

"A little. It was probably a bat or something."

I got some medicated ointment out for her. It left a yellow-purple stain on her forehead, and she couldn't help but grimace when she pulled out her pocket mirror for a look. "Like I'm some kind of Southeast Asian tribeswoman," she muttered.

We kept walking downhill. Occasionally, one or two spindle-shaped stones appeared in the grass, and it felt strange, stepping on them. In the distance, the road looped and wound around the hills, neatly flanked by oak trees about five meters tall. My gaze kept falling on the gaps in the trees—where the chain of green was occasionally broken, glimpses of barren ground showed through. Beyond the shade, sunlight fell on those patches of bare earth. Nearby, there were some old, half-rotten fences, with traces of strikingly white paint on the wooden posts. We had been walking for thirty minutes and were beginning to feel tired. As she walked, my wife took big swigs of water from her water bottle. I glanced at my phone. The sun would set in an hour, and if we didn't hurry, we might not get to the rest stop before nightfall.

"I can't move another step," my wife said. Sweat kept beading at her temples—a rare sight. She dug out her handkerchief and carefully wiped away the droplets.

"What's wrong?" I could tell something wasn't right. Her face was a little flushed.

"I'm… not feeling well," she said. "I feel faint. I just want to sleep for a bit."

I pressed my hand to her forehead. "Ah—hot. You're feverish!" I exclaimed.

"I figured. I feel like I'm made of cotton."

"Why the sudden fever?"

"No clue."

"Is it because of that scratch?" I stared at the mark on her forehead. "Maybe it's infected."

"But didn't we put the ointment on it?"

"Must not be working."

"I can't move another step. I need to rest." With that, my wife sat down. She put her backpack down and leaned against it, half-reclining in the grass. I dug out my phone and looked at the time again. My back was to the west, and the setting sun shone from behind me, illuminating a grey-white stretch of riverbank in the distance. Previously, we'd thought it was a low hill. The river couldn't be far from us, though we hadn't seen any streams on the way here. Perhaps they've dried up. Still, I preferred to shut my eyes and imagine endless schools of fish, both big and small, crowding the waters, pushing the river towards its banks with their shining bodies.

"Let's just camp here tonight," my wife suddenly said.

"No way," I answered. "This area is dangerous. What if there are leopards?"

"If there are, we would have been eaten already."

"Just because we haven't seen one doesn't mean we won't."

"What if we do see one?"

"That's just it. It's best if we don't encounter one at all, but if we do, I'll grab it. You run."

"Wouldn't it be better to be eaten together?"

"And be reunited in its belly?"

My wife couldn't help but giggle. She looked a little more alert, but it was also possible that she had grown weaker. "Let's keep going," she said, getting to her feet. "Maybe we'll run into a doctor at the rest stop."

We didn't have any fever medication, or even anything for a cold. I was frustrated just thinking about it. Taking my wife's backpack, I carried it in my arms, walking behind her. I rarely had the opportunity to look closely at her back. For the last few months, she's stuck to a careful diet and had lost about five kilograms. She was already tall and slender to begin with, and when she walked, her legs swung back and forth like pendulums, her neck drawing back with every step. That wasn't her usual gait, but perhaps she was subconsciously trying to relieve the weight of her neck. The sky was growing dark and I turned on the torch, catching up to walk with her side-by-side. She glanced quickly in my direction, almost like she was looking at a stranger—a stranger who had approached to illuminate her way. She turned her head away and suddenly quickened her footsteps, as if to leave behind the circle of light I was casting. I followed tightly on her heels, but she sped up, almost to the point of running. Just as I was thinking about how I could stop her, she suddenly staggered and almost fell.

"Are you alright?" I took her arm.

"My legs are going to give out," she said, panting.

"You grab the backpacks. I'll carry you."

She climbed onto my back, and we walked a little further. Her body felt like some kind of insect, curled in its damp and warm cocoon. It was quiet all around, save for the sound of wind gradually climbing the hills. Then from maybe three or four hundred meters away came a flash of red—a sign passing its light through the oaks.

"It's the rest stop!" my wife said.

"I see it too."

"But don't you think it's a bit strange?"

"What?"

"Look, the GPS says the rest stop's still two kilometers away."

"It's probably wrong."

"Mm."

We walked towards the rest stop, its glow gleaming brighter and brighter. By the door were two orange trees in pots, wreathed in little multicolored lights. My wife had me put her down—she felt like she could walk again. She grabbed my hand and we went ahead together, her palms a little rough and wrinkled from sweating so much. As we made our way across the manicured lawn, I swore we could both make out a tune. It sounded like funk music with a tight drumbeat, but it was very faint. We figured it was coming from inside the building.

My wife pressed the doorbell. The two-story rest stop was shaped like an overturned ashtray, with a two-meter-tall aluminum door that seemed to be the only breach point in the enormous, mechanical structure.

The bell rang five times, and from where we stood, we could hear the jangle mixing with the music from inside. But no one answered the door.

"But there are people inside, right?" my wife said. "They're just refusing to open the door for us."

"Why?"

"No idea. But I just know it."

"Maybe we can climb in from that window."

I pointed out a small window in the upper right corner of the building's facade, which looked like it would open into a corridor. My wife glanced at it and coldly said, "Let's not."

We circled the perimeter, and found some stairs leading to the basement near the left side of the building. The stairs were very steep, and when we slid down to the bottom, we saw lights embedded in the floor. Further ahead was an elevator, and as we rode it up, taking a scant ten seconds or so, my wife became oddly apathetic. She raised one leg and leaned back, pressing the sole of her foot against the wall, lifting her gaze to the ceiling. It seemed like she had stopped sweating, and her face was suffused with a rigid, pink color. The elevator door opened. In the doorway, there was a cloth squirrel. We gave it a curious glance before stepping out into the lobby. It was unusually silent, and the music seemed to have completely vanished. I even wondered if I had misheard it in the first place. All the lights were on, and not a single speck of dust could be seen. There were two shelves against one wall, neatly stocked with food, drinks, and emergency medical supplies, all looking as though they had never been touched. A basket behind the door was crammed full of black umbrellas, and beside it hung a planter with several sunflowers inside. The soil was damp, showing that the blooms must've been watered only a few hours ago. Everything was in perfect order, except for the squirrel at the elevator door.

"There's no one here," I said to my wife, completing my circuit of the lobby.

She didn't respond. She had lain down on a yellow sofa to try and catch her breath. The look on her face was starting to scare me.

"How do you feel?" I asked.

"I'm okay."

"Like hell you are." I touched my hand to her forehead. "Your temperature's gone up."

"But I feel pretty clear-headed."

"You'd better take some medicine."

I grabbed a box of ibuprofen off the shelves and got her a cup of water from the dispenser. She took the cup, but just stared at the bubbles in the water for a while. It was some time before she swallowed a few capsules, and as I watched her, it felt like her movements were completely alien. She drained the cup in one go. If I had gotten her another ten cups, I'm sure she would have gulped them all down. As I sat on the yellow sofa, I had no idea why my mind was filling with such thoughts.

After some time, my wife began to yawn. She told me that she was just yawning, that she wasn't actually sleepy. It was for fun, she insisted, just like how some people like to shake their legs. They don't have to, but they want to. I knew she was just being stubborn—she just didn't want to doze off in front of me. I could leave. I got up and went over to the reception. There were some books there: a wuxia novel by Gu Long, two English dictionaries, a heavy edition of *Modern Rock Music in China*, and a notebook with a black cover. The notebook was the guest register, and in it were names, phone numbers, and the durations of stays. I turned to a clean page and wrote down our names, as well as the date. As for how long we would stay, well, that depended on how long she would take to recover, but I estimated we would probably leave the next day, or at most the day after—depending on my wife. After I finished, I flipped through the book, looking at the details of previous guests. I'm not sure if there was some subconscious purpose or if I was merely doing it out of boredom, but when I got to the sixth page, a name caught my eye: Yang Jinli. I said the name to myself a few times before realizing that, in looking through the register, I'd been searching for this very person all along—even though the name was unfamiliar. The accompanying information indicated that he had come to this rest stop a week before us, staying two days. I dug out my phone, and dialed the number he had left.

The call connected. After four or five rings, a man's voice came through.

"Is this Mr. Yang Jinli?" I asked.

"Yes. You are?"

"I'm your friend. You know, you sent me an email a week ago."

"An email?"

"Yes," I said, lowering my voice. "You suggested that we should go on holiday, right?"

"I don't know what you're talking about." He was beginning to sound annoyed.

"I took your advice! My wife and I are traveling, just the two of us. We came to Hunan. And guess what? We're at the same rest stop that you stayed at just a week ago. I realized it when I looked at the guestbook. Isn't it too much of a coincidence? Just a week ago, you sent me that email from this exact rest stop..."

"Fuck off, you're crazy." He hung up on me.

I hadn't anticipated that he would hang up so quickly. I didn't even manage to ask him about the "little reunion." Feeling a bit listless, I rifled through the drawers and found a pack of cigarettes, but as soon as I had one between my fingers, the urge to smoke left me. I scrutinized the packet and realized that the picture on the front didn't quite match my memory of it. Maybe it was a knock-off. Just then, the soft sound of my wife snoring caught my attention. I looked over the countertop towards the sofa and saw her slender, curled-up form. There was a kind of soft, plush feeling about her body. I went and sat down beside her, carefully listening to her breathing, a music of distant tides. Previously, she'd been a very quiet sleeper. She never made a sound, nor was she ever woken up by any noise I made. The shape of her sleeping struck me as a subtle and delicate piece of performance art, a fragile, ephemeral artwork that invited the viewer to both peep at and protect her. The sound of the tides ebbed and flowed, and the whole lobby appeared to sway along, growing hazier. Something about her body kept urging me to go to sleep, and I involuntarily yawned once or twice.

Suddenly, a sound came from the elevator, startling both of us awake. Two men wearing balaclavas rushed out, each carrying a long knife. They ran up and ordered us not to move. We were frozen with fear and confusion. When my wife realized what was happening, she began to scream.

"Shut up!" one of the men barked. "Stop it!"

We knew we were in trouble. What were these thugs even doing here? My wife and I embraced tightly, trying to control our panic. One of the men—the shorter one—kept his knife pointed at us. The other prowled around the lobby, ransacking it. After a while, he walked over and shot a meaningful look at his companion.

"Anything?" the short thug asked.

"Nothing," said the other.

"Search these two."

That asshole actually came over to search us. He even went over us twice, but couldn't seem to find what he was looking for. They took all our money and valuables, and sneered at a picture of the two of us that they found in my wallet. A chill went through me at the looks on their faces. Then they told us to strip.

"You're going too far," my wife said angrily. "We're just tourists, we don't know anything, and we've already given you everything we have!"

"Not everything," one of them leered. "Aren't you still wearing your clothes?"

The guy who searched us kept his knife pointed at my wife. He ordered me to strip first. I closed my eyes, first taking off my pants, then my shirt, and finally my underwear. I stood there completely naked, and the two men began to laugh. The whole time, my wife kept her eyes on me. She had her teeth set firmly in her lower lip, as though she was thinking of something else. I was worried for her, but we were several meters apart, and the thugs wouldn't let us get any closer. I tried to catch her eye, hoping to convey that she shouldn't do anything rash, but to no avail. She took her top off, then made a mad dash for the elevator door. But one of the men caught up to her easily and hit her in the face. She struggled against him and even made to bite him. Enraged, he aimed a heavy blow at the back of her head with the knife handle, and punched her in the neck. She slid silently to the floor. At the same time, the short thug kicked me in the ribs. I also went down, and he rained blow after blow on my back, stomach, and head. I felt like every part of my body was being pierced through. As I lay there groaning, I could see my wife in my peripheral vision. She lay face down, unconscious. The men laughed loudly and walked past us, disappearing out the door.

III. KINGDOM

My wife said: A-Li. I said: What? A-Li A-Li. Who is A-Li? A-Li wore a big green quilted jacket with polka dots, and before he went to America, he said that he would come to see me. Did he come see you? No. But after he went to America, he wrote to you. He didn't write to me. He did—every day he wrote, and at the end of each letter he would take a blue pen and draw a fish, something between a silver carp or a crucian carp, which was supposed to represent you. Because my last name is Yu. That's right, he wrote you letters every day but he never sent them, instead he stuffed them into a pillowcase, and when that pillowcase was full, he needed something else to shove his letters into, so he bought more pillowcases, so many that his room was filled with pillows of every color, and they were all stuffed with letters, letters to you. What a touching story. I'm not telling a story. But you're a natural storyteller, have you forgotten? I've never felt like my writing was particularly brilliant, on the contrary, I hate my work. Why? Because I'm suspicious of myself, I suspect that I don't have the talent for writing, that I've lost all sense of taste, any ability to tell good from bad, and I'm not sure if what I write is the "best" according to my standards. You're afraid that your work is trash. No, I'm not afraid, that's not what I mean, I'm scared because every time I look at the words I've written, I feel like they haven't come from me, but I also know that they're not by anyone else—they don't look unfamiliar, but I still have the unshakable sense that they have nothing to do with me. But you still write, you write on time every day, after dinner you always shut yourself up in your room, coming to bed only at two in the morning, and you always wake me up. Actually, I only manage to write for about an hour. And the rest of the time? Just getting into the rhythm that the plants or the stars move to. What do you mean? Plants are elements of silence, growing their quiet spokes through the shadows of the day, turning into spice-spattered cogs of wind at night, and they infiltrate your body, losing their shape, and it hurts. No wonder you cry secretly when you get into bed at night. I cry? You didn't know?

I didn't think you knew. You cried, but I couldn't see your tears. Let's not talk about that just yet... My chest hurts, how about you, you've lost a lot of blood. My head's been split open, the blood in my hair feels sticky and awful. Then don't sleep on the floor—go to the sofa, there's a place for you there. What's the difference between dying on a chair and dying on the floor? If you die on a chair, it means that you were once a member of society, but you're nothing if you die on the floor. Then I should die in the bathtub, like a great man, a hero. But you don't have a skin disease, and you're not a revolutionary. I've always been a revolutionary—the subject of my revolution is myself, and I've always been a feminist, even though I never talk about it and I'll never make a big deal out of it, but I know I am. You shouldn't talk so seriously about that. I know, it's not appropriate to talk about it now, just like I've never talked about it before. To go back to what we were discussing earlier… I cried. Yes, why did you cry? I don't remember—right, once it was because I dreamt of someone. But you weren't asleep, your eyes weren't even shut. I dream as soon as I lie down. Who did you dream of? I dreamt of Chen Ruiyin. Who is Chen Ruiyin? An old classmate of mine from the same hometown, I've talked about him before, the one who drowned in the river while fishing. I remember now—didn't he have a wart on his eyelid? You've never met him before. No, but I feel like I know him so well—I could picture him in my mind's eye the minute you brought him up. His eyelid did have a wart on it, maybe more than one, even. God. Honestly I don't really remember what he looks like anymore, the last time I saw him was seven or eight years ago, but it feels like even longer—it's like when he was alive, we hadn't even landed on the moon yet, and anyway, he had forgettable features, it's been like that ever since he was born, wart or no wart. What was your dream about? I dreamt we were sitting together on the riverbank, fishing, and honestly, it's weird, because I've never gone fishing with him before, and I have no idea how he looks when he's fishing, but as I sat there, I felt so close to him, I can't describe it, it wasn't just him, or the fishing, or the scenery, but it was as though I had experienced all of it a hundred thousand times before. Yes, all these fragments seeping through, throwing the hippocampus into disorder—it creates a sweet sense of strangeness, the sharing of memories, the mistaken imaginings of the mind. We chatted endlessly, he kept talking, so did I, we must have said almost everything there is to say in this lifetime, but the minute I opened my eyes and sat up in bed, it was as though all the words had been scraped from my mind, and I could only remember the few lines he used when describing something we didn't know about yet. Like what? The shared space of our imagination—he said to me—exists beneath all the rivers, under the rush of the water, and as with any kingdom, it follows a set of rules… I asked him how he knew, and he answered that fishing is the way to make contact, the hook catching at the shreds of order slipping out from that space, like how on a rainy day you can only catch yellow croaker and on a sunny day only lizardfish, or that the fish you catch in the rapids will have a more delicate texture, which the fish in other areas never have, and also, some kinds of fish must be kept alive for three days before you can eat them, and some must be released back into the water, otherwise it's bad luck. Ha ha ha. Do you think he's right? No, I'm not concerned with notions of right or wrong. Then what do you think of his idea? What idea? The kingdom under the water. He's provided a new method of investigation, and it's true that fishing is about observation, about making contact, so if you don't fish, you'd be completely ignorant of the kingdom under the water, but then why can't we just fish without any meaning behind it? Fishing meaninglessly. Yes, meaninglessly—after all, I'm very familiar with fish, even though I've never gone fishing, because I grew up in a fishing village, and there, our people didn't fish with rods and bait but with nets, and a whole school of fish is much more meaningless than a single fish. If I get a chance in the future, I'll charter a boat out to sea and give it a try... I think I've lost feeling in my neck. I feel like that in my scalp, like the top of my skull's been lopped off and given to Venus as padding for her new clothes. Venus never wears clothes. We're also not born wearing clothes. So we shouldn't wear clothes when we die. But we need to wear clothes while we're alive. We're not wearing clothes now, aren't we living? We've gone through something horrible and we're in the vortex of the storm. Under these circumstances, I don't think we have to follow the rules about wearing clothes. We're about to die, is it okay to not wear clothes because of that? No—*about to die* and *dead* are two completely different things, it's only the dead who don't need to wear clothes. Why do we have to follow the rules? That's the kind of kingdom you're in, my love. Is there such an existence? You can't feel it? I've thought of something. Tell me. One summer, when I was still a child, my third uncle had a bad seizure, so my dad killed a wild boar and took out its gallbladder, but we needed someone to deliver it to my uncle, and no one else was free, so dad asked me to go, since I'd been to uncle's house to play with my cousins, so I set out happily with the gallbladder, and I walked for an hour on the main road before realizing that I could take a shortcut through the mountains instead, and I could even pick some fruits to share with my cousins along the way, and even though I didn't often walk that way, it wasn't a difficult path, so I went, and it was smooth-going at first, I remember the moss gleaming oil-slick green along the stones, and I went carefully down to the guava trees, laden with ripe fruit the size of ping-pong balls—the wild kind was especially sweet, and my mouth was watering, so I put the wrapped gallbladder down at the foot of the tree, took off my shoes, began to climb, and when I got to the top, I picked one, wiped it clean on my shirt, ate it straightaway, and then I ate another, and another before plucking a few more and stuffing them in my pockets for my cousins, thinking that I should get on with my task, but would you believe, just as I was about to come down, a strange feeling came over me, I can't even remember what it was, but maybe the tree full of fruit caused a strange kind of loathing, even though I had just eaten so many, and after I climbed down, I got a stick and clambered up again, and one by one I knocked every single guava off the tree, turning it barren in an instant, and I felt so relieved, even though I didn't understand where the anger had come from, but afterwards when I went on my way, gallbladder in hand, somehow I got lost, I turned left and right but couldn't find the way out, there was only one path, but I wandered back and forth, not even able to find the way home, and by then the sky was darkening and I was getting scared, the fruit I had stuffed in my pockets had long fallen out somewhere, and finally, after a very long time, I somehow found the way, and I hurried towards my uncle's house, running ahead with the precious gallbladder clutched to my chest, and as I went over the filthy ditch near their house, I heard weeping, an impossibly sad sound, and when I crossed the threshold, I saw my aunt standing under the eaves, wiping the tears from her face, and the moment she saw me, she cried, aiya, ai, your uncle's gone. Aiya, ai. I still remember how her voice sounded, saying those words. Even if you had delivered the gallbladder to your uncle in time, he still would've died, he couldn't have escaped it, so it had nothing to do with you, it's not like he would've lived if you had managed to give him the gallbladder—he had to die, do you get what I mean? No, you've misunderstood, I'm telling you this to prove that the kingdom exists, that order exists—think about it, it all makes sense, if we go back to that guava tree: if I hadn't knocked all the fruit off, I wouldn't have violated the order of things and angered the mountain god, who wouldn't have punished me by making me lose my way, and if I hadn't been lost, I would have reached my uncle in time, and if I had reached him in time, he wouldn't have died, that's the entire chain of events. You've gone a bit too far. I haven't, only I know what I know, because only I was on the mountain that day, and when I climbed the guava tree, guess what I saw, a sight I'll never forget: the rice paddies at the foot of the distant hills, the unbroken red earth dotted with tufts of fluff, the water buffalo swimming like fish, people going back and forth across the ridges, as measured and orderly as machines, never ceasing, and the ones laboring in the field were bent over, revealing the round and shiny backs of their heads, occasionally they would lift their eyes to the sun, and the light would cling to their backs, crawling imperceptibly slow, sometimes they sang, and sometimes they were silent, sometimes they spoke in intimate whispers to their wives, and though I was far away, it was like everything was taking place right beside me, thanks be to Prometheus, an electric current ran through me, and although I didn't have the words to describe it then as I do now, I definitely felt it, a macroscopic order, tradition, or awareness, akin to the skeleton of the kingdom, expanding outwards from my body, slowly enveloping the entirety of the southern skies, ah—the kingdom of grain, the kingdom of agriculture, the kingdom of farmers. The kingdom of fishing. The kingdom of those who fish with nets. The kingdom of those who fish with rods. The kingdom of sleep. The kingdom of memory. I'm going to sleep now. Goodnight, Meow-mie. Goodnight, Genki Electric Dog. Before you fall asleep, think back to where the water runs and the grass grows green, you've sat there countless times, and beside you is your friend, your lover, your servant, and a sweet wind is sweeping past your ears. Talk to them about making love. Masturbate. Eat. Piss. Amen. Amen. Amen. Amen. Amen. Amen.

李嘉茵

TRANSLATED BY
HELEN LEI JIANG

*Li
Jiayin*

波密人的历史时间

HISTORY IN BOMI TIME

I. THE BOOK OF DREAMS

To this day, the origin of the Bomi people remains a contested topic among academics.

They were first given this name by the English scholar Lady Brookfield. During a trip to Coconut City with her husband, her private plane encountered a sudden hurricane, and after dodging numerous cliffs and peaks, they were forced to make an emergency landing in an extensive valley of coconut trees. The fire and smoke from the burning plane attracted the members of a nearby prehistoric tribe; they arrived wearing leather masks, their bodies painted all over, and crooned as they danced around a disoriented Lady Brookfield and her wounded husband. "Bomi, bomi," sounded the hide drums, like wind rustling through the leaves. An elder who appeared to be a witch doctor daubed their foreheads and wounds with a sweet-smelling green paste—what looked like a concoction of sugarcane, noni, and other plants—then covered the injured areas with freshly peeled bark from a dragon tree. Purple smoke rose from a medicine stove, lulling them into deep sleep. While she convalesced, Lady Brookfield studied the tribe extensively. Their houses were woven from tropical plants; they were knowledgeable of the rainforest's every plant and living being, including their value and utility; and they worshiped a totem of an aggressive-looking, lake-dwelling beast that closely resembled a crocodile. While attempting to learn their dialect, she discovered that it was derived from a tangle of language families. Furthermore, it had no present tense, only past and future. This is one possible explanation as to why Lady Brookfield always felt that, compared to other places, time went by faster among the Bomi.

Studies show that prior to the mid-nineteenth century, this dense jungle located deep in the Nanyang region was yet unknown. Then, between March 1854 and April 1862, the English naturalist Alfred Russel Wallace visited the Malay Archipelago multiple times, traveling between its islands. In those eight years, he covered a distance of fourteen thousand miles and collected one hundred and twenty thousand specimens, including three thousand feathers and over twenty thousand samples of various insects, mammals, and terrestrial mollusks—which included nine hundred never-before-seen species of the longhorn beetle. Later on, during a period of illness, he proposed a theory of evolution and a hypothesis on the geographical distribution of animal species based on the tenets of natural selection. Six years after Wallace returned to England, these experiences became a book entitled *The Malay Archipelago*.

The Malay Archipelago describes a long, arching volcanic belt that winds like a train through Sumatra, Java, Bali, Lombok, Sumbawa, Flores, and other islands, all the way to Morotai. Composed of tens of active volcanoes and several hundred extinct volcanoes, it alternates between slumber and wakefulness. On December 29 1862, for example, "after two hundred and fifteen years of perfect inaction, [Mount Makian] again suddenly burst forth, blowing up and completely destroying the greater part of the inhabitants, and sending forth such volumes of ashes as to darken the air at Ternate, forty miles off. … Volcanic eruptions and earthquakes wash away memories of history; they represent both an end and a beginning. In many of the islands, the years of great eruptions form the chronological epochs of the native inhabitants, by the aid of which the ages of their children are remembered, and the dates of many important events are determined." (Alfred Russel Wallace, *The Malay Archipelago*, 1978, p. 126).

After Wallace, several Western expeditions traveled to the region in search of this seldom-seen tribe, but were continuously thwarted by compass malfunctions. Upon their return, tests of the soil samples concluded that the ground contained large amounts of minerals and calcium, suggesting that metal ores in the area had interfered with the compass's accuracy. Further analysis of the calcium microparticles pointed to their provenance as the human body. The anthropologists may well have chanced upon an ancient burial site, speculated to be the remains of an earthquake-stricken village.

In a well-known tribal song of the region, the following lines appear: "Tribesmen vanish as the winter deepens / Awaiting spring, the coming year awakens like a snake from hibernation." As these verses have undergone numerous translations by various linguists and lexicographers, the present iteration is for reference only.

—excerpted from *Field Report on the Origins of the Austronesian Bomi People of Southeast Asia*

♋

There's nothing to explain.

I had made up every single word in that report. My sources were a fragmented edition of an Austronesian-language text I'd found at a flea market, and a dream I had one afternoon.

I handed in my made-up report as if it were a work of genuine academic research, slipping it into my professor's letter box at the university. As the bound pages slid to the bottom, light as an icefish entering the water, a brief spell of satisfaction passed through me—but it was quickly replaced by apprehension. For some inexplicable reason, a voice told me not to panic. I was doing nothing wrong. After all, it was only coursework for Professor Y.

Professor Y had taught me during one of my university electives, later becoming my dissertation supervisor. I'm a third-year student at a coastal university in southern Fujian, majoring in Anthropology. Malinowski, Lévi-Strauss, and Lim Hooi Seong populated the bookshelves of my dorm room for years, but I never had the courage to crack open any of those thick tomes. I was originally pushed into anthropology for purely administrative reasons, and to this day I still can't muster any interest for it. I just wanted a degree. In my third year, with my head empty and the term drawing to a close, I was obliged to start thinking about my thesis.

For Professor Y's class, I had planned to do a study on a rarely-seen Southeast Asian tribe. A few years ago, during a clearance sale at the local flea market, I found half a tattered copy of some book written in an Austronesian language, no publication date. I uploaded photos of the day's finds to Facebook—a piece of scroll-patterned batik, a Thai amulet of a see-no-evil Buddha, and the book—earning some positive feedback from my friends. An Indonesian person politely messaged me about the book after seeing the photos; he said that he had come across the language as a child, but hadn't seen it since his grandfather passed away. A tiger dies and leaves behind its stripes, an elephant dies and leaves behind its tusks—his grandfather had left this world so quietly, and he told me he found that regrettable. His profile picture was a photo of Mount Bromo erupting, rose-colored flames sputtering in all directions before a blue and purple sky. When I asked him if he could understand the contents of the book, he told me that the writing was a mix of Old Javanese and the more obscure Kawi, a language widely used before the establishment of the Mataram Kingdom, which he could understand only partially. He agreed to my request to summarize the parts he could make out, but said it would take some time.

I didn't renew my VPN when it expired a few days later, mostly because I was busy with other things. I was in the middle of moving between campuses, swamped with the million trifles that came with the process, and after I'd settled down, I spent my days wandering aimlessly around the university. It wasn't until I was staring down at my completely blank research paper at the end of term, panicking, that I thought of the book again. I looked through my luggage, but no luck. When I logged back on to check my Facebook albums, a couple of weeks-old messages from the Indonesian person popped up. He said it was a rough translation, he'd forgotten the exact meaning of many words that couldn't be found in Old Javanese dictionaries, and some parts could only approach the gist of the original. I thanked him and saved the translation. He said he wouldn't mind translating a few more pages if I needed. I didn't reply. He added that he didn't require payment, but he would like to buy the book from me, if I was willing. I silently closed the chat window.

Recently, I've begun recalling parts of the book. It stated that for centuries, the Bomi people survived on hunting, gathering, and fishing. They wove baskets and hammocks, carved wooden canoes, made lances, bows, and arrows, leading a nomadic life in the depths of the rainforest, unbothered by the passage of time. They were a peaceful peo- ple with a very faint sense of hierarchy, naturally disposed to share all they had. In other words, theirs was a society in which the concept of private ownership did not exist.

To them, there were no clear boundaries between dreams and reality. If a boy dreamt about a girl, he would give her a flower upon waking. The Bomi were also known as the Dream People; they learnt how to control the realm of dreams, and foresaw real-life events in them. They had a profound conviction that events contained in dreams even- tually found their way to reality.

I found a twenty-minute black-and-white film on YouTube called *The Dream People*, in which a director of Malay descent documented their search for the Bomi people. The algorithm then recommended several videos that captured the shoot behind the scenes, which showed the director using elephants to transport equipment. The elephants swayed along with their eyes closed, unfurling their trunks to reach for the leaves at the side of the road, where green bananas hung from the branches in garlands. There was also footage of natives riding on elephants—a wholly choreographed fantasy, since natives of that region don't actually ride elephants.

At first, in the futile hope of retrieving something from the vaporous depths of history, I tried searching through academic materials for possible causes of the tribe's extinction, formulating theories about war and displacement and natural disasters as though I were chasing down an ancient myth. The truth is, the Bomi people may have disappeared naturally, like a flock of migrating birds, scattering.

The rainforest blocks out the sky, the sun. The light of modernity shines on everything, leaving nowhere for anything to hide.

Around that time, I revisited the works of R. G. Collingwood. In *The Idea of History*, he posits that historical narratives do not hinge on fixed points, but are perpetually shifting and sliding. Encouraged by the fact that "imaginative reconstruction" had become a relatively common approach in microhistory studies, and pressed by a dearth of fieldwork data and a looming deadline, I settled on using fiction to represent this entangled, nebulous period. History is but the product of a linguistic fabrication, I thought. Between cognition and memory, memory and reconstruction, reconstruction and narrative, there had never been any clear boundaries to begin with.

I have to admit that my decision to fabricate my report had something to do with the elective itself. It was a perplexing course. If I'm being honest, I'd slept through most of my classes that term, but Professor Y's classroom was the only one in which I couldn't get any proper rest. He would occasionally burst into song during lectures, and I'd be startled out of my slumber to tap my knuckles against the desk, knocking out an accompaniment to the music. One day, the setting sun cast a diagonal shadow into our classroom, severing space and time, half vivid orange and half dark copper, the boundary between the two slowly gliding over the edges of desks and chairs. I had been sleeping in the dark, braced over my desk, when the sunlight fell along my eyes, waking me. Professor Y had stopped teaching, and stood with a pensive look on his face. Then, he began singing a low, somber song, and everyone quieted, holding their breath to listen. After the song ended, he was silent until the bell rang, signaling the end of class. He looked up, as if suddenly surfacing from a different realm. He just remembered a mourning song, he said, and began singing it on the spot, without rhyme or reason. He asked everyone in the classroom to forget what just happened.

It was nearing twilight by the time I sat down to write my report. Feeling tired, I lay down to rest a while. I dreamt I was lying on a river, where the sound of laughter reached me from some distant shore. They held long machetes to cut nipa palm leaves, their faces painted red, and led me through a path crowded with rambutan and durian trees towards a cave. In front of the peeling paintings covering the walls, they offered up sacrifices and beat their drums. From the outside came a blast of mining explosives, and the cave promptly collapsed. I woke up and sat in a daze for a while, mulling over the dream. I finished my report overnight, borrowing from my unconscious visions and making a point to tack on a long and pretentious English-language bibliography, taken from various non-existent foreign publications. With no time to go over the finished report, I dashed to the faculty building to drop it—an hour before the deadline—into Professor Y's letter box. As I watched the manuscript slip through the long, narrow opening and into the dark interior, I breathed a long sigh of relief.

The next term, I ran into Professor Y on campus, sitting on a stone bench with his head bowed, seemingly lost in thought. I tried to walk by surreptitiously, but he intercepted me. Wide-eyed, he said that he'd never seen the quotations in my essay. I insisted they were real, and dutifully told him about the Old Javanese book I'd found at the flea market several years ago. Professor Y shook his head, smiling, then stood up and walked away. I let out a defeated sigh, knowing full well that he wouldn't buy my story. After that encounter, my days became lost to anxiety. One night, I dreamt about Professor Y tearing up my report in front of the whole class. Pieces of paper floated about us, suspended in mid-air, while he sang a somber mourning song, looking at me with those solemn eyes. So, when I logged into my university account two weeks later to check my grades, I was overjoyed to find that I'd only just passed. With the disquietude finally tempered, I reverted to my scattered, carefree ways, and resumed my daily schedule of aimless wandering.

I ran into Lynx on a hot, stuffy day, in a small video rental shop near the university. Lynx, who'd started at the university two years before me, was Professor Y's teaching assistant—a Singaporean Chinese whose family came from Quangang, he had enrolled as an overseas student and spoke fluent Mandarin. He had copper skin and deep-set eyes, large and listless. According to him, there was some Filipino heritage on his paternal grandmother's side. We'd only met a few times before that, during department-wide electives, so though I could recognize him, we weren't close. I'd never been especially engaged in Professor Y's ethnology classes, nor had I ever contacted Lynx in private.

The video shop was on the third floor of a street-facing commercial building, reachable by a narrow staircase winding and twisting as if headed towards the sky, wide enough for only one person to pass at a time. Only a handful of people were there for the screening, sitting scattered about the room. They were showing *Shamans of the Blind Country*, a documentary by the anthropologist Michael Oppitz that recorded the nomadic everyday life and shamanic rituals of the Nepali Magar people. To make it, Oppitz had lived in a Magar village for two years, eventually assembling the footage into a nearly four-hour-long film.

The projector started up and the lights dimmed, transforming the space into a darkroom. Half an hour into the film, a few people silently got up and left. An hour later, to keep from dozing off, I went to the bar, got a martini, and poked the green olive at the bottom of the triangular glass again and again with a metal skewer. I let myself drift off another forty-five minutes later, unable to fight the drowsiness any longer. The last thing I remember seeing before falling asleep was a boy sitting in front of me, his back as straight as the trunk of a palm.

I awoke to the sight of a row of toes: long and slender, almost ape-like, sticking out from a pair of flip flops the color of floating weeds. I looked up to see a smiling face half-way between familiar and unknown. Still in a daze, I nodded to him out of politeness. It took me a while to remember who he was. They're closing for the night, Lynx said, let's go back to campus together. How was the documentary? I asked. He said it was pretty good, very illuminating for his current research on semi-nomadic peoples. We made our way down the long and winding staircase, and as I walked behind him, my face to his back, he turned towards me slightly, eyes sparkling, and warned me about the steps, they were steep. Standing on that grim and narrow underworld passage of a staircase, I was instantly moved by his gaze; it reminded me of Orpheus, who had also turned back to look.

Out on the street, we stood under a streetlamp and smoked. For a brief spell of silence, I watched the moths flying around the post in circles. Lynx stubbed out his cigarette and said, I saw the report you submitted last term, Professor Y asked me to give preliminary scores to all the papers. Thank you, I said, it's only because of you that I managed to pass. I'm curious about what drove you to write a fake report, he said, and does that book really exist? I told him the background story in detail, to which Lynx said, smiling, We have stories like that back home, too. Let's talk about this someplace else.

We went to a nearby Mexican-themed bar that served small plates, with walls covered in intricately patterned Talavera tiles. Lynx chose a window seat and ordered a Loch Lomond whiskey and a hookah, leaning against a curtain splashed in bold colors. Where I'm from, he said, there are lots of islands, and on one of them, some fishermen once found the remains of a settlement, a cluster of prehistoric huts like the stilt houses of the Dayak people. They were dilapidated—a mere shadow of what had once existed there—and surrounded by lush greenery. The people who lived in them long ago are nowhere to be found.

In the muted yellow glow of the bar lights, the four tubes sticking out of the hookah made it look like a spongy deep-sea jellyfish. Every time Lynx took a drag, it looked like he was sucking on one of its tentacles. He said that he'd done some research on foreign websites but hadn't found any conclusive answers, only scattered data and vague conjectures. He exhaled some smoke and stirred the straw in his drink. The mint in his peacock-blue glass floated up and fluttered back down.

"The enigmatic silence of all things," I said.

Using the keywords and foreign databases Lynx provided, I found two articles, each offering a different hypothesis. The first suggested that the Bomi settlement ruins were located close to Lak Sao, where jungle-dwelling natives had once sought temporary refuge from violence. On the banks of a nearby river, two ancient boulders that were used to sharpen knives marked the starting point of the local residents' hunt for the natives. Natives who were captured were then enslaved, deprived forever of freedom. The elderly were killed, while the children were adopted into modern society, where they would grow up to forget their identity and ancestry. During the hunt, the terrified natives escaped into the depths of the rainforest and built a new settlement in a remote, unknown location. The second hypothesis proposed that the Bomi may have been related to the upstream-dwelling Dayak people, but were forced to migrate due to an earthquake that occurred a century ago. The article then took a geological turn to explain the correlation between tectonic shifts and the appearance of settlements, even including a cross-section of the earth's crust and a geological model illustrating its movements. That article was funded by a student research grant from the Society of Economic Geologists.

When I was offered an internship at M Securities a few days later, I promptly abandoned these unresolved and impenetrable historical riddles to spend my days crossing the city south to north, plopping down into a cubicle to print, photocopy, write reports, and translate documents. To cut down on the commute, I moved out of my dorm and rented a place in an old residential building closer to the company. In the muggy summer heat, the building's outer walls grew a layer of moss, and the showerhead in my bathroom intermittently dripped with a yellowish-brown liquid. While living there, I always felt that I would eventually start to fester and decay alongside the building. There was a fruit stand open year-round on the corner of the street, run by a granny who pushed her cart in from the village every day. She was short and stocky, with skin tanned auburn—she reminded me of a dried persimmon splayed out under the sun. Whenever I walked by her stand, I would buy mangoes, jackfruit, and other tropical fruits to store in the cupboards of my rental. If there were java apples, I'd get them while fresh. Throughout the summer, I ingested large quantities of sweet fruit to combat that inner decay. Maybe they were too high in sugar, or ripened too fast, but the fruit in the cupboards always went rotten within a day or two, prematurely filling the air with a smell of putrefaction. Somehow, it never felt like time was going by that quickly. After Typhoon Meranti passed through the country, a flower shop opened up opposite to the fruit stand, bursting with color. Fresh flowers are always in bloom on this tropical island.

With the arrival of the rainy season in August, my roof started to leak, so I made a deal with the landlord to get back part of my rent, and started looking for a new place to live. On the day of the move, my repeated trips up and down the stairs barely made a dent in the sprawling number of things, which wordlessly returned my gaze from their piles on the floor. All the course mates I usually got along with had, one by one, politely turned down my appeals for help, and so without much hope I messaged Lynx, asking if he had already gone back to his hometown.

Fifteen minutes later, Lynx replied, saying that he planned to leave in two weeks— there were still some documents he had to sort through at the university. I briefly explained my predicament and asked if he could come to the north of the city. No reply. By the time I'd used every ounce of strength to lug my collapsible wardrobe down the stairs, I noticed that Lynx had texted ten minutes earlier to say he was on the BRT, and that he would be there in twenty minutes.

We went out for seafood at Bashi Market after we finished moving. From that day on, I often received texts from Lynx, inviting me to exhibitions or screenings of obscure documentaries. The galleries were sparsely attended and extremely air-conditioned; the documentaries were grainy and full of long, sleep-inducing takes. Lynx always seemed to enjoy himself, while I fought to stay awake. Things progressed smoothly from there: we met every week, and slowly grew closer. I realized one day, watching him nonchalantly reach for my glass of absinthe to taste its anise notes, that we had entered the early stages of a young, tentative romance.

We spent a few nights together at the seaside, where Lynx told me many stories of the jungle he had heard as a boy—about his grandfather's burial, the demon king of Penang, sorcerers dwelling deep in the rainforest, soldiers turning to crocodiles, and so on. He then said, avoiding my gaze, that he would be going home in two days. I was briefly caught off guard, then nodded slowly. The waves washed over my feet, drenching the bottoms of my shoes. Not far from where we stood, a bright, round seashell washed ashore. I picked it up and inspected it in the moonlight: palm-sized, hard-shelled, shaped like a coin with a five-petaled flower blooming in the center, and covered in down-soft thorns. I cupped this amazing creature I'd never seen before in my hand, marveling. That's a sand dollar, Lynx told me, something he and his friends often found on his childhood beaches. Sand dollars only wash up after they die; they turn white, and that whiteness is their skeleton. He had a biscuit tin full of sand dollars under the mattress back home, because there's a wilted flower on the back of each one.

A pale, solitary moon rose up behind him, allowing me to study his face. The left side was thicker-set than the right, and hidden in the musculature of his left cheek was a small, sweet dimple, tinged light pink.

Lynx looked at me and asked if I wanted to go on holiday with him to the tropics— we could visit the Bomi settlement ruins he'd told me about. He wanted to submit a proposal for a study on Southeast Asian ethnic minority settlements, to support his PhD application next year. He said, with a wink, that he would be willing to share the findings of the trip with me, if any came up. I agreed to it with a nod. If nothing else, at least I would get an idea of what to write for my dissertation.

Strangely, after I made up my mind to go on that trip, I stopped having dreams at night. I realized that dreams don't follow people around as faithfully as shadows do. Lynx once told me that whenever he couldn't sleep at night, he would get up and play basketball. Summers in southern Fujian are marked by an abundance of rain and the frenzied growth of plants. One midnight, I got up and walked into the corridor, where a big clump of feathery oil palm leaves peeked in, blocking the way like an unfurled, thorned tuanshan. I gently pushed the leaves aside, causing their dark shadows to ripple along the floor. Cold blue light flooded the space between the sky and the earth. The temperature had dropped slightly, and the night wind carried a note of chilliness. I propped my elbows on the railing and looked out into the night, listening to the sounds that rose from the basketball court downstairs. In the dark, I imagined that the silhouette obscured among the layers of leaves belonged to Lynx. The basketball's rubber surface bounced off the concrete court with a blunt, muffled sound, rising and falling until the break of day.

≈

I was worried about sanitary conditions in the wild, so I cut my hair short ahead of the trip to avoid becoming a playground for insects. I also wanted to meet with Professor Y; not only was he proficient in several languages and well-versed in Hakka and Fujian dialects, he had also gone deep into the Shennongjia Forestry District in search of wild men and their traces, visited the remote mountainous regions of Yunnan to study reproduction amongst the Lisu people, and had a wealth of fieldwork experience. I wanted his advice, but all my emails went unanswered. In the faculty building, I found the door to his office locked shut, leaving me no choice but to go next door and question a colleague of his. Looking up from a book with eyes framed by golden wire, the young professor told me that Professor Y was in the hospital after having a stroke; his daughter, who was in England, hired a professional care worker to look after him daily, but he had yet to wake up.

We took a plane, then a train, then a south-bound passenger liner to arrive at Lynx's hometown, on an island in southern Singapore which floated separate from the country's principal landmass, a star within the constellation that was the Nanyang archipelago. A clear and serene sea, nipa palms shaking their slender, feathery leaves, the raised backs of islands in the distance: everything within view appeared translucent and luminous under the sun.

It was starting to get dark by the time we left the pier. Having planned to spend the first night by the harbor, we strolled along the twilit coastline after dinner, bare feet on the sand, bodies almost weightless. In the distance, where the sea met the shore, a gathering of people was pushing a colorful barge onto the water. It's an Ong Chun ceremony, he said, to honor the gods of the ocean. There's a Chinese village nearby, so some customs from Fujian and Taiwan have been preserved here.

The waves rolled back, taking with them an animal head wrapped in a red sack—a sacrificial offering—bearing it all the way into the sea's depths. The kindling ceremony followed: the barge stationed on the beach, the colorful drawings that covered it, its lion-shaped prow and dragon-shaped stern, all were engulfed by scarlet flames which, as the wind picked up, jumped and danced in tandem with the waves. The parts of the barge that hadn't yet burned down remained stranded on the beach. They usually burn for a long time, he said, and when the tide rises tomorrow morning, the water will wash away the ashes. After we'd walked a long way off, I looked back, searching for the burning barge. The crowd had dispersed, but the flames burned feebly on, scattering ashes all over the ground. The sea swept in, mixing it all into a soft, wet quicksand.

A few stalls at the seaside market were still open. Some were laden with the day's spoils, which the fishermen sorted through, while others displayed strange ornaments: oddly-shaped corals; desiccated, shrunken starfish; jungle lizard specimens; and a row of dried, yellowing crocodile teeth, strung together and hung on a wooden stand. I held the necklace up for a closer look: a thin crack ran down the middle of one tooth, filled with dust and grime and emanating a faraway jungle gaminess. Lynx explained that the crocodile was an indigenous totem, that the locals firmly believed its teeth would bestow divine protection upon their wearer.

At dusk, I leaned against the hostel bed and leafed through academic papers, while Lynx listened to music next door. The song, Wu Bai's "Tangled Passions," filtered in through the door and the windows. I stared at the tamarind tree, centered on the map of the settlement site and surrounded by a hexagonal arrangement of huts. I thought back to my made-up report:

> In the book *The Peoples of the South Sea*, written by members of the Western expedition after they had returned to their respective countries, the descriptions of the Bomi people are completely at odds with the records of the English scholar Lady Brookfield: "The area is populated by a people of uncertain race: they have high cheekbones and upturned noses, the tips of which remind one of a gull soaring over the sea with outstretched wings. They are brown-skinned and black-haired, clad in ancient Chinese garments—a tribe of Tatars migrated to a tropical rainforest. Their fences and stilt houses are built out of bamboo and wood, their leader is a white-haired Elder, and pearls of varying quality, as well as differently shaped pebbles, are used as currency within the tribe."

> This settlement, hidden deep within the mountains, does not reveal itself lightly to outsiders. The Bomi lie snugly in the embrace of towering mountains that seamlessly surround them on three sides, connected to the outside world only through a hidden cave; water pools in the cave intermittently, while storms flood it completely, cutting off the path. It is likely the most remote and isolated human settlement on earth.

> Driven by the tides of history to this corner of the world, the Bomi inhabit the depths of a jungle that has lost its temporal dimension, removed from their ancestry and forgotten by language. Their speech is a mix of several: Minnan, Hakka, English, Malay, Hindi, Burmese, with an accent of untraceable origin. Afraid of being identified by invaders as one tribe or another, the Bomi buried their native tongue while their new language gestated, amalgamating flavors as in a cocktail, and twisting together like the entangled branches of a tree, rendering its provenance unknowable. Their speech is occasionally punctuated by gestures

imitating those of prehistoric animals, or even the way that prehistoric plants such as nipa palms, oil palms, wild plantains, and monsteras dance in the wind.

I closed my eyes and drifted off to the music. "Let the wind become fire / And set everything alight / Let it submerge you and me." I dreamt I was visiting the settlement site's volcano memorial, at the center of which lay two charred bodies entwined in each other's arms, their palms merging like a confluence of waters. The song's melody and lyrics echoed in my head, then cut off abruptly, like a piece of silk torn down the middle.

I woke with a start. My bed was shaking and the walls were trembling. I got up and met Lynx in the corridor, he held my hand tightly as we ran out. We followed a crowd onto the semi-circle plaza in front of the local mosque. Lynx refreshed his newsfeed over and over while I asked him for details, thinking of my own phone under my pillow. A Facebook notification popped up on his screen: a 6.0 earthquake had triggered the eruption of a volcano on a nearby island. He clicked on it, quickly scrolling through before closing the window, focusing on the messages from friends and family. I caught a glimpse of his profile picture, a photo of Mount Bromo erupting. He phoned the pier and canceled our booking for that afternoon, then put the phone back in his pocket.

Two smaller aftershocks followed, during which I still panicked, but Lynx comforted me, saying that locals eventually get used to the vibrations. Michael Oppitz once said that vibrations created the universe.

The next day, following our original plan, we made our way to the settlement site. Before we set out, Lynx warned me about insects and the bloodsucking leeches lurking on the water's edge. I had no choice, then, but to brave the forty-something degree heat in long sleeves and long trousers, while Lynx looked like a plantation owner in a loose-fitting, short-sleeved beige cotton tee, khaki shorts, long cotton socks, and olive-green hiking boots. He wore a nylon rope pinned to his waist, from which hung an intricately carved dagger with black and green silk threads wound around its handle. The whole getup gave him the air of a jungle tribe chieftain.

We went by the forest path that villagers took to tap resin up in the mountains—the deeper we went, the narrower it became. In the quiet of the rainforest, we heard the hum of insects and frogs, and the occasional hoot of an owl. Don't owls usually sleep during the day and hunt at night? I asked. The ones that come out in the daytime are known to be wobbly fliers—it's like they're sleepwalking, Lynx said, and told me to watch out for any owls falling out of trees.

Once out of the rubber forest, we were barred by a river. We could only backtrack to a village in the upper banks and rent a boat. Our boatman told us that the river, known to the locals as River Ming, was formed during an earthquake several decades ago; it used to flow underground, but seeped above snakelike after the quake, growing day after day until it eventually flowed into the Samunsam River, becoming one of its tributaries.

We got off the boat and walked through a stretch of rainforest until we arrived. A large wooden sign at the entrance read, "Historic Site of the Bomi Settlement." By the entrance, at a ticket booth that had been made to look like a hut, a young woman in a batik sarong stopped us and charged for tickets, then tried to foist some cheap rental audio guides on us. They had six channels—Chinese, English, French, German, Thai, Malay—to choose from, were rented by the hour, and required a deposit of two hundred ringgit. We got one and walked at the same pace; I listened through the right earbud, while Lynx took the left. A row of imitation huts stood before us, with exposed nails in their rafters and varnish still drying on their walls. We weren't expecting tourism developers to have already devised such a thorough and comprehensive commercialization scheme for the site, complete with immersive performances to boot. A middle-aged woman meticulously mending a fishing net beneath a narra tree put down her workand plastered on a picture-perfect smile as soon as she saw us approaching. She was barefoot, wearing a batik sarong and a black-grey top, with large, plump agates hanging from her ears, and bracelets of emerald-green beads adorning her wrists. She spoke a local language I couldn't understand—likely an indigenous resident hired from the area.

The woman led us into a hut, where a sizable crowd was already gathered. A white-haired Elder of indeterminate gender sat solemnly before an old, grimy wooden chest in the center. We walked to a row in the back and sat down. The Elder opened the chest and took out a boar-skin coat with one sleeve torn, a pheasant's red and black crest feathers, and a hide drum painted with a figure that had the head of a fish and the body of a woman. The Elder heated the drum head over the fire, then brought out an instrument made of crocodile teeth, striking it with a small wooden mallet that had been soaked in sacred water. Each of the seven teeth represented a different note, and emitted its own pleasant sound when played.

She stood in front of the crude wooden altar and fixed her turbid gaze on a point in the distance, dispelling evil spirits with a steady flow of curses that bubbled from her lips and densely wove into the surrounding chants of myths and epics. The drumming sped up, then slowed down again once the rhythm repeated, accompanied by the tinkling of the crocodile teeth, gradually sinking us into a trance state. A few middle-aged women sat around the Elder Witch, mending fishing nets or knitting with wool, as if watching an opera performance. Two younger women spoke to each other in whispers. An older woman explained that the Elder had been a wizard in a past life, which is why she was employing men's curses to drive away evil and cast spells.

After the ritual ended, we left the hut along with the other visitors and explorers. I asked Lynx whether he understood the curses we'd just heard. He shook his head, then told me a story from a Nepali legend: a shaman and a Buddhist poet were competing to see who could climb a mountain faster, and the victor would be given a sacred book. The poet won, predictably, because shamans have no need for books; their drums are their scripture. When I asked him where he'd heard that story, he replied that Michael Oppitz had told it somewhere.

At the center of the site, we sheltered from the sun under a tamarind tree. Next to it was a wooden plaque that read "The Last Bomi Man," alongside a photo of an indigenous person. He was bare-chested, with brown skin, black hair, and rings on his lips. His dark eyes gleamed obsidian but appeared empty, as if they beheld nothing.

The plaque read further: "A majority of the tribe's members were gradually killed in the 1970s by unlawful ranchers who had settled in the area. In 1995, an illegal miner attacked six members of the tribe, and this man was the sole survivor. In 1996, the overseer of a plantation found him under a large banana leaf, after which he vanished for a period of time. In 1997, the local government built an indigenous protection zone in this location; the existence of the settlement was kept under wraps for many years, and researchers were allowed to study it in secret. Some researchers speculate that this man had lived alone for at least thirty years. He refused contact with the outside world, viewing any food or supplies brought by the groundskeeper as bait or entrapment. Whenever he sensed danger, he wielded weapons he had made himself, closed off paths using vines and branches, and shot poisoned arrows at bulldozers. Once, a groundskeeper who attempted to carry out a health check-up was shot through the lung with an arrow as he approached the man's hut. In 2001, the man's body was found several months after his death, covered in macaw feathers."

I looked around, imagining what life in the settlement might have looked like in prehistoric times. Numbers were carved onto the huts' stilts, indicating the water levels of each year's flood: 1988, 1993, 2001, 2002, 1996. Beneath each number scribbled in black was a line drawn in blue, covering the stilts in uneven stripes. I asked Lynx if all of it had really happened. He said we couldn't prove that these people had existed any more than the other tribes lost to the course of history. Those who could remember them are long gone, and alleged artifacts cannot serve as abiding proof of their existence. We were, just like them, caught in a vortex of history.

Not far from us glinted a lake, silver-sheened and mirror-like. Could it be, I said, that the world we live in is a reflection of another world, and that in this other dimension, the Bomi people still live here? Lynx narrowed his eyes against the sunlight and spoke no more.

II. THE CROCODILE'S REFLECTION

We waited for our boatman by the river, which was beginning to blur under a layer of mist. The cigarette in Lynx's hand burned down to a stub. We contemplated the implausibility of our respective field projects in silence. After we got on the boat, he suddenly mentioned that the tree where his grandfather is buried was just nearby, we could drop by to pay our respects—then at least the trip wouldn't have been in vain.

Off the boat again, I followed him into a deep, dense forest. It was customary in his family to keep the ashes of the deceased in urns and to hang them on trees. After a long silence, he pointed at the dark, weighty urn slotted into the branches and said, Actually, Grandfather's remains aren't in there, only his belongings are. A red-eyed hornbill perched on a branch, watching Lynx fixedly and solemnly from above, like a faithful gravekeeper.

I asked him, That person who contacted me on Facebook before—that was you, wasn't it? A sheepish look came over his face and he lowered his voice. He never got the chance to explain, but that book might contain clues of his grandfather's whereabouts, and he never had any intention of deceiving me. He told me—

When Grandfather left home, no one knew where he went. After he disappeared, Father found a tattered, worn-out diary in the urn. It dated back to 1933, when Grandfather was fifteen years old. At twenty-one, he was a student at the Navigation College of Jimei University, but he put his studies on hold to volunteer as an overseas Chinese worker on the Burma Road, driving truckloads of supplies to the front lines during the War of Resistance. When Singapore fell not long after he returned home, he disappeared into the jungle with two guns he had bought off a fleeing Brit for eight cents, and was not heard from for a long time.

Lynx walked to the tree and caressed its hollowed-out trunk, saying, There used to be a photograph here, it was like a little shrine. It was of Grandfather when he was young, its corners all rounded from age. When I came back to see it recently, only a small part of his face was still visible, the rest of the image had been eaten away. Maybe the photo paper was chemically altered by insect secretions, or corroded by sap and resin, but either way, it was eventually completely consumed by the tree. I asked what the photograph had looked like. He said it wasn't a very sharp image, you could just barely make it out. Grandfather had a square jaw and a broad forehead, with voluminous, curly black hair gathered at the back, like sails fluttering in the wind.

He continued: According to Father, there was something odd about the diary. The first half was a thin journal of notes written in a foreign language, filled with ink splotches and a squiggly script resembling Old Javanese. The words were densely packed, and every single available space was covered in tiny writing and notations of dates. He didn't think Grandfather knew the foreign language—his own writings bore no relation to those passages, and consisted mostly of his musings on life and records of dreams. The text was written closely together presumably out of necessity, at a time when paper was scarce. The second half consisted of white pages, also brimming with dates and writing, and seemed to have been appended at a later date. The two halves were bound together.

The pages in the second half were dated out of order, ranging from the 1933 of Grandfather's youth to the summer of 1982 when he left home on his own—a deck of cards that had been shuffled at random. The documented occurrences were equally chaotic. It was like having twenty-something billiard balls bouncing around in your head, with no way of telling where the next strike would come from. As the writing jumped back and forward in time, some of the accounts were inconsistent and contradictory. They disrupted the internal temporal logic of events, like two mirrors leaning against each other, refracting multiple dimensions. Father only discovered that the diary had been rebound once he'd read through most of it. The margins occasionally offered up fragments of poems, "A body hangs on the shore / All dreams flow on the river"; "The lakes of the world converge on a blade"; "I encounter a shadow in the depths of a flame," and so on. It was unclear whether Grandfather had written the verses himself, or if he had read them somewhere.

Many of the words were pierced and threaded through with twine, drawn into the darkness of the book's spine. The writing on the last page was illegible, squiggly lines soaked and blurred by tea-colored stains, as if he was smiling through the mist and saying, Don't delude yourselves that you'll get anything certain out of this diary.

To the family's dismay, the diary later disappeared inexplicably during a typhoon. An excess of rain had caused the rivers to overflow and flood everything around, forcing them to flee with their neighbors and seek shelter in the mountains. After things had calmed down, they returned to find their house leaking from all sides and their belongings bobbing up and down in water. Half a month later, sitting in front of a chest of drawers, Lynx's father remembered Grandfather's diary, but it had long vanished—along with the drawer it was in—into the flood's gaping maw.

Based on Lynx's description, the book I'd found at the flea market in southern Fujian may very well have been the first half of the diary. I told him this, and also confessed how I had lost it again. It's split in two, he said, each half drifting out there in the world, with nowhere to return to.

He said his father vaguely remembered that quite a few passages included mention of Mr. Tan Kah Kee, a prominent figure in Nanyang's overseas Chinese community. Grandfather brought up Mr. Tan multiple times, alongside recollections of canned pineapples and pineapple cake (Mr. Tan had made his fortune in rice trading and pineapple canning). The fact that such sugary foods were being sent as supplementary supplies to the front in mainland China seemed like an immense luxury to Grandfather, and regularly awakened in him a nostalgia for the sweet-tasting foods from home. Passages detailing specific interactions with Mr. Tan, on the other hand, were few and far between.

One such passage read:

> It is 1939, and I am one year away from graduating from the Navigation College. I had hoped to find employment with an English shipping company, to brave the seven seas at the helm. But alas, we have been engulfed by war, and when I learned that Mr. Tan was, coincidentally, enlisting overseas Chinese workers to aid the southwestern front, I gathered my belongings and boarded a train headed for the Burma Road.

A later passage read:

> Mr. Tan's glasses had fogged over. He took them off and wiped the lenses. Rain was pouring from the sky, and as he crossed the stream, he stepped on a cold, slippery rock, almost losing his footing. I quickly steadied him.

Lynx said there was one detail that isn't mentioned in Mr. Tan's memoirs, making it difficult to verify. In 1943, the third year of Grandfather's homecoming, he hid in a cave deep in the rainforest. There, by the light of an oil lamp, he put down his memories of the Burma Road on paper.

He had a brief encounter with Mr. Tan, while the latter was supervising work along the Road.

A countryman of Grandfather's—another overseas Chinese worker—had gotten into a drunken brawl and escaped back to Singapore. For lack of anyone to arrest, the authorities ludicrously apprehended Grandfather to be punished in his countryman's stead. He was released from prison in the middle of a damp, cold winter with no money for warm clothes, and had to wear a shirt and sandals on his drive to deliver supplies to the north, during which he encountered Mr. Tan's fleet of trucks by chance. Seeing him dressed so inadequately, Mr. Tan struck up a conversation and, hearing his story, let out a deep sigh and took off his gold-rimmed glasses, bowing his head as he polished them. His eyes held the hint of tears. As they spoke further, Grandfather learned that the Singaporean village where his family lived was just across the river from Mr. Tan's mother's hometown.

When he wasn't working, and while he awaited letters from home, Grandfather would walk around the workers' camp. Having renounced card games and gambling, he often roamed through the wild jungle, where the tree ferns, camphor trees, and firs—the lush greenery and cool, serene dales—fed his constant ache for home.

Later, when Singapore fell and English soldiers started peddling their guns to the Chinese at four cents apiece, the workers huddled together in a jungle cave to work out how to get that kind of money. Grandfather paid a visit to Mr. Tan, who urged them to lie low elsewhere instead of staying and sacrificing their lives for nothing. Through a friend of Mr. Tan's who worked at a shipping company, Grandfather managed to get three steamer tickets and gave them all to his family, putting them on the last ship to Java. He then took the two guns he had exchanged for money and plunged into the rubber plantation, vanishing as if into a distant cloud of grey fog.

Lynx said that for half a year, Grandfather hid in the caves. One afternoon, he heard motors that sounded like warplanes circling above, and as he held his breath, waiting for them to fly away, he heard voices coming from the other end of the cave. He peered inside, but the deeper he went, the fainter the voices became. Having never ventured very far into the cave, he took a branch from the earthen oven he had built, lit it with kindling, and made his way deeper inside, holding his torch.

There, he found a lake connected to an underground river. He walked to the water's edge and saw his own reflection on the surface, illuminated by the fire.

Laughter emanated from the bottom of the lake as if through a passage to another world—one that knew nothing of bombings or death. His reflection puzzled him, and he wondered if there laid on the other side a homeland that had not fallen into enemy hands. When the people in that world looked to the water, did they see the flame-lit, rippling contours of his silhouette?

Beneath his reflection floated a dark, driftwood-shaped mass with a pair of glinting eyes. He took a step back, recalling tales about dark caves that circulated in the villages.

After he returned home, he began writing in his diary about the world on the other side of the water—a resplendent, dreamlike fantasy world. He wrote more than once about wanting to dive into the lake, to find out what it held once and for all. As a Navigation College alumnus, he was a strong swimmer, but reason cautioned him against it. The chances of getting lost in a groundwater system were high, and he could easily suffocate to death, or be carried off into the dark unknown by subterranean torrents.

Strains of song wafted out from the rainforest. We followed the music to find a burial being held in front of a tree, not far from where we stood. An elderly man with white hair and a white beard hoarsely sang a solemn, mournful song that sounded surprisingly similar in melody and rhythm to the one that Professor Y had spontaneously sung in class. I looked towards Lynx, but he didn't seem to have noticed. At my insistence, he translated the lyrics for me line by line.

They sang of a soldier who, under the pursuit of enemy forces, had turned into a crocodile and dived into the rapids. He later became a boatman, and spent his days roaming the river in the underworld. According to local legend, crocodiles have the ability to summon all souls that wander adrift. Lynx said that the elder for whom they were holding the burial was ninety-seven years old when he died. He had fought in the war, and his entire left leg was blackened by a bullet that they never managed to extract. The other elder was singing him a mourning song to cleanse his corporeal form and lay his soul to rest, to help it pass over peacefully into the next world.

He said that if Grandfather were still alive, he would have been around the same age. When he was sixty-five years old, he left the village he called home and never returned. Many villagers saw him heading into the depths of the rainforest with his cane. Later, Father and Uncle went into the forest and found the cane that Grandfather had cast aside, a piece of scale next to it. They took the scale back to the village, where hunters speculated that it belonged to a kind of reptile. The whole family took turns going into the forest, but despite months of searching, they couldn't find even a single scrap of clothing.

After Grandfather's birthday banquet that year, the family had a set of new clothes made for him. They remained neatly folded in a drawer—he was wearing his old, tattered clothes when he left home that day. Grandmother recalled that they seemed to be the very same clothes from when he had re-emerged from the rainforest to come home, so many years ago. She had wanted to throw the tatters away at the time, but Grandfather wouldn't let her, and refused to speak to anyone for several months before coming to his senses. When the family plied him with questions about what he'd been through, his answers were often contradictory. When they asked where he had hidden during the war, he only spoke of a cave in which the ground was often awash in white light. He stowed his battered clothes away, donning them once more, over forty years later, to vanish forever into the vast forest.

Lynx recalled a story his father had told him after drinking: once, when he was young, he had heard someone call out his childhood nickname while swimming in the river. Looking around, he saw a crocodile with a scar on its short snout, slowly swimming towards him. He reached for the rubber-tapping knife in his pocket, but the crocodile only floated once around his raft before swimming away. As far as he remembered, this crocodile with a scarred snout had never hurt anybody.

Decades ago, he said, Grandfather left home and withdrew into the forest. After the family had spent many days fruitlessly searching for him, Father went to the village witch doctor and asked him to divine Grandfather's whereabouts. The witch doctor held Grandfather's abandoned cane and the scale they had found next to it, and closed his eyes in contemplation. Purple smoke from an incense candle filled the room. When he opened his eyes, he advised the family that there was no need to keep looking, that Grandfather would never return. Unable to accept the news, Father fell to his knees and pleaded.

Shrouded in a purple haze, the witch doctor remained silent, but a deep voice rippled forth from the walls of the stone cabin, as if from an ancient oracle: Grandfather had swapped bodies with a crocodile.

⁓

A spotted trilobite beetle crawled over my left shoulder, leaving a string of tiny blood droplets in its wake. Maybe the beetle was poisonous, or maybe I had spent too long in the scorching afternoon sun, but my cheeks started to flush soon after, and I felt slightly faint. A nimble pig-tailed macaque leapt among the palm leaves in a flash, ablaze with fiery sparks. Then I blinked, and the fire was gone. It must have been a hallucination.

We'd reached the edge of the rainforest by then. The riverbank wasn't far, but our boat and boatman were nowhere to be seen. Maybe he took the wrong path in the forest, Lynx said. As I walked through the grass, their tendrils wound around my ankles and made me trip, leaving a mark. I turned down Lynx's offer to carry me on his back and told him to go back to the pier—I would stay and wait for the boat.

I sit in silence, looking out across the water and contemplating the events of the past few days. A diary split in two halves: the first a historical account of unknown authorship, written in an Austronesian language, the second a record of war and dreams, written by Lynx's grandfather. Two completely unrelated volumes, bound together with no regard for order or linguistic uniformity, had subliminally led me here. Time could not illuminate the secrets of the rainforest. Historical truth, ever changing and ever ungraspable, is a shell that has never been pried open. Its smooth, unblemished surface defies the sharpened knives of all who attempt to do so, and its interior remains equally unknowable.

I repeat to myself the words and phrases accumulated in my memory, letting them float among the trees. I can no longer tell whether they are fragments of the made-up report, or barely discernible words from the lost diary:

> Schopenhauer says that "[n]o human being has lived in the past, nor will any live in the future; rather the present is the only form of all life." (*The World as Will and Representation Vol. 1*, passage 54) Many researchers are perplexed by the lack of the present tense in the Bomi language, which means that any utterance would be immediately relegated to the past. The Bomi people split time into many tiny fragments, they have never lived in continuity.

Without a present tense, the Bomi existed as if affixed to a picture card from birth, perpetually being turned over by a pair of invisible hands. Bomi words were destined to become history as soon as they left the lips. The future flows backwards into the past, and Time whirls around in a vortex.

As the sun sets vermilion, Lynx appears on the water. Not far behind him, black smoke billows out of Mount Bromo and the sky blazes, reflecting the volcano's fiery depths.

The mountain fire is here, Lynx says. He squints, and an anxious look edges onto his face, accentuating its lines and furrows, lending it the appearance of a green walnut shriveling up under a scorching sun. A basin of water rests on the bottom of the boat, filled with blue-green shells. His silhouette glides onto that small circle of water, wobbling, shattering, and becoming whole again.

As we sail through the river, the smoke and the fog close in. I catch glimpses of the tamarind tree burning at the center of the settlement site: tall and leafy, shrouded in clouds of smoke, a torch in full blaze. Were it not for this unforeseen eruption, it would have flourished alongside the rainforest until the end of time.

A crocodile glides beneath our boat and emerges from the water's rippling surface. It swims beside our boat like a shadow. The cool water caresses its granite form as it drifts in and out of sight amongst the currents, and the scar on its short snout gives it a look of exceptional melancholy. I am struck by the thought that the necklace I had picked out that day at the seaside market may have held one of its teeth.

I calmly meet the crocodile's gaze as my reflection overlaps with its shape. Lynx is also looking at the crocodile. I laugh and say, Your grandfather must have heard your prayers in the forest. He chuckles, lights a cigarette, takes a few drags, and says, You really believe all that? When the cigarette burns through, he tells me about a passage in the diary written by Grandfather himself. In it, he had made a point of changing the narrative to the third person, to signal objectivity:

> He had been captured after being shot, and was fortunate enough to survive a long period of widespread fever. "Dead as he is in his own lifetime, he is the real survivor," he remembered once reading in a large book at a flea market.

While his captors struggled to decide on his punishment, he agreed to exchange a list of names for the chance to walk out alive. They had spent the entire night devising ways to crack open his skull and replicate his memories, all while keeping him alive, and had finally arrived at what seemed like an infallible solution. But before they could execute their plan, he suddenly gave in and, as if sighing, let the names fall pearl-like from his lips, taking them all by surprise. The sense of time's passage was disintegrating, and he felt hollowed out, like he could no longer change anything. To him, the world no longer seemed real.

In his later years, he made and fired an urn with his own hands—a weighty, pitch black, gleaming vessel. He closed his diary, tore off its spine, and put the loose pages, like snowflakes, into the urn. He instructed his family to burn all of its contents, then walked into the forest. In the long days of waiting for Grandfather to return, Father pieced the diary back together, attempting to find even the slightest clue as to Grandfather's disappearance.

As soon as Lynx finishes his story, the crocodile sinks back silently into the depths, leaving only my reflection on the surface.

The red glow of the sun spills onto our sampan while Lynx stands at the stern and prays, his voice gnat-faint. Grandfather, please forgive me for bringing a stranger here. She wants to learn about our history, please grant us your blessings.

On both sides of the river, the nipa palms shake their broad, feathery leaves, casting shadows that dance amidst the liquid glow of the fire. History, alienated, flows in the resin of the trees, while the absent truth, much like the leaves and branches reflected in the water, remains an illusion. Time whirls around in a vortex here. The water undulates languidly, like pages turning in the wind, in a book that will soon close as night falls. My boat sails upon this vast book. Closing my eyes, I recall my dream about the volcano memorial, where two charred bodies lay entwined. I remember the Wu Bai song, "Let the wind become fire / And set everything alight / Let it submerge you and me." Lava pours in, fire streams over water.

The rainforest crackles and snaps as it burns. By my side, Lynx's prayers grow fainter, becoming the murmurs at the threshold of sleep: in the beginning there was a world in which all things were small, encircled by mountains. Then the vibrations of the earth unleashed a mountain fire, the fire engulfed this first world, and in its place a new world emerged. We all come from the same Mother and Father: they had many children, and we now inhabit the earth's every corner.

马叙

Ma Xu

TRANSLATED BY
ZUO FEI &
JENNIFER FOSSENBELL

诗三首

Stop at One, and No More

Stop at one. It's a tough start.
I don't want to talk about two or three. No more. Not even 1.1.
But now, I'm up to 0.7. All this has to be handled carefully.
Say it on the outside. Don't get your heart involved.
Don't talk about the past, its happiness or unhappiness.

Don't talk about any astronomical figure,
not even that lonely thief wandering in the distance.
Wipe the dirt from your face. Put away your hands.
Catch the shuttle bus before dawn. Sit by the window.
Gulp down a few parts of the passage. Don't think. Don't try to digest it.
Get off halfway. The bus will take away the rest.

Go to a small station. Make the unfamiliar familiar.
That girl in the dark corner—oh, she's selling groceries.
If you get to one, will the dawn break?
Don't say anything else. Nothing more than the grocery. Nothing at all.

No more buses at the station. The parking lot has been emptied.
All is stillness. It's about time to move beyond one.
But no more talk.
Stand outside the desolate station. Choose not to speak.

Endless Rain

The endless rain whittles him down,
whittles his limbs,
whittles his stuttering tongue,
whittles his fire.
But he—
he always keeps that one small part dry.

Meanwhile, the endless rain
whittles the backdrop, flowers, the halves of clouds,
the poeticism of the reader,
and the meaning of endless rain.
Look, by touching the dry part
—that hard core of revolution—
he's still yearning for
a bourgeois storm.

Standing in the dry part,
he watches
the endless rain
whittle away the world of the proletariat
and whittle down
the world of the bourgeois.

The endless rain
whittles this strange world.

Once I Mistook the Moonlight on the Sea

The bodies of the waves darkened the sea.
I think of my heart as a vessel for sensitive matters.
In fact, I often mistake what's going on around me.
Once I even mistook the moonlight on the sea,
while also mistaking one wave for another.

Oh, once again I mistook things,
and not even the sea corrected me in time.

You think I can be beautifully erroneous.
You are too quick to believe the fables of mermaids.
Let me tell you the truth:
In fact, that night there was no moon.
In fact there was no moonlight.

Nor was I at the sea at all.
I was but the body of a wave myself.
And when I came to understand this,
my heart went dark.
At that moment, a woman passed by.
At that moment, the space around me filled with darkness.

AUTHORS

Chen Chuncheng 陈春成 was born in 1990 in Fujian. The novella 《音乐家》won the *Harvest* Literature Novella Award in 2019, and the short story collection 《夜晚的潜水艇》was named the best novel in the Douban Annual Awards, as well as one of the top ten works of the year by *Asia Weekly*. In 2021, he was awarded the Blancpain-Imaginist Literature Award.

Da Tou Ma 大头马 was born in 1989 in Anhui. She was one of the writers included in Nanjing's Project to Promote Young Literary Talent, and her publications include the fiction collections 《谋杀电视机》,《不畅销小说写作指南》, and 《九故事》. She has been awarded the first prize in the Douban Essay Competition, the first prize in the Global Chinese Diasporic Youths Screenplay Competition, the first prize in the Macau Literary Awards, the best work of the year in the first Zhongshan Star Awards, and the Emerging Writers Award at the seventh Purple Mountain Literary Awards. Her works can also be found in 《收获》,《小说选刊》,《花城》,《十月》, and more.

Du Lulu 杜绿绿 is a poet and a critic, born 1979 in Anhui. Her collections include 《近似》,《她没遇见棕色的马》,《我们来谈谈合适的火苗》, and 《城邦之谜》. She has received the Young Poet Award at the Pearl River International Poetry Festival, the *October* Poetry Award, and has been named one of the Top Ten Contemporary Chinese Poets. She lives in Guangzhou.

Fu Wei 付炜 was born in 1999 in Henan. He has won the Global Chinese Youth Literature Award for Prose, the Guanghua Poetry Award, the He Jingming Literary Award for Poetry, the Li Shutong International Poetry Award, and the Sakura Poetry Awards.

Hei Tao 黑陶 is a poet and essayist, born in an ancient pottery town at the juncture of Jiangsu, Zhejiang, and Anhui to a farmer and a ceramicist. His essay collections include 《泥与焰：南方笔记》,《漆蓝书简：被遮蔽的江南》,《二泉映月：十六位亲见者忆阿炳》, and 《夜晚灼烫：凝定的时间肖像》. His poetry work includes a collection inspired by Bruno Schulz, 《在阁楼独听万物密语：布鲁诺·舒尔茨诗篇》, as well as the collection 《寂火》. He has been awarded *Poetry Magazine*'s Outstanding Works Award, the *October* Literature Award, the Ai Qing Poetry Award, the Sanmao Prose Award for Best Collection, the Wansongpu Literature Award, the Purple Mountain Literature award, and the Yang Sheng'an Literature Award for Prose.

Huo Xiangjie 霍香结 is the penname of Li Hongxing. He was born in the 1970s in Guilin, and his works include the novels 《灵的编年史》,《铜座全集》, and 《日冕》, as well as the epic poem 《黑暗传》 and the poetry collection 《灯奁》. He co-authored the monograph 《明清篆刻边款铁笔单刀正书千字文》 (One Thousand-Character Essays Written in Iron Upon Seals of the Ming and Qing Dynasties), and was one of the main contributors to the catalogue for the thirteenth Shanghai Biennale. He has received the Houtian Novel Award, was shortlisted for the Blancpain-Imaginist Literary Award, and has been twice nominated for the Mao Dun Literature Award.

Jia Wei 葭苇 is a poet, a translator, and a teacher of poetry to children, living in Beijing. She is the author of the collection 《空事情》.

Jiang Li 江离 is the penname of Lu Qunfeng, born 1978 in Zhejiang. He is the author of 《忍冬花的黄昏》 and 《不确定的群山》, and the co-founder of 《野外》 and 《诗建设》. He has been awarded the Liu Lian Poetry Award, the *October* Literary Award, the Zhejiang Province Award for Outstanding Literary Works, the *Yuhua* Literary Award, the Su Shi Poetry Award, and more. He lives in Hangzhou.

Li Hongwei 李宏伟 was born in Sichuan and lives in Beijing. He is the author of the collections 《有关可能生活的十种想象》 and 《你是我所有的女性称谓》; the novels 《信天翁要发芽》,《平行蚀》,《引路人》; the novella collections 《假时间聚会》, 《暗经验》,《雨果的迷宫》; the essay collection 《深夜里交换秘密的人》; and more. He has received the Yu Dafu Novel Award, the Wu Chengen Novel Award, the *October* Literature Award, the Chinese Young Writers Award, the Xu Zhimo Poetry Award, and more. His works have been selected for the *Harvest* Literature List, the *Yangtze River Review* Literature List, the Chinese Novel Society Rankings, and the *Asia Weekly* Top Ten Novels.

Li Jiayin 李嘉茵 was born in 1996 in Shandong. Her works can be found in 《收获》, 《天涯》,《小说界》, and more. She has received the fourth Zhongshan Star Award for Outstanding Young Writer and the Biennial Award for Short Stories. She lives in Beijing.

Lu Yuan 陆源 was born in 1980 in Guangxi. His works include the short fiction collections 《大月亮及其他》 and 《保龄球的意识流》; the novels 《童年兽》,《祖先的爱情》,《范湖湖的奇幻夏天》, and more. He is also the translator of Bruno Schultz's *Sanatorium Under the Sign of the Hourglass* and *Cinnamon Shop and Other Stories*, as well as Herman Melville's *The Apple Tree Table and Other Sketches*. His poems have appeared in 《诗潮》,《诗歌月刊》, and more. He lives in Beijing.

Ma Xu 马叙 is the penname of Zhang Wenbing, born in 1959 and currently lives in Zhejiang. He is a member of the Chinese Writers Association. His works have appeared in《人民文学》,《十月》,《中国作家》, and《大家》, among others, and they've been selected for many domestic anthologies. His collections include《伪生活书》,《他的生活有点小小的变化》,《乘慢船，去哪里》,《在雷声中停顿》,《错误简史》, and many more. He has been awarded the *October* Literature Award, the Poetry Prize at the God of Poetry Awards, and the Chu Jiwang Literary Award.

Mao Jian 毛尖 was born in 1970 in Zhejiang. She is a writer of film, contemporary culture, and modern Chinese literature. Currently a professor at East China Normal University, a researcher at the Urban Culture Research Center of the Institute of Modern Chinese Thought, and the Vice President of the Shanghai Film Critics Society. She is the author of《非常罪，非常美：毛尖电影笔记》,《当世界向右的时候》,《乱来》,《这些年》,《例外》,《我们不懂电影》,《有一只老虎在浴室》,《夜短梦长》,《遇见》, and《一寸灰》.

San San 三三 was born in 1991. She works by day as an intellectual property lawyer, and her works have appeared in《收获》,《人民文学》,《花城》,《十月》, and more. She has been awarded the Zhongshan Star Youth Excellence Award, the Qinghua Lang/People's Literature Award for New Writers, the Yu Daju Novel Award for Short Story Collections, the PAGEONE Jury Award, the Jing'an Literary Prize, and the Red Cotton Literary Award. She is the author of the short story collections《晚春》,《山顶上是海》,《俄罗斯套娃》, and《离魂记》.

Suo Er 索耳 was born in 1992 and currently lives in Guangzhou. He has been an editor, a producer, and a curator. His publications include the novel《伐木之夜》and the collection《非亲非故》. He has received the Po Xiansheng Award, the Zhongshan Star Literary Award, and the Hong Kong Youth Literature Award.

Tan Lin 檀林 is a poet and translator working with form poetry.

TRANSLATORS

Irene Chen is from Harbin, and has translated stories, essays, and poems from the Chinese.

Liuyu Ivy Chen is a poet, writer, and translator based in New York. Her translation work has appeared in the *Washington Square Review, The Margins, Asymptote, Spittoon Literary Magazine,* and *No Tokens,* among others. She is studying pre-modern Chinese literature and culture at Columbia University.

Michael Day is a traveler, translator, and writer who lives in Los Angeles and Mexico City. His awards include the 2015 Bai Meigui Translation Prize and the 2020 Jules Chametzky Translation Prize. His work has appeared in *Georgia Review, Massachusetts Review, Words Without Borders,* and *Chicago Quarterly Review,* among other publications.

Shangyang Fang is the author of the poetry collection *Burying the Mountain* (Copper Canyon Press, 2021). He is an Assistant Professor of English and Creative Writing at the University of Massachusetts, Boston.

Bernie Feng has worked in localization for games such as Genshin Impact. He has a fascination for stories, languages, and cultures. He is currently based in Shanghai.

Ana Padilla Fornieles (Spain) graduated in Translation and Interpreting Studies from the University of Granada before continuing her Chinese language and culture studies at Beijing Foreign Studies University. Her translations have been published by Penguin, De Gruyter, *Books from Taiwan, Journey Planet,* and *Spittoon Literary Magazine,* among others. She also translates nonfiction regularly for *The World of Chinese.* Her writing has been featured in *Womanhood, The Shanghai Literary Review, Voice & Verse Poetry Magazine, Sledgehammer,* and elsewhere. She lives in Beijing.

Jennifer Fossenbell lives in Denver, USA, where she works as a web editor, writer, and mother. Her poetry and other linguistic experiments have appeared in *Alluvium, So & So, Black Warrior Review, The Hunger,* and *where is the river,* among others. She has also co-translated poems from the Vietnamese and Chinese, which have appeared in various anthologies and journals.

Dave Haysom has been translating, editing, and writing about contemporary Chinese literature since 2012. Managing editor of *Pathlight* from 2014 to 2018, he has translated novels by Feng Tang, Li Er, and Xu Zechen, in addition to *My Tenantless Body*, a collection of poetry by Yu Yoyo, and *Nothing But the Now*, a short story collection by Wen Zhen. His essays and reviews have appeared in *Granta, Words Without Borders, The Millions, China Channel,* and *SUPChina*; his portfolio is online at spittingdog.net.

Aiden Heung (He/They) is a Chinese poet born in a Tibetan Autonomous Town. His English poems have appeared or are forthcoming in *The Australian Poetry Journal, The Kenyon Review, The Missouri Review, Poetry International, Harvard Review, Cincinnati Review,* among many other places. He is an MFA candidate at Washington University.

Zhi Hui Ho, born and raised in Singapore, is a budding translator who completed her M.A. in Translation and Interpretation at Nanyang Technological University in 2021. Her translations include essays and short stories for online journals such as *Alluvium* and the Nanjing Normal University literary journal, *Chinese Arts & Letters*.

David Huntington's poetry, translations, and short fiction have been published in *Literary Hub, Lucky Jefferson, Post Road,* and elsewhere. As a PhD candidate at the University of Arizona, he studies critical theory and Anglophone and Chinese literary modernisms.

Helen Lei Jiang is a Brazilian-born translator working in English and Chinese. She studied translation and business interpreting, but literature is her one true love.

Yiqiao Mao is a history student with a penchant for languages. Originally hailing from Beijing, he now resides in the UK.

Xiao Yue Shan is a writer, editor, and translator. *then telling be the antidote* was published in 2024. *How Often I Have Chosen Love* was published in 2019. Her work can be found in *Granta, Poetry, Asymptote,* and *The Kenyon Review*, among others. She is the English-language editor-in-chief of *Spittoon Literary Magazine*.

Simon Shieh is the author of *Master* (Sarabande Books, 2023), winner of the Kathryn A. Morton Prize and the Norma Farber First Book Award. His poems and essays are published in *Poetry, American Poetry Review, Best New Poets, Guernica,* and *The Yale Review*, among others, and have been recognized with a National Endowment for the Arts Literature fellowship and a Ruth Lilly and Dorothy Sargent Rosenberg Fellowship from the Poetry Foundation. Simon co-founded *Spittoon Literary Magazine* in 2016 in Beijing.

Sean Toland is a high school literature teacher based in Beijing, where he moved in 2020 after completing a PhD in German Literature at Princeton University. When not reading or teaching, he can be found jogging the hutongs, practicing piano, and performing in community theater productions.

Austin Woerner is a writer and Chinese-English literary translator whose work has appeared in *Ploughshares, Poetry, The New York Times Magazine*, and *Best American Essays*. He is the translator of *The Invisible Valley* by Su Wei, and two volumes of poetry by Ouyang Jianghe. He currently teaches at the University of Leeds, and would like to thank the student participants in the Poetry Translation Lab @ Leeds, as well as the attendees of a workshop hosted by the Oxford Comparative Criticism and Translation Research Centre in May 2024, for their invaluable contributions to these translations.

Zuo Fei 昨非 is a Beijing-based university English teacher and writer who runs a poetry platform on WeChat, introducing foreign poetry to Chinese readers. She serves as the Chinese-language editor-in-chief of *Spittoon Literary Magazine* and was the featured poet of *Spittoon Monthly* in May 2020. Her recent works include a poem in *Mingled Voices 8: The International Proverse Poetry Prize Anthology 2023* and a piece of fiction in Paper Republic titled "Notes from the Consulting Room". Her essay collection, *The Reed Cutter*, was published by Guangxi Normal University Press.